# The Mystery of the Missing Brooch

The Salisbury Murders:
Book 1

by

WENDY BOYNTON

THE CHOIR PRESS

Copyright © 2024 Wendy Boynton

All rights reserved. No part of this publication may be reproduced or transmitted in any form or by any means, electronic or mechanical including photocopying, recording or any information storage or retrieval system, without prior permission in writing from the publishers.

The right of Wendy Boynton to be identified as the author of this work has been asserted by her in accordance with the Copyright, Designs and Patents Act 1988

First published in the United Kingdom in 2024 by
The Choir Press

ISBN 978-1-78963-494-5

This book is a fictional story set in the beautiful and very real city of Salisbury in Wiltshire. I lived in the Salisbury area for many years and still return regularly to visit family and friends there.

Whilst I have tried to stay faithful to the real locations, I have altered or invented certain aspects for the sake of the story. For instance, there is no care home called The Cedars, nor does the old rectory in Harnham exist as described. All the characters in this book are entirely the products of my imagination, and any similarity to real people, living or deceased, is coincidental.

# Acknowledgements

First, I must thank my wonderful husband for all the support he's given me throughout the writing process, and for the countless cups of tea. Not to mention the occasional bar of chocolate when he could see things weren't going so well! Then there's the friends and family members who I inflicted the first draft manuscript on; without your encouraging praise and helpful criticism, this book would never have developed into the book it is today. My particular thanks to Patsy, without whom the character of Lauren would have fizzled out instead of developing into a key figure in this and the books to follow. Grateful thanks also go to Dawn and Izzy, who spurred me on when I was ready to give up. Without their motivation, this book would never have made it to a publisher! And a special shout out to Andrew Skiller, who proof read my first manuscript and then proof read it again once I'd finished re-writing it.

Huge thanks to everyone at The Choir Press for guiding me through my first experience of publishing, especially David Onyett and Rachel Woodman. I hope we will be able to work together on many more books to come! I am eternally indebted to my copy editor Ann-Marie Lowery who picked up all the errors that Andrew and I both missed, and for her glowing praise which made all the difference to my self-confidence.

And finally, very special thanks to Heather Bowditch for providing the amazing artwork used on the cover.

I dedicate this book to you all!

# Prologue

*Monday 11th April 2022*

It was one of those wet Mondays in early spring that throws a damper over everything. Heavy and persistent rain fell from leaden grey skies, soaking everything in its path. Water trickled steadily from the guttering around the house. It dripped from the trees and bushes in the garden. It splashed into puddles in the driveway and bounced off the dark grey van that was parked there, reversed up to the front entrance with its doors wide open. It kept the solemn residents inside, silent and locked in their private thoughts as they watched two men manoeuvring a black gurney into the back of the transit.

Marianne gave a faint gasp and wiped a sodden handkerchief across her eyes. Annie moved closer, putting an arm around her shoulders. Muriel stood silent, tight-lipped and disapproving. Sylvia looked sad and confused. Albert and Jack were silent for once, their petty squabbles temporarily forgotten as they mourned their loss. Only Janet wasn't with the group standing in the bay window, confined as she was to her wheelchair. But they were all united in their grief at Harry's sudden departure from their tight-knit little care home.

In the hallway, the staff stood silently respectful as the corpse was loaded into the van of Hill & Sons Funeral Directors. Dr Philip Baker comforted the grieving daughter, who had just become an orphan at the age of fifty-nine. No one spoke until Chris Hill, one of the aforementioned sons, asked if it was okay to depart with their cargo safely on board. Phil looked at the bereft Kathy, who mutely nodded, and he gave the go-ahead. The doors were slammed shut, the engine revved and a disrespectful puff of exhaust heralded Harold Leadbetter's departure from The Cedars.

Whilst Harry's tragic passing was an upset to the other

residents, a shock to the staff because of its suddenness and a bolt from the blue for his only child, most of them were able to console themselves that at least Harry had passed peacefully in his sleep and not suffered a lingering, painful death. Dr Baker had not hesitated to sign off the death as natural causes, having found nothing to suggest otherwise and having seen his patient only a few days previously. Knowing Harry's history of high blood pressure and cardiovascular disease, he determined the cause of death to be straightforward heart failure.

Only one person there knew that was not the truth.

# Chapter One

*Tuesday 16th August 2022*

Lauren wasn't quite sure if she was excited or terrified. Butterflies tumbled in her stomach as she hesitated on the kerb. Opposite her, an open gateway revealed a gravelled sweep of drive flanked by wrought iron gates that looked like they hadn't been moved in years. Tall trees, she guessed they must be cedars, stood either side of the driveway, and twin signs proclaimed this to be The Cedars Residential Care Home. She took a deep breath before striding across the road and onto the driveway. This was it. Her first day in her first full-time job.

Instead of heading for the front door, she made her way to the left of the mellow-bricked building, round a corner to a small car parking area, and found the back door as per the orientation email she'd received from the home's matron, Mrs Brenda Wollstonecraft. She remembered meeting this motherly woman at her interview. Middle-aged and plump, with curling shoulder-length brown hair that appeared to be completely unstyled. She had put Lauren at her ease and made her questions seem more like friendly conversation. Not so her husband, who'd leered at her a little too intensely, or the home's care manager, who'd barked out questions, making Lauren dither with uncertainty.

She tapped nervously on the wooden door, which was opened by a carer in blue uniform tunic and trousers. Her fine mousy hair was swept into a bun from which tendrils escaped, framing a kindly face. 'Hi, I'm Sally,' smiled the woman, opening the door widely. 'And you must be Lauren, I assume?' She nodded her agreement and followed Sally into a modern extension housing a staff changing area with lockers and a kind of utility room. To her right, she noted two large chest freezers, two washing machines and a huge tumble dryer along one wall and cupboards with an enormous old-fashioned sink across the end wall, under the windows.

Sally guided her to the lockers along the third wall and opened one, before giving her the key. 'Here, this is your locker. You'll find all your uniforms in there ready for you. There's a changing cubicle there,' she indicated a curtained alcove, 'then you put all your personal stuff into your locker. I'll wait while you change.' Lauren did as instructed then slipped her locker key into her pocket along with her phone. Sally had advised her to put her phone in her locker too, but no way was she doing that! What if one of her friends messaged her?

Sally led her through a pristine kitchen and introduced a giant of a chef called Andy, before entering a long corridor leading into the original part of the building. This was now familiar from her interview, with its swirly green carpet and magnolia walls. Wooden doors were labelled with discreet signs, gents and ladies on her right, whilst a grandiose staircase descended on her left, then a treatment room opposite metal lift doors. As the corridor opened out into a spacious hallway, an archway on the left revealed a view of the dining room, with a few residents eating breakfast. The scent of bacon teased Lauren's nostrils and reminded her she'd been too nervous to eat before leaving home. Next came a door marked private and then the staff office, opposite the huge oak front door where Lauren had entered previously. To one side of the door was an antique carver chair next to a table with an artificial flower arrangement, an assortment of leaflets reminiscent of a doctor's waiting room and a pay-telephone unlike anything she'd seen before. On the wall was a notice board with details of upcoming events, a fire evacuation plan and various other notices. Double doors stood open at the end of the hallway, leading into a sunny day room, where a couple of residents were ensconced in cosy-looking armchairs, one dozing and another reading a newspaper. Sally steered Lauren towards the office, tapping lightly before entering.

The intimidating care manager was seated behind a light

oak modern desk with papers strewn across it and a biro carelessly abandoned. But her attention was clearly focussed on the man standing close behind her, one hand casually caressing the woman's shoulder. His head had been bowed close to hers, but he straightened up and took a step back as they entered. The care manager startled, pursing her lips in annoyance. 'You should wait for a response after you knock,' she reproached sternly.

'Sorry, Ms Trainer,' Sally grimaced. 'I've brought our new carer along for her induction.'

'Ah yes, Lauren Peachy, isn't it?' smarmed the man, easing a lock of wavy black hair from his forehead as he rounded the desk and grabbed her hand for an unwanted squeeze. 'I expect you remember me? Brian Wollstonecraft.'

Lauren muttered a polite response and quickly withdrew her hand. Whilst the care manager snapped at her to take a seat, Brian slinked out of the door, pausing only to cast a wistful glance in Ms Trainer's direction. Lauren sat on a chair at right angles to her, listening as the manager rattled off information. She tried her hardest to appear interested but found her mind wandering. Just what had been going on when they'd entered the office? Was something hinky going on between Mr Wollstonecraft and the care manager?

❀

Having spent the morning reading policies and procedures in the office, Lauren was beginning to wonder if she'd ever get to see any of the residents. She'd become a carer to look after people, not to be shut in a stuffy office!

Three years ago, she'd been about to start her GCSEs when her dad had died in a car accident. Her exam-focus lost, she'd floundered for a while, adrift in a sea of grief. Her plan of A-levels followed by a nursing degree shattered, she hadn't been able to face going back to school. Eventually, her mum had coaxed her into going to college instead, where she'd taken the essential GCSE subjects alongside an NVQ in Health and Social Care. She'd just started her A-levels at college when disaster struck again: her mother had an abnormal smear test, resulting in a pre-emptive hysterectomy. Stubbornly, Lauren had insisted on staying at home to look after her mum, and studying had once more been thrown out of the window. But with her mother almost recovered now, and finances at home tighter than ever, with her mum getting only basic sick pay, Lauren had insisted that, at the age of nineteen, it was high time she got a job and contributed to the household bills. And being a carer had seemed a suitable alternative to nursing.

She was roused from her daydreaming by Sally's voice. 'Are you ready to come to lunch, Lauren?' With relief, she fetched her lunch box from her locker then followed Sally upstairs to a small staff lounge equipped with a microwave, kettle and mini-fridge, and two battered but surprisingly comfortable sofas. Over lunch, she discovered that Sally was thirty-four and married without children. 'The problem is, we're stuck in a rental property,' Sally explained, 'and every spare penny goes into our savings towards a deposit for a mortgage. Darren doesn't want to start a family until we have a place of our own. But I'm beginning to wonder if that'll ever happen.'

'Mum and I live in a rented place too,' Lauren sympathised.

'Is it just the two of you?' Sally asked.

'Yes. The rent is so expensive, and then there's all the bills. I don't know how Mum ever managed on her own, but at least now I can pay my share.'

'Shouldn't you be at university, having fun clubbing and stuff? Not many people your age are thinking about rent and bills.'

'Yeah, but university isn't for everyone,' Lauren sighed with a frown. She was saved from having to explain further by the arrival of another carer, a tall girl with olive skin and a dark brown ponytail, who introduced herself as Kiera. Sally glanced at her watch and stood up.

'Come on, Lauren, it's time I gave you the tour and explained the daily routines.'

She left her lunch box on the small table alongside Sally's and meekly followed her.

# Chapter Two

As Lauren was getting a tour of the care home, one of the residents was making her way from the dining room towards the front door for her usual afternoon perambulation around the gardens.

'Ah, Margaret, just the person I wanted to see.'

Meg sighed. Felicity Trainer, the care manager, had appeared from the office door and was looking at her condescendingly. 'Really?' Meg murmured quietly, raising a questioning eyebrow at the officious manager.

'I was just looking at the Activities List and I see you haven't signed up for the Nails and Wigs session next month.'

'No, I haven't,' Meg replied tartly, turning to make a quick getaway. Or as quickly as she could for someone with an arthritic hip.

'We do like all our residents to participate in our specially chosen activities, if we're going to make them financially viable,' Felicity continued brightly.

'I thought the cost of all these optional activities was already included in our fees?' Meg enquired scathingly, glancing back over her shoulder as best she could.

'They are, of course they are! But we wouldn't like you to feel left out, now, would we?' enthused Felicity.

'Well, you needn't worry about me: I shan't feel at all left out!' Meg asserted, completing her turn and setting off determinedly towards the door.

'Wouldn't you like to have beautifully manicured nails?' continued Felicity, before realising that she might as well be talking to herself. 'Oh well, of course you don't have to participate if you really don't want to,' she muttered crossly.

*I know*, thought Meg, carefully closing the reassuringly solid door and wondering, not for the first time, why she felt so compelled to obstruct Frau Flic whenever she could. She knew she would probably join in the proposed session with all the others. After all, she had nothing else in her diary, did she?

She took a deep breath of fresh air tinged with the scent of newly mown grass. She looked up at the pale blue sky where little white wisps lingered in the still air and felt the warmth of the summer sun on her wrinkled skin. Her warm brown eyes took in the curvaceous borders filled with lilac and pink asters. She remembered planting asters in her own garden, so long ago. She smiled, and the smile lit up her intelligent face, nicely framed by grey curls that had once been as deep a chestnut as her eyes. Today marked four months to the day since she had arrived at The Cedars, and she was feeling decidedly content.

She set off at a more relaxed pace, following the perfectly flat stone-paved path round the corner of the building, leaving the traffic noise of the main road behind. Wheelchair friendly, she nodded in approval. Not that she needed one of those contraptions, thankfully. Her walking stick, tap-tapping along the path, seemed to taunt her: *not yet, not yet.* Well, it would come eventually, she supposed, unless the hospital could be persuaded that an eighty-one-year-old was worth the time and cost of yet another operation to sort out her badly replaced hip. What was it that young registrar had said on her last visit? *Let's wait and see how it goes, Mrs Thornton. We'll review you again in six months.* What he probably meant was *let's wait until you've departed this earth and then we won't need to waste precious resources on someone so old*. Well, good riddance to him; she fully intended living at least another ten years!

She rounded another corner of the mellow-bricked former rectory, which blended in quite naturally alongside Harnham All Saints' Church, and headed down a smaller path that meandered between beds of roses on one side and colourful dahlias the other. It looped round the main lawn until it found an ornamental fishpond nestled besides a weeping willow. It was a peaceful south-facing spot, not frequented by many of the residents. But, to her annoyance, she saw that her favourite reading spot was already occupied. She came to an abrupt halt with a minor curse that was not as quietly whispered as she had intended it to be. The interloper looked up, startled, a cloud of concern passing over her face.

'Oh, it's you, Meg,' flustered Marianne. 'I didn't think you'd be outside until later. But, of course, it's probably already later than I realised!'

Meg studied the petite eighty-nine-year-old fellow resident with untidy white hair sticking out in all directions, delicate features and a permanent expression of anxiety on her forehead. She was wearing a skirt and blouse that really didn't belong together and a cardigan that was buttoned up incorrectly, creating an uncared-for appearance.

'What on earth do you mean?' The words escaped her lips somewhat harshly, before she could stop herself.

'Oh dear, I didn't mean to sound so muddly.' Marianne looked fit to burst into tears. 'It's just that I usually sit here for a while, to admire the view ... until I see you coming, of course ... and then I go up to the patio to join the others.' She paused. 'If any of the others are there, which they aren't always, you know ...' she trailed off sadly.

'You mean to tell me,' Meg jumped in, 'that you also like to sit on this bench here?'

'Yes.'

'And yet you leave when you see me coming?'

'Well, yes. Everybody knows how attached you've become to this bench since you arrived ... and I wouldn't want you thinking ... well, you know ...'

'No, I don't know!' Meg retorted. 'Am I such an ogre that you feel you can't sit wherever you please?'

'Oh no!' Marianne stood up. 'This is your special place, and I wouldn't dream ... oh!' She put a hand to her mouth in horror. 'No, no, of course I don't think you're an ogre!' She looked more flustered than before, if such a thing were possible.

'Marianne, do sit down, please, before you wet your knickers with worrying so much.'

'Oh,' wailed Marianne, sitting down as abruptly as a well-trained puppy, with big brown eyes to match.

Meg took a deep breath, crossed the invisible chasm between them and sat on the opposite end of the sun-worn wooden bench. 'Yes, this is the bench where I like to come and read if the weather is pleasant enough,' she explained in a kinder voice, 'but, Marianne, this isn't my seat, however much I like it. And you are quite entitled to use it if you happen to get here first.'

'Oh! I didn't mean that this was actually your bench ... y-y-you know ... i-i-it's just ...' Marianne stuttered.

'Yes, I know,' Meg smiled, reassuringly. 'And there really is room for both of us, if we happen to both come down here at the same time.'

'Thank you.' Marianne visibly relaxed, a little smile playing nervously at the corners of her mouth. 'You're so kind!'

'Thank you, but I'm not really that kind, am I? I do tend to rush in and say the first thing that pops into my mind, without thinking it through.' Meg surprised herself with her sudden openness towards her feather-brained fellow resident.

'Well, some people do say that you're a little ... well, er ... sharp-tongued ... I suppose ... not that I agree with them,' Marianne hastened. 'I expect it's because you used to be a teacher, didn't you?' She looked at Meg, who nodded. 'I just wish I could be more like you, you see. I can never think of clever things to say, like you just did. I simply stutter and stumble until I just know that people are thinking what an idiot I am.'

Meg suppressed a nod of agreement. 'Whatever did I say that you thought was supposedly clever?'

'You know. That thing about ... wetting my knickers with worry!'

'Oh Lord ... I'm so sorry ...' Meg started guiltily.

'No, you see, you're so very right! I do worry about every little thing, and you saw that immediately.'

'I didn't mean ...'

'Of course, I don't actually wet my knickers ... well, only if I cough suddenly, or, you know, something like that.' Marianne blushed slightly.

'Oh, I suspect every woman here knows that feeling! A

sudden cough can be disastrous! And God forbid, we sneeze!'

The two ladies each caught the other's eye and burst out laughing. They continued chatting together like old friends. Well, they were both old, and Meg hoped they were becoming friends. She was surprised to find that Marianne, when she wasn't apologising for being alive, had a surprisingly good sense of humour. They contentedly compared notes on their fellow residents: ship-shaped Albert (never Bert), prim and proper Miss Muriel, scatter-brained Sylvia and the others. One of the pleasures of such a small retirement home as The Cedars was the fact that you soon got to know all the other residents. Not like her last home... so huge and impersonal ... but she mustn't think about that. It didn't do to dwell in the past.

Having dispensed with all the residents, they began on the staff. 'What do you think of Felicity?'

'Miss T-T-Trainer?' stuttered Marianne, surprise on her oval face.

'Ms Trainer, you mean!' Meg replied, studying her friend's reaction.

'You know, I've never really understood the way some women insist on being Ms and not just plain old Miss or Mrs. I mean, what's she trying to hide?' Marianne mused thoughtfully.

Meg hesitated; what to say next? 'I expect she's divorced, isn't she?' she asked cautiously.

'Oh, how clever of you,' exclaimed Marianne. 'I expect that'll be it, won't it?'

'Not that I can really imagine anyone being married to our Frau Flic.'

'Oh, I do wish people wouldn't use that dreadful nickname,' frowned Marianne.

'How did she get landed with it?'

'That was Jack's idea; he'd just been watching repeats of *'Allo 'Allo!*

'Ah! Herr Flic of the Gestapo!' Meg smiled.

'Yes, exactly. But I think, well ... despite her bossiness, Felicity is quite attractive, don't you agree?'

'If you like skinny and angular!' Meg bit her lip; better not go down that road. Just because her first husband had run off with someone so remarkably similar to Frau Flic was neither here nor there. You shouldn't judge a book by its cover, and all that.

'Well, don't you think she's just a little too officious?' she suggested carefully.

'Oh yes! And so efficient, too! If there was a Mr Trainer, he'd probably have his day planned out on a roster.' Marianne giggled slightly at the thought.

'And his shirts would be filed by colour in the wardrobe!' Meg joined in the fun.

'And his socks would probably have the days of the week on them ... you know, all arranged in the correct order!'

'And woe betide him if he wears the wrong ones!'

'And as for making love ...' Marianne giggled nervously, wondering if this was a poke too far.

'It would be just like our Saturday exercise classes!' agreed Meg.

'Up, down, up, down, up, down!' they chanted together, before collapsing into hopeless laughter. In that moment, Meg felt that the warm camaraderie that had been developing with Marianne had now blossomed into full-blown friendship.

# Chapter Three

'Are you alone?'

A disembodied head appeared around the office door and hissed rather than spoke. Felicity looked up, tutting with impatience. Why couldn't he just open the door and come in? She raised a neatly plucked eyebrow.

'I thought we might spend a little time together,' he added suggestively.

Her employer sidled stealthily into the room. His black curly hair was untidily ruffled, greying at the sides and slightly thinning on top. But his face was not unattractive as he smiled warmly at Felicity, and she felt a sudden rush of tenderness for him.

'Brenda's gone to the hairdresser's,' he explained. 'She won't be back for hours!'

'Yes, but it's the middle of the afternoon. The residents are mostly up and about,' she objected.

'And most of them are deaf anyway,' he said, softly closing the door and coming to stand behind her. He massaged her shoulders lovingly and a slight frisson of annoyance tingled down her spine. She put a hand up to cover his.

'Later,' she warned.

'He slid his hand under the buttons of her blouse and lifted the gold sweetheart locket that hung discreetly out of sight.

'I thought you appreciated my little gift,' he reminded her.

'Oh, I love it,' she soothed.

'So perhaps we could just slip upstairs now,' he murmured seductively into her ear, his hand moving lower.

'I've got next week's staff rota to finish.' She removed his hand from her breast and tossed her immaculate blonde bob a little impatiently.

'But, darling!'

He wasn't being put off and a flicker of exasperation crossed her face. *Careful*, she thought, swivelling her chair and masking her face with apparent regret.

'I really am very busy,' she pleaded, lips pouting provocatively. He planted a gentle kiss on her waiting lips and reluctantly edged away.

'Later, then. I'll come to you tonight, as soon as Brenda's asleep.'

'Later,' she agreed, 'I'll look forward to it.'

She watched as he straightened his tie and cautiously left the office, before sighing. He was beginning to get a little too ardent for her purposes.

❀

Lauren had just finished her tour with Sally and was about to knock on the office door when Brian all but walked into her. 'Hello again,' he murmured, his face a little too close for comfort. She took a step backwards, only to be subjected to a long lecherous look that swept from her head to her toes and back again. If he hadn't been her employer, she'd have given him what for in no uncertain terms!

'I was looking for Miss Trainer,' she uttered coldly.

'She's in the office,' Brian muttered, before striding off in the direction of the kitchen. Lauren hesitated as she watched his back for a moment and then tapped on the office door, entering as she heard an irritable 'What now?' from inside.

'If you've come to pester me again ...' the care manager began, without looking up from her paperwork.

'Miss Trainer,' Lauren began, wondering what on earth was going on.

Felicity's eyes snapped angrily onto Lauren's as she shot back, 'It's Ms Trainer and don't you forget it.'

'Sorry, Ms Trainer.'

'Well?' Felicity regarded her new care assistant suspiciously. Elfin-like short blonde hair, aquamarine blue eyes and a doe-like expression that she knew only too well would be a fatal attraction for any red-blooded male. She'd have to watch this one, she knew. But then, hiring staff was getting harder and harder these days, and a care manager could hardly afford to be choosy. Lauren was, she admitted, at least keen to learn even if she wasn't the brightest of students.

'Sally says she's finished with me, and I should see you to find out what you want me to do next.' If Lauren had hoped that might involve some actual nursing, then she was disappointed as Ms Trainer launched into yet another lecture. *She certainly likes the sound of her own voice*, Lauren thought.

❁

Lauren finally escaped from the office, having been sent to help Sally with the afternoon teas. She paused outside the office door to quickly check her phone. Oh good, she had a text from Jed. She was in the middle of tapping out a reply to her friend when Mrs Wollstonecraft emerged from the kitchen, two shopping bags in each hand, closely followed by a somewhat flustered-looking Mr Wollstonecraft. Brian was speaking. 'Look here, Bren, you can't . . .'

Lauren managed to slip her phone back into her pocket, just before Brenda spotted her. 'Brian, can we discuss this later, please?' she hissed at her husband. When he seemed about to argue, she lowered her voice further. 'Not in front of the staff!

'Hello, Lauren, how are you settling in?' Brenda beamed at her.

'Okay, I think, Mrs Wollstonecraft.' Lauren smiled nervously.

'That's good. Now, will you take this bag into the day room and give it to Janet, please.'

'Janet?'

'Mrs Smith. She's in a wheelchair, in the corner by the French doors to the garden —'

She was handing one of the bags to Lauren when Brian butted in crossly. 'You haven't been shopping for the residents again!'

'Yes, of course I have,' Brenda replied calmly.

'But you shouldn't run around after them like that, dear. They take advantage of you.'

'I do it because I want to,' she explained patiently, 'and Janet has no visitors to bring her treats.'

'Yes, but —'

'And she is a hundred and one! If she can't enjoy life's little pleasures now, then when?'

'But who pays for these little pleasures?'

'I'll take it out of Janet's purse later, of course. With her knowledge. She wouldn't dream of letting me pay for her things!'

Brenda headed through a door marked private that led down to their personal quarters, leaving Brian outside the office door looking disgruntled and vaguely worried. Lauren started towards the day room but glanced back as she heard the office door open. She couldn't believe the change in Brian's tone of voice as he murmured, 'Felicity!' She whipped round the edge of the day-room door and continued to spy on them.

'Not now, Brian. I need to sort out the treatment room and order some stock.' Felicity blew him a kiss and side-stepped his tentative embrace.

'Later.' She smiled provocatively at him.

'Later!' he returned with a suggestive twitch of his eyebrows.

'Later?' asked Brenda, returning noiselessly and bag-less from their basement flat, much to Brian's surprise.

'Uh, yes,' he stuttered, 'we're going to ... um ... yes, I'm going to check the staff rota ... er ... later.'

Brenda glared at him angrily as he sidled round her and all but ran into the office, slamming the door as if to stop her following.

*Well, that was very interesting*, Lauren thought, as she went to find Mrs Smith.

Mrs Smith turned out to be a wizened old lady with terribly deformed hands reclining in a very fancy-looking wheelchair. She beamed a toothless smile as she thanked Lauren, who couldn't help but think that she was remarkably alert for a hundred and one years old. Lauren paused on her way to the kitchen to dash off a quick WhatsApp message to her mum to tell her about the very aged resident. When she finally got to the kitchen, Sally was just putting a huge pot of tea onto an already laden trolley. 'Come on,' grinned the older carer, 'it's time you met the residents!' Lauren perked up as she followed Sally back to the day room.

※

'I'll pour and you can play waitress,' Sally commanded, pouring tea into a mug decorated with a pretty countryside scene and adding a generous splash of milk.

Lauren nervously approached the resident Sally had directed her to. 'Your tea, Mrs Thornton.'

'Oh, thank you, my dear. And do call me Meg. I don't like all that formal Mrs this and Mr that nonsense.'

Lauren relaxed a little and smiled. 'Would you like a biscuit too, Meg?' she enquired.

'Yes, please, that would be lovely.'

'I'll just go and get you one.' Sally had the next drink waiting for Lauren, as well as the plate of biscuits, which she'd forgotten on the previous trip. 'This one's for Albert Grimshaw.' She pointed as she handed over a mug decorated with a cricketing scene.

'What-ho? Teatime already!' Albert took the proffered mug and then looked at it suspiciously. 'Did you put sugar in it?'

'Um ... I-I-I don't know,' Lauren stammered.

'Well, either you did, or you didn't,' began Albert, a petulant note in his voice.

'Albert, stop messing around. Sally has already sugared your tea, and well you know it,' Meg intervened, smiling reassuringly at Lauren.

'Of course, of course, just my little joke,' chuckled the curmudgeonly old man.

'Would you like a biscuit, Bert?' Lauren offered.

'Bert!' Albert roared indignantly, almost causing Lauren

to drop the plate in shock. 'My name is Albert! Captain Albert Grimshaw, Royal Navy, retired! Always Albert, never Bert, and I'll thank you to remember that!'

'Albert! Do calm down and stop intimidating the poor girl,' scolded Meg sternly.

'Well, these things matter, don't y'know,' Albert muttered as he helped himself to a Rich Tea.

*Being ex-navy explains a lot*, thought Lauren, noting his proud bearing, well-tanned bald head, and comic-book beard and moustache.

'Thank you, Meg,' she whispered, as she turned away from Albert.

'My pleasure.' Meg winked, a friendly twinkle in her eye as she took a chocolate digestive. Lauren decided she liked this resident.

# Chapter Four

'Where's my tea?' demanded a thin lady with a sleek steel-grey bob, as Lauren walked past her. 'Nae-one ever asks me if I want a tea,' she grumbled, her heavily accented words unmistakeably Scottish.

'But . . .'

'I'll take it strong with one sugar, thank you,' she continued, as though Lauren hadn't spoken at all.

'It's okay, dear.' Meg put a reassuring hand on Lauren's arm. 'She's as deaf as a post, is Muriel.'

'I'll just go and get your tea,' Lauren all but shouted into Muriel's startled face.

'There's nae need to shout at me, lassie,' snapped the rather prosaic woman, her spinsterish features frowning at the carer.

'Don't mind Miss MacIntosh,' Sally imparted, as she passed a china cup filled with dark mud-like tea to Lauren. 'But you don't need to shout, either. Just get her attention first, then speak slowly and clearly while she's looking at your face.'

Lauren offered the appropriately thistle-decorated cup and saucer to the prim woman.

'Thank you, m'hen.' Muriel nodded appreciatively at her but refused the plate of biscuits.

*I bet she was a teacher*, Lauren thought. *She looks the type.*

'Ah might be a Scot but I'm nae Miss Jean Brodie,' corrected Muriel, almost as though she had heard the teenager's thoughts.

'Who?' she mumbled.

'Although I doubt you'll know who I mean.'

Lauren's mouth dropped open.

Sally pressed another two mugs into Lauren's hands.

'That one's for Annie Featherstone,' she indicated a salt-

and-pepper grey-haired lady sitting on one end of a small sofa, 'and that one's for Sylvia Pratt, the lady next to her with the walking frame.'

'Mrs Featherstone?' Lauren offered a stout pottery mug with a cartoon on it.

'For goodness' sake, call me Annie. You're new here, aren't you? First day?'

'Yes, Annie. I'm Lauren.'

'Now that's a pretty name. Perhaps I'll suggest that to my Mandy when she pops out her next little 'un.'

'Oh,' Lauren replied, uncertain how to react.

'Is she expecting a girl this time?' interjected Meg from behind her.

'Oh yes, didn't I tell you? She had her scan last week. Look, I've got a picture here, somewhere.' Annie fumbled in a capacious bright purple handbag as Lauren offered the remaining delicate china mug to the other occupant on the sofa, a beautifully coiffured and blue-rinsed lady.

'What's this, dear?'

'It's your tea, Mrs Pratt,' she smiled.

'Oh, it isn't teatime yet, is it?'

'Yes. It's after four,' she replied.

'Really? I thought I'd only just had lunch.'

'That was more than three hours ago, dear,' Annie explained to Sylvia. 'She's a bit forgetful,' she directed to Lauren, 'well, more than a bit, really. Poor dear.'

'Did you say someone's having a baby?' Sylvia looked round-eyed at Annie. 'Is it one of the staff? You don't suppose it's that nice Sally, do you?'

'No, Sylvie. My granddaughter Mandy's expecting her second.' She looked up at Lauren. 'This'll be my third great-grandchild,' she announced proudly.

'Great-grandchild?'

'Yes, dear, I've got six children, three of each. Fifteen grandchildren. And two great-grandchildren, with another one on the way!' Lauren reeled at the thought of such a huge family.

'How ever do you manage Christmas presents for that many?' she burst out.

'Oh, I'll get busy with my knitting needles as soon as the cooler weather comes along. They all know what to expect from me.' Lauren smiled at a sudden memory of hand-knitted jumpers from her own grandmother.

'Did you say that Felicity was expecting a baby?' mused Sylvia. 'Only I don't think she's married, you know.'

'No, Sylvia. I said Mandy, my granddaughter.'

'You know, you don't have to be married to have a baby these days!'

Sylvia looked shocked at Meg's suggestion, but Annie just chuckled, 'Oh, I know that.'

Bewildered, Lauren returned to the tea trolley to find Sally waiting for her. 'Just a tip, Lauren, try not to get chatting to the residents until after all the teas have been distributed. The last one'll be cold at this rate!'

'Sorry.'

'No need to apologise, but if I don't tell you, you won't learn, will you?' Sally explained, wearily brushing a tendril of hair away from her face.

'And these two?' Lauren nodded towards a pretty china cup with dusky-pink flowers on it and a rather odd-shaped plastic beaker with a lid and spout, which looked suspiciously like something you'd give to a toddler.

'The china cup is for Marianne Chadwick, over by the bookcase. The beaker is for Janet—'

'Oh, I know which one's Janet!' interrupted Lauren, pleased to show that she at least knew this one small fact. 'She's the little old biddy by the French doors!'

There was a moment of disapproving silence from the residents. Lauren coloured under their gaze and looked to Sally for reassurance.

'We don't use language like that in front of the residents,' Sally explained quietly.

'Language? It's not like I said fuck or something!'

There was an audible intake of breath around the room.

'No, but you have done, now, so let's hope you haven't given anyone a heart attack! And if Felicity had heard you ... well, you'd be out of the door already!'

Lauren had the grace to look taken aback at her gaff.

'Lauren, we never call any of our ladies a biddy, it's really disrespectful. And we certainly never call anyone old!'

'But ...'

'Listen, I know it, you know it ... they all know it ... but old is a word we just don't use here!'

Lauren's head dropped and she delivered the two drinks in silence, getting a shaky smile from Marianne and a disapproving frown from Janet.

'Is that it?' she muttered sullenly to Sally.

'One more,' replied Sally, pouring into a large Union Jack mug as she spoke.

Lauren looked round the day room with a puzzled frown. 'But they've all got tea!'

'Not yet,' Sally smiled. 'Wait a moment ... and ... three, two, one ...'

The day-room door was pushed open with such vigour that it crashed into the arm of Muriel's chair. 'Whatever now?' she protested indignantly.

''Just me!' grinned a short and slightly rotund figure, winking broadly at Muriel, who surprised Lauren by simpering like a teenager.

'Look here, Jack! You could've hurt someone badly by throwing the door open like that, don't y'know!' Albert positively simmered with indignation.

'Nonsense,' bantered Jack, 'better I hurt someone badly than I hurt them really well, don't you think?'

'What?' Albert barked at him.

'Isn't that right, Sylvia?' Jack flashed a cheeky smile across the room.

'Oh, um, I'm not really sure, Jack. I don't think anyone should be hurting anyone else.'

'But better I'm bad at hurting someone than really good at it, eh?' he said with a wink.

'Well, yes. I suppose so.'

'Damn nonsense!' Albert growled at Jack.

'Jack, come and get your tea before it's completely cold,' intervened Sally, before Jack, a mischievous twinkle in his eye, could reply.

'Albert, don't you have something you wanted to say,

now that everyone's here?' Meg calmly reminded him, drawing his attention away from his protagonist.

'Ah yes, well remembered, m'dear.' He put his empty mug carefully onto a side table before pushing himself unsteadily to his feet and clearing his throat. Jack, meanwhile, circled round to sit beside Sylvia, much to her obvious delight.

'Now then, as you all know, we have a new member of staff with us today.'

Lauren glanced up in surprise.

'Fantastic news!' exclaimed Jack. 'Just what this place needs, some new blood.' He winked at Sylvia, who giggled.

Albert fired daggers from under his bushy eyebrows but declined to acknowledge the interruption to his carefully prepared speech.

'And being such a tight-knit little family as we are, I propose we welcome her in our usual way.'

Much to Lauren's embarrassment, the residents of The Cedars started a round of applause, some struggling to their feet, others staying as they were, knowing they wouldn't get on their feet before it was time to sit down again. She blushed, unsure how to respond. Sally prodded her gently. 'This is where you introduce yourself.'

'Thank you,' Lauren began, then abruptly stopped.

'Come on, m'dear. Speak up and don't be shy!' encouraged Albert.

'Yeah, no need to be shy around any of us!' chortled Jack. 'After all, once you've wiped all of our bums, you'll be part of the family!'

'Jack!' several voices groaned together, as Lauren blushed an even deeper shade of rose.

'It's okay,' reassured Sally, 'you won't really have to do that. Some of our residents,' she glared at Jack, 'are quite capable of wiping their own bums!' Lauren gulped and nodded. 'So, just tell everyone your name and where you live. Perhaps a little bit about your previous job, if you like. And your family. Stuff like that.'

'Well, I'm Lauren Peachy,' she began.

'Looking very peachy to me,' murmured Jack.

'... and I'm nineteen.'

'Oh, to be so young again,' sighed Marianne.

'... and I live in Downton with my mum. There's just the two of us.'

'Poor dear, no other family?' sympathised Annie.

'After I left school, I did an NVQ in Health and Social Care at the college. I've always wanted to work with people.'

'So nice to know we've got such an enthusiastic carer,' put in Meg.

'What's she saying?' demanded Muriel irritably. 'I do wish people would stop mumbling so.'

'Thank you, Lauren,' intervened Sally. 'And thank you to Albert for welcoming her.' Lauren breathed a sigh of relief.

'Now, if you collect up the empty cups, I can get rid of the tea trolley while you spend a little bit of time getting to know our residents,' instructed Sally.

# Chapter Five

Just then, Mrs Wollstonecraft came in, so Lauren busied herself collecting the cups and returning them to Sally's trolley. Brenda crossed the room, nodding at or exchanging a few friendly words with each of the residents, before sitting quietly beside Janet, who immediately scrabbled around in her specially made wheelchair, looking for something. Lauren decided to leave the beaker, afraid of interrupting.

'Why don't they all have the same type of cup?' she asked Sally, curious about the odd assortment of crockery.

'It's all part of treating them as individuals,' Sally explained, 'we offer them a choice when they first arrive, cup and saucer, or a mug. Some of our ladies can't handle a heavy mug, whereas others prefer it. And we encourage them to provide their own mug.It's so much more personal then.'

'And Janet's beaker?'

'Have you noticed how her hands tremble when she lifts anything? It's due to her medication. A beaker is safer, so she can't spill hot tea all over herself.'

'Oh, I didn't notice.'

'Well, in this job it pays to notice all their little habits and mannerisms. When something changes, that's when you worry. Now, go and talk to some of the residents.' Sally pushed the trolley out into the hallway and headed for the kitchen.

Lauren looked around the day room and made for the resident she'd felt an instant affinity to: Meg. 'Do you mind if I sit a while with you?' she asked awkwardly.

'Not at all, my dear,' smiled Meg, indicating the chair recently vacated by Albert, who had just left the room. Lauren sat down.

'Tell me a bit more about yourself,' suggested Meg.

To her surprise, Lauren found herself confiding in Meg about her dad's accident and her mum's cancer diagnosis. These weren't things she usually felt comfortable talking about, but there was something about this resident that inspired trust. She was a good listener and she seemed to genuinely understand.

'What did you used to do?' she asked.

'I was a secondary school teacher for all my working life. I taught English. Although I was also the SENCO, that's the Special Educational Needs Co-ordinator, for many years. And I became deputy head towards the end of my career.'

Lauren wished she'd had a teacher like this to talk to when her dad had died. Maybe she wouldn't have dropped out of school if she'd had someone like Meg around to support her.

'What about family?' she asked shyly. 'Do you have children and grandchildren, like Annie?'

'I was married twice but we didn't have children,' Meg stated in a matter-of-fact voice, 'which, in the case of my first marriage, was a good thing because my husband left me for another woman.'

'Oh, I'm so sorry,' gasped Lauren.

'Water under the bridge, now, dear,' Meg reassured her. 'My second husband was a much nicer man. But he had a responsible job and worked all hours, like me, so we decided that having children wasn't a good idea.'

'He was a teacher too?' asked Lauren.

'No.' Meg paused. 'I don't tell everyone this, but he was a detective chief inspector.'

'Wow,' Lauren replied in awe.

'Yes, I used to love hearing about all his cases and trying to help him to solve them. Not that he was supposed to tell me any details, of course. But he knew I wouldn't tell another soul.'

At that moment, Brenda approached. Apologising to Meg for interrupting, she addressed Lauren. 'Do you remember, I asked you to take a bag to Janet earlier?' Lauren nodded. 'Did you happen to see Janet's purse lying around when you were with her?'

'Oh, I found a little black purse on the floor after I gave the bag to her.'

'And?'

'I picked it up and put it on the table next to her.'

Brenda looked across at a small black table covered with magazines and newspapers, with several packets of sweets amid the muddle.

'Ah, that explains it! Only Janet was sure she'd tucked it into her chair.' Brenda tidied the items on the table, retrieving the purse, before turning to pass the plastic beaker to Lauren. 'I think you missed this; you'd better take it down to the kitchen before Sally finishes the washing-up.'

Lauren grabbed the beaker and hurried down to the kitchen. She came back a great deal more slowly, wondering why caring for the elderly included boring things like washing up. She leant against the wall by the office and checked her phone, having felt a ping in her pocket.

'Lauren?' queried a worried-looking Brenda coming from the day room. Lauren jumped and quickly hid her phone.

'Did you open Janet's purse when you found it?'

'No,' she replied defensively. 'Course I didn't.'

'Well, Janet swears there's a ten-pound note missing.'

'But how would she know? She's so old . . .'

'Don't go there! Janet might be our eldest resident, but she has more wits about her than most of the others put together.'

Lauren swallowed uncomfortably, the back of her eyes pricking just a little. It was so unfair! She was trying really hard, but she couldn't seem to get anything right. She opened her mouth to protest then left it hanging open as she saw the dishiest bloke ever come out of the kitchen.

'Evening, Mrs W,' he beamed at Brenda. 'Ooh, and who do we have here?'

He looked down at Lauren and she felt her knees buckle slightly. A little above medium height with a nicely sculptured body, blond hair sticking up in little spikes like a hairbrush, though she could see the dark roots underneath, and the most amazing green eyes.

'Hi there,' she said, smiling flirtatiously.

'Hi there, yourself.' He offered his hand. 'Paul.'

'Lauren,' she replied. Perhaps this place wasn't going to be so bad after all.

'Evening, Paul. Can you just give Lauren and me a moment, please?' interjected Brenda.

'Anything to oblige, Mrs W, you know me!'

Lauren's heart sank as she realised that she wasn't off the hook yet.

'I told you, all I did was pick the purse up off the floor,' she protested.

Paul stopped at the door to the day room and spun round on his heels.

'Whose purse is that, then?' he breezed cheerfully.

'Janet appears to be missing a ten-pound note from her purse,' Brenda explained, much to Lauren's shame.

'Really? Well, I didn't see a tenner in her purse yesterday when she asked me to take her lottery money out. Just two fivers and a few coins.'

Lauren could have cheerfully kissed him for that. In fact, she'd really rather be kissing him instead of standing there like a lemon.

'Thanks,' she began.

'That still doesn't explain why Janet is missing a ten-pound note,' warned Brenda.

'She probably just got confused,' protested Lauren.

'I told you, Janet doesn't get confused, does she, Paul?'

'Oh no, she's amazingly with it, is dear little Janet. If she says there was a ten-pound note in her purse, then there was a ten-pound note in her purse. No doubting it at all!'

'Exactly,' said Brenda.

'Oh-kay,' replied Lauren hotly, feeling tears prickle her eyes, 'but I didn't steal it.'

'I never said you did,' Brenda exclaimed, 'I was only going to ask if you had seen it there or not, which question Paul has now adequately answered.'

'Oh,' muttered Lauren.

'Ooh,' bantered Paul, 'were you jumping to the wrong conclusions there, Pixie? Once you get to know Mrs W, you'll find that she's nothing if not fair.'

'Sorry,' Lauren muttered, embarrassment flushing across her face again. Whatever must he be thinking of her?

'C'mon.' He linked his arm through hers and pulled her into the day room. 'Let's go and play detectives.'

Brenda stifled a smile. Pixie was an appropriate nickname for the elfin-like girl, but she hoped she wasn't getting any ideas about Paul. She'd soon be disappointed there.

# Chapter Six

After dinner, Meg wandered into the day room and made her way purposefully towards Janet, who had been restored to her favourite spot with its view of the back garden.

'Janet?' Meg said softly.

'Yes, dear,' she replied, with twinkling eyes and a remarkably firm voice. At a hundred and one, her brain had far outlasted her body, which was grotesquely contorted with osteoarthritis and now weakened by severe osteoporosis.

Meg sat down in the chair where Brenda had sat earlier and leant forward conspiratorially. 'Did Brenda find out where your ten-pound note had got to?'

'No, I'm afraid she didn't. And although those two young carers have promised to search my room for it, I doubt I'll see that again,' Janet said quietly. 'I know it was in my purse when they brought me down yesterday morning, but it wasn't there when Paul took my lottery money yesterday afternoon. So, it disappeared from here, in this day room.'

'You don't think ...?'

'Oh no, Paul wouldn't do a thing like that!' Janet exclaimed. 'Paul always takes two pounds on a Tuesday afternoon. He gets my lottery tickets on his way home. He's such a kind lad.'

'Sorry, yes, I didn't mean to accuse Paul. I was just wondering ...'

'Yes?'

'Is there any other staff member who you think might have taken it?'

'You already have someone in mind, perhaps?' Janet suggested.

'Well, what are your views on Ms Trainer?'

'You think there's something off about her, don't you?' asked Janet.

'Yes, I'm afraid I do.'

'What is it?'

'Oh, I really shouldn't say!'

'Hmm! I would hazard a guess that you've come across our care manager somewhere before you moved here.' Meg jumped a little at Janet's perspicacity. 'Oh yes. I saw the shocked expression on your face when you first arrived. And you've been studiously avoiding her ever since.'

'You don't miss much, do you?' Meg remarked carefully.

'No, I don't,' replied Janet modestly.

'Confidentially?'

'Of course. I don't like idle gossip.'

'Well, I'm sure Ms Trainer used to be a certain Mrs March I came across a while ago.'

'So, she's divorced then?'

'Yes, possibly. That would explain the change of surname.'

'But why would you suspect her of stealing?'

'I lived in another care home before coming here, in the New Forest. I used to meet up with a friend of mine for afternoon tea in Lyndhurst from time to time. You know, they serve the most delicious homemade jam in that tearoom in the town centre.'

'Go on.'

'Yes, well, Patricia, the friend I mentioned, was telling me about a suspicious death in the care home where her sister lived.'

'A suspicious death?'

'Yes. According to Pat's sister, a resident named Tony was found dead in his bed one morning.'

'Hardly that suspicious, in an old people's home!' Janet cackled.

'No, of course not. But the night staff swore that he'd been as hale and hearty as usual when they'd taken in his early cup of tea.'

'A sudden heart attack? Or a stroke, perhaps?'

'Apparently, they did a post-mortem, because his daughter insisted on it, and they couldn't find any sign of either.'

'Most peculiar.'

'Yes, that's what Pat said. Well, I wasn't really listening all that carefully. I mean, I'd never met Pat's sister, let alone this Tony who died.'

'Quite.'

'But just as she was describing the senior care assistant at her sister's home, a Mrs March, I heard someone enter through the street door behind me and poor Pat's face went as white as a sheet. I asked her whatever was wrong.'

'It was this Mrs March?'

'Yes! She whispered to me that Mrs March herself had just walked into the tearoom!'

'So, was she involved in this Tony's death?'

'That's what Pat thought. Of course, I thought she was being a little fanciful. Anyway, she was rambling on about money going missing and a book that disappeared and other little mysteries. And I said, even if the woman was dishonest enough to steal things, it didn't make her a murderer.'

'Of course not! What changed your mind?'

'Apparently, Tony had caught this Mrs March in the act, so to speak. Trying to steal his watch when she thought he was asleep! He was going to report her to the matron.'

'And then Tony mysteriously died before he could?'

'Yes, exactly.'

'Probably just a coincidence.'

'That's what I said. But the following week, Pat phoned me in floods of tears, to cancel our afternoon tea.'

'Oh dear.'

'Her sister, Mary, had just passed away that morning. Suddenly and inexplicably, just like Tony. And the care home had announced they were going to launch an investigation, seeing as they'd had two unexpected deaths in a week.'

'And what was the outcome?'

'Unfortunately, I don't know.' As Janet looked disappointed at the anti-climax, Meg hastily continued. 'You see, that was just at the beginning of the COVID pandemic.'

'Ah, I see.'

'Yes, you remember how that turned all our lives upside down. The home was shut off from the outside world for so long, all outside things were forgotten. It was like we were trapped in a prison for months on end.' She shuddered at the memory. It was one of the reasons why she'd decided to move to a smaller care home.

'Yes, indeed,' Janet nodded, 'those were terrible times. But why do you think our Ms Trainer is your Mrs March?'

'I saw her, you see, in a mirror on the wall behind Pat. She had longer, darker hair, which is why I'm not completely sure, but she had exactly the same skinny and kind of angular-looking body. You know what I mean, all elbows and shoulders and no curves to speak of.'

'I see. Well, she could quite easily have cut and dyed her hair, of course.'

'That's what I thought!'

'Interesting.'

'You will keep this to yourself, won't you?' Meg asked anxiously, looking around to check no one in the day room was listening. Apart from Jack and Marianne watching TV, the others all seemed to have gone elsewhere.

'I told you, I don't like gossiping,' Janet bristled.

'Of course, I'm so grateful. I just thought that, perhaps, we could keep an eye on Felicity between us to see if she does anything to give herself away.'

'Don't you worry,' said Janet firmly, 'I've been watching Ms Trainer for quite some time already.'

'Really?'

'Yes, but I won't say any more than that, for the time being.'

'But you have seen something amiss?'

'Oh yes.'

※

Brenda and Brian were in their basement flat with the TV on. Brenda wasn't so much watching TV as listening to it whilst she surreptitiously studied Brian's face. He was lounging on the sofa, feet up on their coffee table. His hair was combed neatly, and he appeared to have washed his face since dinner, as the smudge of curry sauce had disappeared from his chin. And she was sure she could detect a slight whiff of toothpaste. Very suspicious. His face was relaxed as he chuckled occasionally at the sitcom they were watching, and she thought wistfully of how they'd met, all those years ago on holiday in Tunisia.

He had been lounging just like this in the hotel bar, feet up on a table, when she'd accidentally barged into him on her way to the bar. Brian had jumped up, apologising furiously. And, being ever so slightly drunk, she had fallen about laughing at him. He'd bought her a drink and chatted her up. Eventually, they found themselves strolling along the water's edge. A huge golden moon had been shining romantically across the sea and she had fallen in love.

She shook her head furiously, silly idiot that she had been. But she had loved Brian then, without a doubt, and he had loved her every bit as much. The early years had been happy, despite Brian losing first one job and then another. Their son, Dominic, had come along in '88 and her life had been full; working, raising Dom, housework, gardening, and propping up Brian every time another great business idea had failed. After Dom had left for university, she contemplated leaving too. But, in the end, she couldn't bring herself to do it. Then, Brian's dad had died, leaving what seemed like a small fortune. That's when Brian had proposed his greatest business idea of all: opening a residential care home. With her nursing experience and his business acumen, what could possibly go wrong?

They'd trudged around old houses, eventually finding this one on the outskirts of Salisbury. It was an old rectory in what had once been the village of East Harnham, though it was now no more than a suburb on the southern fringes of the city. They'd scrubbed and decorated and polished until the woodwork sang. Proudly, they had opened to their first five residents. They had extended since then, adding three bedrooms above a big bright new kitchen on what had once been a vegetable plot. They'd also had the lift installed.

At first, she had managed everything herself, working sometimes fourteen hours a day. Then, with the money coming in steadily, the lovely Miss Bell had responded to their advertisement for a live-in care manager. Brenda had continued managing the accounts, covering her care manager's off-duty hours and ensuring the home retained its warm family feeling, whilst Tessa Bell organised the staff and managed the daily running of the home. It was a good arrangement that allowed her to spend more time with her beloved residents. But, two years ago, Tessa had moved up north with her new husband and Ms Trainer had arrived in her place. Oh, her references had been glowing all right, and she was undoubtedly very efficient. But she had seen the way Brian looked at Felicity. It was the same look she had seen on that beach, long ago in Tunisia.

At that moment, the programme Brian had been watching finished. He switched off the TV and stood up. 'Just going to pop upstairs to finish those statistics for the Health and Safety people,' he said airily.

'What, at this time of night?' Brenda asked incredulously.

'Well, they won't do themselves, will they?' he snapped.

'Do you want me to come and help?' she offered.

'No need, you get yourself off to bed. Don't wait up for me.' He rushed off before she had time to reply.

Her heart thumped uncomfortably under her ribcage. He was going to her again, wasn't he? *Don't be so silly*, she told herself. *You don't know that he's having an affair. This could all be in your imagination.*

# Chapter Seven

Meg had settled off to sleep quite quickly for once but woke about an hour later with cramp in her left calf. She tried straightening out her leg and wiggling her foot, but that just made the pain worse. Reluctantly, she swung her legs over the side of the bed and reached down to massage her calf until the pain had subsided. But now she'd moved, the inevitable happened and she needed the bathroom. She shuffled into her ensuite, grateful that she didn't need to leave the warmth of her bedroom. As she sat in the dim glow of the safety night light, she thought she heard someone calling 'Hello!' How strange at this time of night! She washed her hands and softly went to her bedroom door, easing it open just an inch to peer into the hallway.

'Hel-lo-oh!' called a male voice more clearly and this time she recognised it.

'Brian,' whispered back a female voice on the stairs, just out of sight.

'Why are you trying to avoid me?' Brian hissed from downstairs.

'I'm not. I thought it might have been Brenda in the office.'

'Well, it wasn't,' he said, coming up one stair.

'Where do you think you're going?' whispered the female through clenched teeth.

'I promised I'd come to you later.' He ascended another stair. 'Guess what!' He came closer still. 'It's later!'

Meg heard a groan. 'I suppose you'd better come up then.'

Brian positively jumped up the next few stairs and there was the sound of kissing and a little shriek of shock, or was it delight? 'Shh!' giggled the woman, 'someone will hear.'

'You've been drinking.' He sounded disappointed.

'Just the one,' she reassured him.

'Without me?'

'Well, of course, without you. You could hardly have come with me, could you? I think Brenda would've noticed that.'

With a shock, Meg recognised the female voice as Felicity.

'Who were you drinking with?' Brian demanded.

'Just some friends.'

'Which friends?'

Felicity groaned in frustration. There was a brief pause, a sigh of ... was that pleasure? ... and then Felicity giggled. 'C'mon. Let's go up to my room and have some fun!'

'Come on then,' Brian murmured throatily, leading her up the stairs. Meg drew back into her doorway as they came into view, behaving in a most unseemly way. They turned the lower staircase light out and hurried up the second staircase, putting that light out too as they reached Felicity's second-floor flat. Meg breathed a sigh of relief when she heard the door shut above her, grateful that she hadn't been spotted.

What was all that about? Clearly, Brian and Felicity were having an affair. Maybe that was what Janet had alluded to earlier. *Poor Brenda, I wonder if she knows.*

Shivering a little, she allowed her door to quietly close itself and returned to her nice warm bed. No sooner was she comfortable than she thought she heard another noise.

She sat up and turned her lamp on. Did it matter? Of course not, she told herself. It could be one of the night staff or another resident moving around. Or maybe it came from upstairs. She shuddered at the thought. Or what if it was Brenda, downstairs? Unable to contain her curiosity, Meg slid out of bed again, wrapping her summer dressing gown snuggly around herself this time. Once again, she eased open her bedroom door a crack. She listened but the house was silent. She proceeded cautiously along the landing to stand outside the staffroom, her back to the wall, listening. No sound at all. She risked a little peek around the door, trying to think of an excuse in case one of the carers was awake. But the room was empty. Could they still be in one of the other rooms, settling a restless resident?

She continued along the corridor, listening outside each room but, apart from a few snores, there were no other noises to indicate where the carers might be. Perhaps they were downstairs. Without really knowing why she was so doggedly pursuing such a trivial matter, she headed back to the top of the stairs. She would normally use the lift, but that would be too noisy at this time of night. She peered uncertainly down the staircase, wondering if her hip could cope with going down and still get her back up again. The sound of a door clicking shut on the top floor brought her to her senses. It wouldn't do to be caught standing there! She tiptoed as fast as her stiff legs would allow back in the direction of her bedroom, but she was too slow. Feet pattered lightly down the stairs and Meg turned to see Brian, just in the same split second that he realised that someone was on the landing.

'Meg!' he spluttered, clearly shaken.

'Good night, Brian,' she said firmly as she reached her bedroom.

'Do sleep well,' she murmured politely as she pretended to close her door.

'Shit!' Brian swore loudly and was answered by Brenda calling softly from the hall below.

'Brian?'

Meg's heart was in her mouth. As she heard Brian hurry down the stairs, she tiptoed back out onto the landing so that she could hear them.

'What are you doing?' Brenda asked anxiously.

'I was going to ask you that,' Brian retorted indignantly. 'I thought you were tucked up asleep in bed,' he complained, as though it could only be her fault that she wasn't.

'Where have you been?' insisted Brenda.

'I was just checking something with the night staff,' he said airily as he descended a few more stairs. 'Why? Where did you think I'd been?'

Meg could scarcely hear Brenda's muttered reply. She risked descending a couple of stairs and gingerly sat down on the top step, just able to peer through the balusters to see the lower half of the staircase.

'You weren't having silly, suspicious thoughts about me, were you?' Brian demanded, his hand grasping Brenda's jaw so that she was forced to look into his eyes.

'Of course not,' Brenda demurred, pulling away from him. Brian let her go, watching her scornfully. Meg could see from the heaving of Brenda's shoulders that she was probably crying, and her heart went out to the poor woman. Once Brenda had disappeared from sight, Brian slowly descended after her.

Meg struggled to stand up and was returning to her room when she heard the voices of the two night carers, Sonia and Jan, coming up the stairs behind her. Evidently, they hadn't seen either Brenda or Brian. But it confirmed what she had known already, namely that Brian had told Brenda a bare-faced lie when he said he'd been upstairs to talk to the night staff.

They rounded the turn in the staircase, steaming mugs in hand, stopping when they saw Meg. 'Are you all right, Meg?' solicited Sonia.

'Just thought I heard a noise,' Meg replied innocently.

'I'm sorry,' replied Jan, 'that was probably us going down to the kitchen to get a decent coffee. They only put that instant stuff in the staff lounge, but Andy's got one of those pod machines in the kitchen. He doesn't mind us using it.'

Meg nodded her understanding.

'It does a nice hot chocolate too, if you'd like us to go and make you one?' offered Sonia.

'Oh no, thank you so much, but another drink now will only have me up to the bathroom again before the night's out.'

'Well, get yourself back to bed and try to sleep,' advised Jan.

'I will. Goodnight.'

'Sleep tight,' called Sonia as Meg closed her door.

# Chapter Eight

*Tuesday 6th September 2022*

In the chilly early morning, Lauren was walking along Harnham Road towards The Cedars, hands in pockets, earbuds in place listening to Dua Lipa. She'd been at The Cedars for three weeks now and was beginning to settle in. She was getting to know the staff and residents better. The only person she couldn't fathom out was Paul. She got along well with him, but despite all her flirting he still hadn't asked her out.

She didn't see him waving from across the road, so when he rushed up behind her and tapped her shoulder, she nearly jumped out of her skin.

'Morning, Pixie!' he grinned.

'You scared the shit out of me then!' she complained, taking her buds out and shoving them in her pocket.

'Ooh, touchy, aren't we?' he mocked.

'No.' She grinned back at him. 'And if you're going to insist on calling me Pixie, you need a nickname too.'

'Who, me? Oh, I don't think so!'

'So you say!' She took a deep breath and put on her most seductive face. 'How about we grab a pint after work tonight? We can discuss it some more then.'

Paul hesitated, an invisible cloud passing across his eyes.

Oh God, he obviously didn't fancy her. 'Of course, if you've already got a girlfriend ...' she backpedalled.

'Not at the moment, and not bloody likely!' he chuckled.

'What then?' She stared at him. He pulled a few faces at her.

'Oh!' she gasped.

'And the penny drops!' he chuckled.

'Me and my big mouth!'

'S'okay. We can still be mates,' he said with a wink. They continued in silence until they reached The Cedars, Lauren wondering how on earth she could have missed noticing that Paul was gay. No wonder all her best chat-up lines had fallen flat!

They turned onto the driveway and made their way round the house to the back door. Inside, they kept up the banter as they took turns in the changing cubicle then went through the kitchen to the office, where Paul knocked on the door. Felicity issued a curt 'Come in,' and they entered the dragon's lair. 'You're both here? Good. Paul, I want you to work upstairs with Lauren this morning. But leave Janet in her room, for now. She's not feeling so well.'

'Nothing serious, I hope?' Paul asked, genuinely concerned.

'Probably not, but I've called Dr Baker, just in case. He'll drop in sometime in the next hour or two.' With that, Felicity's attention returned to the computer monitor, and Paul beckoned Lauren to follow him.

'Oh, now there's a treat. You'll get to meet the delicious Doctor Baker, at last,' said Paul as they went up the stairs.

'Who?'

He rolled his eyes at her, moving to one side as Jack came thundering down the stairs. 'Good morning, Jack, and how are you?' Paul asked.

'Fine, Paul, thanks for asking. And how's our lovely Pixie this morning?' He winked at Lauren, who blushed. 'Have you seen old Stone-face this morning?'

'Not yet but he's probably in the dining room, overseeing breakfast.'

'Well, I'd better get on down there, then, before Andy runs out of bacon. Can't miss my morning bacon, can I?'

Jack trotted downstairs and Lauren remembered what she'd been about to ask Paul.

'How come I haven't met this Dr Baker before?'

'He's been on holiday for the last three weeks. All right for some, isn't it?'

It was ten to ten before Dr Baker finally arrived, by which time all the residents, apart from Janet, were in the day room. Paul, who'd been showing Lauren what was where in the treatment room, bounced into the hall as soon as he heard his voice.

'Good morning, Doctor Phil!'

'Morning, Paul,' the doctor replied.

'Did you have a good holiday?'

'Yes, thanks, the weather was excellent.'

'You were cycling in France, weren't you?' Paul asked.

'Yes, that's right. A group of us were following La Vélodyssée, that's the Atlantic Coast Cycle route from Roscoff down to Santander in Spain. It was—'

He was interrupted when Felicity appeared from the office. 'Ah, hello, Doctor. Nice of you to grace us with an appearance at last. Janet's up in her room.' With which she abruptly turned before he'd had time to reply and all but marched up the stairs.

'Good luck,' mouthed Paul.

'I might just need it, with her in that mood,' muttered the doctor as he followed behind.

Lauren stared open-mouthed at Paul as he returned to the treatment room.

'You fancy him, don't you?' she demanded.

Paul coloured slightly, considered arguing then sighed.

'Yeah, but I've got about as much chance there as you have with me!' He gave a wry smile, and Lauren, feeling sorry for him, gave him a quick hug.

※

Ten minutes later, Felicity and the doctor returned, chatting earnestly as they entered the treatment room.

'... and I'll check all the prescriptions today, save me coming back on Friday, if that's okay with you, Felicity?'

'You won't be coming on Friday then?' she replied tartly.

'Not unless any of the residents need me,' he replied. 'Oh, I'm sorry, I don't think we've met?' His friendly gaze fell on Lauren, who realised that the doctor was, indeed, almost as dishy as Paul had intimated. In a kind of Harrison Ford way.

'This is Lauren Peachy, our new care assistant.' Felicity waved a hand in her general direction.

'Lauren, this is Dr Baker.'

'Hello.'

'Dr Baker usually visits us on a Friday to check that all our residents are well, and no one needs a new prescription for anything.'

'That's kind of you,' began Lauren.

'Stuff and nonsense, it's his job,' snapped Felicity. Just then, the phone rang in the office and a flicker of annoyance crossed her face.

'Shall I get that?' offered Paul.

'No, it'll be Janet's granddaughter. I left a message for her to call me back.'

'Well, don't let me stop you,' sighed the doctor, with evident relief. Felicity gave him a black look then hurried over to the office.

'Right, prescriptions, please, Paul.'

Paul passed a yellow folder down from one of the shelves and watched as the doctor checked each prescription against the items in the locked medicine cupboard, before opening the padlock on a small fridge and searching in there.

'Problem?' asked Paul.

'Not really, I just can't find any spare insulin for Jack,' he replied. 'I'd better write a prescription, if you could make sure someone takes it to the pharmacy, please.'

'Of course I will,' answered Paul.

The doctor looked at Lauren and smiled.

'Now then, young lady. Do you know what insulin is used for?'

'Diabetes,' she promptly replied.

'Very good!'

Paul looked at Lauren in surprise.

'I've been learning about all the patients' medical conditions,' she explained.

The doctor finished scribbling his signature and handed the script to Paul.

'I'll see you next week, I expect.'

He left the treatment room in a hurry, clearly hoping to escape the house before Felicity finished on the phone, but he ran into Brenda in the hallway.

'Brenda,' he beamed.

'Phil!'

'How are you?'

Brenda's lip wobbled but she swallowed and managed a croaky 'Okay, thanks.'

'Oh, like that, is it?' sympathised the doctor. 'Well, if you ever need a shoulder to cry on ...'

'... I know where to find you,' finished Brenda, with half a smile. They held each other's eyes for a few seconds longer than was strictly necessary, before Brenda excused herself and slid into the office. The doctor gazed wistfully after her for a moment then turned and left the house.

'Did I just see that?' breathed Lauren, who had been watching.

'What?'

'The doctor's got the hots for Mrs W.'

'Nonsense,' said Paul, stomping out of the treatment room and almost running into Marianne in the hallway.

Lauren had intended following Paul, but he'd already disappeared by the time she came out of the treatment room. Then she spotted Marianne feeling through her pockets and patting down her clothes. 'Is everything okay?' she enquired.

'Oh my, how kind of you to ask ... it's just ... I can't seem to find my brooch.' Marianne looked close to tears.

'Is it very precious to you?'

'Yes, it was my mother's ... and her mother's before her ... and her mother's before her too ... I think.'

'Were you wearing it today?' she asked.

'Oh, now that's a good question,' flustered Marianne. 'Do you know, I can't really be sure ... I mean ... I usually wear it all the time.' Her voice trailed off hesitantly.

'How about you go and check your room to see if it's there?' Lauren suggested.

'Oh, that's a good idea!'

'Would you like me to come and help?'

'Oh no, dear, I'm sure it'll probably turn up.' And, with that, Marianne trotted off to the lift. Lauren shrugged her shoulders and went down to the kitchen to get the trolley ready for the morning coffee round.

# Chapter Nine

*Wednesday 7th September 2022*

The next day, Paul was in the day room, tidying a bookcase crammed with books, board games and jigsaw puzzles, when Brenda walked in. 'Mrs W!' he hailed cheerfully.

'Morning, Paul.' She forced a wan smile back.

'You're looking a bit peaky this morning, is anything wrong?'

'Oh, nothing much, I just haven't been sleeping all that well.'

Before he could ask any more questions, she addressed the room. 'I'm just popping into town for something. Is there anything anyone would like me to get for them while I'm out?'

'Would you pick up a *Telegraph* for me, please, Brenda?' Albert looked up from the newspaper on his lap.

Confused, she asked, 'But isn't that the *Telegraph* you're reading?'

'No, it's some dreadful old rag,' he complained, 'it was all that was left on the hall table when I finished breakfast.'

'If you hadn't eaten your breakfast at such a snail's pace, you might not have been last out of the dining room,' teased Jack, waving his copy of the *Sun* at Albert.

'At least I don't shovel my breakfast down my throat as disgustingly fast as you,' bristled Albert, 'nor do I read that kind of gutter press!' he added, wagging a finger at the offending paper.

'Gentlemen! Let's keep it friendly, shall we?' soothed Brenda.

'Sorry, Mrs W,' winked Jack, not in the slightest abashed.

'Disgraceful!' Albert muttered.

'Don't worry, Albert, I'll get you a *Telegraph* while I'm out.'

'Thanks, m'dear. You're an absolute angel.'

'Does anyone else want anything?' she asked. No one replied so she let out a long sigh and decided to head off straight away. She really didn't feel up to work today.

Paul finished tidying and dusting the bookshelves and strolled over to Sylvia, in her usual spot on the settee. 'You okay, love?' he enquired, noticing the slightly puzzled frown on her forehead and plonking himself down beside her.

'Oh, hello, Paul. No, there's something not quite right with my paper this morning.'

'Uh-oh!' He turned down the corner to check its title. 'Yes, I thought so! That's not your paper, is it, Sylvia?'

'Isn't it?' she quavered.

''Fraid not.'

Paul took her paper and silently handed it to Albert, then picked up the *Express* that he had flung on the coffee table in disgust, and quietly dropped it into her hands.

'Oh, good show, young man,' beamed Albert.

Jack let out a guffaw of laughter and Albert glared at him disapprovingly.

'Is this mine?' asked Sylvia in a bewildered voice.

'Yes,' smiled Paul. 'And now I'd better go and try to catch Mrs W,' he said, leaping up.

❁

Brenda was already walking away from The Cedars and down the hill towards Salisbury. She needed the space and fresh air to think. Brian was becoming more and more distant towards her, and he seemed to be spending a lot of time with Felicity. Of course, he denied that there was anything going on. But he would, wouldn't he? Were they really just friends and work colleagues as he insisted? Her head wanted to believe him, but her heart was telling her that something was amiss. What was worse, she was pretty certain she'd spotted him giving Felicity some kind of a present the other day. Should she challenge him about it? But he was so good at twisting her words around and making her feel the fool for asking.

Anyway, that's why she'd decided to go to the bank today and request copies of their statements for the last three months. If he was spending money on that bitch, she would be able to spot any unusual transactions. Of course, it would have been a whole lot easier if she could've just looked at their statements online. But she'd tried twice, and both times nearly been caught by Brian. She didn't want to have to explain to him why she was looking at their personal accounts. That would only spark another row.

※

Lauren had finished her morning tasks upstairs and was just heading downstairs to the day room when, to her surprise, she saw Marianne standing outside the office door, her ear pressed against it. Marianne put a finger to her lips to signal to her not to speak, so she waited, bemused at the old lady's behaviour. Suddenly the door was flung open, and Marianne sprang backwards, startled.

'And what's that supposed to mean?' Brian said angrily to someone in the office, his back to Marianne and Lauren.

'You know very well what I mean! I can't afford to go losing this job as well,' Felicity snapped back at him.

Brian spun round, exasperated, then pulled up short as he saw the two of them. 'And what do you want?' he growled at them.

'I only wanted to check what time the Nails and Wigs session starts this afternoon,' Marianne quavered, on the verge of tears.

Brian pulled himself together. 'Half past two, in the dining room.' He tried to smile reassuringly, before striding off towards the kitchen, completely blanking Lauren.

Marianne looked terribly upset, so in an effort to distract her, Lauren asked, 'Marianne, did you find that brooch you were looking for yesterday?'

'Oh no, dear. I ... well, I confess, I went upstairs to look for it and when I got there, I couldn't remember what I'd gone upstairs for! I only thought of it again this morning when I wanted to put it on ... but I was already running late for breakfast ... so I didn't have time to ... um, you know ...' She sighed loudly.

'Shall we go upstairs and search for it now?'

'Ooh, can we? Thank you ever so much, dear, you really are too kind.'

❃

Lauren gazed around Marianne's room wondering where on earth to begin. Every piece of furniture was all but hidden under a pile of clutter; it made her own room look tidy by comparison, and that was saying something! 'Where do you usually keep your jewellery?' she enquired.

'Well ... the things I wear every day are in that little trinket box on my dressing table ... but I've already looked in there. I do have another box in my underwear drawer, though.'

'Well, let's start there then.'

But having systematically worked their way through both the box and the drawer, they'd had no luck. They were just searching the top of the dressing table when Paul passed the doorway, did a double take and came in. 'What on earth are you two up to?'

'Oh, Paul, I can't find my brooch,' wailed Marianne.

'Not the pretty one that looks like a flower?' he asked.

'Yes, that's the one.'

'Well, when did you last have it?'

'Um ... let me think. I was definitely wearing it on Sunday when my daughter visited. And I remember transferring it to this cardigan on Monday morning when I put the old one in the wash. Then, yesterday morning, I realised it wasn't there.'

'Yes,' jumped in Lauren, 'I saw her searching for something, and that's when she told me it was missing.'

'I presume you've already reported it?'

'Um,' Lauren flushed slightly, realising that perhaps she should have done just that.

'You didn't, did you?' Paul was looking at her quite sternly now. 'Policies and Procedures ... all missing items must be reported to the care manager immediately.'

'Sorry, I didn't think about that yesterday, as Marianne was going to come straight upstairs and look for it herself. I did offer to help her!' she finished hotly as she caught Paul's expression. For a moment, she thought she was really in trouble, but then his face creased into a smile.

'Got ya!' he grinned. 'Tell you what, I'll go and report it to Frau Flic now, if you like, while you carry on searching with Marianne.'

Lauren nodded gratefully and turned back to the dressing table with its assortment of ornaments, perfume bottles, books, letters and all sorts of random junk. But try as she might, she couldn't find the brooch.

# Chapter Ten

Meg was sitting at a table in the bay window of the day room quietly doing a jigsaw puzzle, when a shadow suddenly fell across her pieces. 'Oh, hello, Marianne.'

'Am I disturbing you?' Marianne sounded worried.

'Not at all,' Meg smiled, 'pull up a chair and tell me what's on your mind.'

'It's been a really strange couple of days,' Marianne began hesitantly, settling into a captain's chair at the end of the table, her back to the room.

'Oh? In what way, my dear?'

'I'm not quite sure where to begin.'

'Well, go back to when it first got strange.'

'Well, I was in the hall after breakfast yesterday morning, checking the notice board.'

'Yes.'

'There was a new event posted, but I couldn't read it because I didn't have my reading glasses.' She paused and shook her head. 'But that's not what I wanted to tell you.'

'Well, carry on,' Meg encouraged.

Marianne frowned. 'It's just ... as I was standing there, I saw the doctor with Brenda ... and what Lauren said afterwards was quite shocking ... and then I discovered my brooch was missing. And today ... I overheard something ... they were having the most awful row, you know ... and then he nearly bit my head off! And Lauren helped me look for it, but we still can't find my favourite brooch!'

Meg pulled a face, not following the disjointed discourse at all.

'Why don't you start again at the beginning and tell me all the details you can remember,' she suggested calmly.

Their two heads drew closer as Marianne unburdened her heart to the attentive Meg.

Brenda returned from her walk, disappointed that the bank statements had shown nothing unusual. Maybe she was just imagining things. She hurried into the day room and dropped a newspaper into the hands of the now-dozing Albert.

'What? What?' He jerked his eyes open. 'What's this, then?'

'Your *Telegraph*, Albert,' she smiled.

'But I've already read my *Telegraph*.' He sounded indignant at being disturbed.

She frowned and looked around the room in exasperation, noticing the carefully folded *Telegraph* on the coffee table. How did that get there? She was beginning to think she was losing her marbles!

Then her eyes alighted on the grey and white heads closeted in animated conversation in the bay window. What on earth were Meg and Marianne gossiping about? she wondered. At that moment, Marianne glanced up, caught Brenda's look and immediately flushed.

*That's strange*, she mused. *Anyone would think they were gossiping about me. Oh, good grief, perhaps they are!* She turned away in confusion and thought back, trying to identify exactly what Marianne could be telling Meg. With a sudden start, she recalled Marianne being in the hall when she'd bumped into Phil yesterday. *Oh no! Whatever must they think of me?* She hurried out of the day room, colouring with embarrassment. Though, when one thought about it rationally, there was really nothing to be embarrassed about, was there? She knew that Phil had a soft spot for her, but unlike her husband, Brian, she had no intention of having an affair. That's if he was having an affair and she wasn't just imagining things!

Brian peered round the day-room door cautiously, checking who was there. He needed a word with Brenda but had no wish to bump into Felicity again after their recent argument. She really was being quite unreasonable about everything, and with Brenda getting more suspicious, it was getting to be quite the balancing act. He wasn't sure how much longer he could carry on with things the way they were.

He too noticed Meg and Marianne at the table. He glowered as he watched Marianne confiding in Meg. Damn it! Just how much of their row had the nosy old woman heard? And why the hell had she been listening at the office door in the first place? He grimaced. Marianne was well known as the home's biggest gossip. It would be all over the place by tomorrow. That wouldn't do at all. He backed out thoughtfully into the hall.

※

A few minutes later, Felicity glanced around the day room, searching for Brian. She wanted to put things right with him, worried she'd been a little too sharp. She needed to keep him sweet for a bit longer. But it was so exasperating when Brenda was obviously getting suspicious and he didn't seem to see the need to keep their affair a secret. He'd even admitted that one of the residents had caught him coming down from her room a couple of weeks ago and had had the audacity to brag that he'd successfully fobbed her off. What if meddlesome Meg had told Brenda what she'd seen? She shuddered at the thought. She had so much more to lose than he did.

That's when she noticed the two ladies at the table, with Meg chatting and Marianne listening so intently that neither of them noticed her. Botheration! What if Meg was even now telling Marianne what she'd seen? It would be all round the home by tomorrow and was bound to get back to Brenda's ears. That was all she needed!

※

Marianne finished unburdening herself to Meg, who was now determined to solve the various mysteries presented to her, such as where was Marianne's missing brooch? Could it have been stolen? Was Brenda having an affair? Did she suspect that Brian was? And why was Felicity worried about losing this job as well?

Those last two words seemed to suggest that Felicity had lost a previous job, maybe in suspicious circumstances. But, of course, that was assuming that Marianne had heard her correctly. Meg would never have said this out loud, but Marianne was easily confused. Maybe she'd misheard.

Just then, the chef, Andy, announced that lunch was imminent. They joined the usual slow-motion stampede to use the toilets, with Albert and Jack faring somewhat better than the ladies, who needed to queue.

✦

In the dining room, Lauren was supervising the residents with Paul. He whispered to her that he'd reported the missing brooch to Felicity, and she confirmed that it still hadn't been found.

As everyone settled down to their soup, Lauren looked round at all the faces and was relieved to see that Marianne was looking more relaxed than she had done earlier. It must help knowing that Frau Flic would be taking the matter in hand. She wondered if the police would be called in.

# Chapter Eleven

When lunch was finished, there was another undignified scramble for the toilets but, when the men ambled off to the day room for their afternoon naps, the ladies all returned one by one to the dining room, a buzz of excitement building in the air. It was their monthly Activities afternoon! The lunch things had been cleared, and the tables were now covered in large white tablecloths. Sally and Kiera, who were both working the late shift, joined them, along with Felicity and a curious Lauren.

A clinician from a local beauty salon arrived and started unpacking a large box. First, she placed a standing mirror and two mannequin heads in front of each pair of ladies. Then she laid out a large array of wigs, from black to bleached blonde and from Rapunzel long to Pixie short.

'Now then, ladies,' she said in a warm melodious voice. 'We've done this before, so I'm sure you all remember. We're going to help you to choose and style a wig of your choice: perhaps remembering what you looked like as a young girl, or at the height of your career, or perhaps a different style or colour that you've always fancied. Don't forget, later on, we'll want you to tell everyone why you've chosen that particular wig for your mannequin! Then we'll get your nails trimmed and shaped and you can choose your colour of nail varnish. There's plenty of us here to help you today, so let's get going.'

A buzz of excited chatter broke out, and Lauren felt herself drawn into a world of memories.

'I remember my hair was all the way down to my waist when I first started work,' announced Muriel, choosing a long jet-black wig, much to Lauren's surprise.

'What job did you do?' she dared to ask, remembering to speak clearly and slowly.

'I was a librarian,' replied Muriel, 'in the main university library in Edinburgh. It was a very responsible job, y'know.'

Sylvia reminded everyone that she had been a hairdresser, but then couldn't remember where she had lived or worked. She rifled through the wigs before choosing a long blonde one. 'Perhaps I can make a beehive out of this,' she stated dubiously. 'I remember having my hair like that a long time ago.'

Meg seized on a wig with shoulder-length chestnut curls. 'It reminds me of how I looked when I first started teaching in 1962,' she said. Lauren's mind boggled. That was way back in history! She couldn't imagine Meg as a young woman at the time of the Beatles and miniskirts – those being the only two things she knew about the '60s. She watched as Meg deftly rearranged the curls and realised that she must've been very pretty when she was younger.

Marianne had chosen a bright auburn wig with glorious tumbling curls. Lauren suddenly realised that they had each had a life about which she knew nothing, and suddenly she wanted to find out more. 'What did you do when you worked?' she asked Marianne with genuine interest.

'Me? Oh, I started out as a shorthand typist, but I ended up as personal assistant to the managing director,' Marianne boasted proudly. 'It was in a factory making fireworks, up at High Post. You won't remember that. It burned down quite a few years ago. You can't imagine the explosions and all the fireworks going off all at once.' Lauren wished she had seen that; it must've been quite a spectacular sight!

She discovered that Annie was ninety-five and had started off life as a bus conductress, a job she'd never heard of. All the Wilts & Dorset buses she travelled on were manned only by a driver. She listened in fascination as Annie described her uniform and ticket machine, how she'd been responsible for keeping order, and woe betide any young lads who thought they could sneak a quick grope in the back seats. Lauren laughed at the thought of it.

To Lauren's surprise, the afternoon raced past, and she was late going off shift because she'd completely lost track of time. Who knew you could have so much fun in an old people's home!

※

Much later that evening, long after the day staff had gone home, after dinner had been served and TV watched, after the night staff had taken over and distributed the bedtime medications, the house was finally calm and quiet. Most of the residents were already in bed, some snoring and others reading. Meg alone was in the day room, reading by the light of a strong lamp that she preferred to the one on her bedside table. Finally, she lowered the book with a sigh and gently closed it. Just as she'd deduced! There was rarely a book she read these days where she hadn't worked out the whodunit before reaching the denouement. With an effort, she levered herself out of the armchair and placed the book on the bookshelves; it had been a birthday present but someone else could read it now. She turned off the lamp and made her way into the hall. The office light was off, and the door firmly closed; it looked as though both the Wollstonecrafts and Ms Trainer had long since gone offduty.

Meg pressed the button for the lift then heard a slight sound from the treatment room. She turned slowly but was only able to see a thin sliver of the room through the part-open door. She watched as a pair of hands lifted a vial from a small under-the-counter fridge and placed it carefully on the worktop. Whoever it was then took a needle and syringe and began to draw liquid into it. The lift pinged and the person in the treatment room hastily pushed the door closed.

Slightly disconcerted, Meg stepped into the lift and pressed the button for the first floor. A cold feeling came over her as the lift rose smoothly, and she had the distinct feeling that she had glimpsed something she shouldn't have. She frowned then gave herself a little shake. *That's what you get for reading a murder mystery just before bedtime, Margaret Thornton*, she thought. *You start getting fanciful ideas.*

# Chapter Twelve

*Thursday 8th September 2022*

It was Sonia who made the discovery early the next morning, but it wasn't long before the whispers spread quickly like ripples from a stone. Marianne was dead.

Dr Phil was called. At eighty-nine years old, death was hardly a surprise. He examined his patient and could find no signs to suggest that the cause of death was anything other than natural. As he had seen her within the statutory fourteen days, he saw no need to contact the coroner's office. He signed the death certificate and hurried off. Brenda phoned the next of kin, who were happy for her to contact the funeral directors and arrange for the body to be taken away, as they wouldn't be able to get there for several hours.

✿

When Lauren arrived at the back door for her day shift, it was Sally who broke the news to her and gently asked if she would like to join the other staff in prayers around the deceased. Lauren's eyes opened wide and the colour drained from her face.

'Do I have to see her dead body?'

'You don't have to as you've only been here a few weeks, but you're bound to see a dead person sooner or later, in this line of work.'

Lauren gulped. 'Will she be all bloated and black?' she whispered.

'No, Lauren. Death isn't like that when someone has recently passed away. She will just look like she's sleeping, except you can sense that her spirit has left her body.'

Lauren looked sceptical.

'Learning how to recognise death and what to do when a client has died will be part of your training, Lauren. It's early days yet, but you will have to see a dead body at some point.'

Lauren nodded. 'Okay. But I won't have to touch it, will I?'

Sally smiled reassuringly. 'Her, not it. But no, not this time.'

Lauren followed Sally upstairs and joined a group of staff members who were gathered on the landing. She was surprised to see Paul in on his day off. He squeezed her hand. 'You don't have to come in,' he said, 'but Brenda sends a text round and most of us do, if we can, especially when we've known the client for a long time.'

Brenda silently handed out laminated prayer cards, and the staff respectfully filed into Marianne's room.

It wasn't nearly as awful as she had expected, but Lauren was surprised to find that there did indeed appear to be something missing; it was like Marianne was smaller after death than she had been before.

Afterwards, Brenda took Lauren's arm and said quietly, 'Sally has to wash and lay out Marianne now, so I'll work with you this morning.'

Lauren was relieved to have been spared that, whatever it was.

As they visited each resident in turn, checking the occasional blood pressure where it was under observation, replacing dressings as required and helping them to wash and dress where such help was needed, Lauren was impressed by how gentle and compassionate Brenda was. She sat with each resident to break the sad news, although it turned out they all knew already. She comforted those who wept, listened to those who needed to talk and offered reassuring words of condolence. This was the kind of caring that Lauren aspired to.

It was Meg's reaction that was the most surprising. She seemed totally distraught and for some reason held herself personally responsible.

'Meg, it's not your fault,' soothed Brenda.

'But I could have stopped it!'

'Of course you couldn't.'

'If only I'd said something last night.'

Eventually, hesitantly, Meg explained how she had seen someone preparing a syringe the night before. Brenda shook her head, puzzled.

'I doubt it's related, but perhaps you'd like to talk to Dr Baker about this? I'm sure he can set your mind at rest.'

'Yes, please.'

Brenda and Lauren withdrew from the room. 'Is she a bit gaga?' asked Lauren.

'It is possible for a bereavement to exacerbate someone's level of confusion,' Brenda explained, 'but Meg had no previous signs of dementia so it's unlikely. And she only moved here a few months ago, so I can't believe she was all that close to Marianne. I'm going to phone Dr Baker and ask him to call in, when he's got a moment.'

She leant towards Lauren slightly. 'Oh, and Lauren ... gaga is not a recognised medical term.' She moved away from a very contrite-looking Lauren.

❀

Dr Baker arrived mid-morning after his surgery had finished and was closeted with Meg for over half an hour. When he emerged, Brenda was hovering outside Meg's room. She immediately led him to the staffroom and closed the door.

'I've tried to convince her that Marianne's death was natural, but she's not having any of it,' he said.

'I know, it's really disturbing,' Brenda replied. 'I've never known anyone to react to a death quite like this.'

'And she's adamant that she saw someone drawing up a syringe late last night.'

'But she couldn't have done, not at that time of night. She must be confused about the time.'

'She seems entirely rational, so I have to say that she's beginning to make me wonder if I've overlooked something.'

'Oh, Phil, no!'

'I know. It's highly unlikely. I checked everything methodically and thoroughly like I always do. I can't believe I would have missed anything.'

'Phil, you are such a good doctor, you can't doubt yourself!' she exclaimed, before unexpectedly bursting into tears. 'I really can't handle this just at the moment,' she wailed.

Phil put an arm around her shoulder. 'Hey, what's this all about?' He was shocked to see the cracks in her usual professional detachment. She leant into him and sobbed silently for a while, before eventually pulling away, taking several deep breaths to calm herself down.

'What was all that about?' enquired Phil gently.

'Oh, I don't know. It all seems to be getting to me today.'

'But you've lost residents before.'

'Yes, I know.'

'So, is there something else?'

'Perhaps.'

'Tell me about it?'

'I can't.'

'Is it Brian?'

She looked at him with an agonised expression on her face, and before she could stop herself, it all came tumbling out, as though someone had released the floodgates. Phil listened patiently.

'He's a class-A bastard,' muttered Phil angrily, when she had finished.

She looked at him in horror.

'Sorry, but I've been watching the way he treats you like a doormat for too long now.'

She looked into his eyes, not knowing what to say. An invisible thread appeared to pull her towards him. She allowed him to draw her into an embrace. Nestled into his soft jumper, she felt warm and protected and ... something else ... a strange feeling she hadn't felt in a long time. She couldn't put a name to it, but she was in no hurry to move away from him, and he seemed in no hurry for her to go.

So intense were their feelings and so preoccupying, they didn't hear the door open.

Eventually, he kissed the top of her head and murmured,

'You know, I will always do whatever I can to protect you.'

They didn't notice the door quietly close again as someone withdrew from the room.

# Chapter Thirteen

The dark grey van from Hill & Sons had come and gone before lunch. The day was not as grey as the one five months previously when they'd collected Harold Leadbetter, nor was it raining. But with the black gurney bearing its tragic load, the staff lined up in the hallway and the residents standing in the bay window, it felt much the same. The lack of grieving relatives to oversee Marianne's departure was more than made up for by the profound sense of loss among the residents. Meg particularly was inconsolable, blaming herself as she did. But hers were not the only tears being shed.

After the van had gone, Meg wandered across to Janet.

'She'd been here nearly nine years, you know,' said Janet sadly, wiping her eyes.

Meg smiled sympathetically. 'You must have known her well.'

'I did.'

They sat in companionable silence for a while.

'Can I ask you a question, please, Janet?' Meg began softly.

'Of course.'

'And you will tell me if you think I'm being totally ridiculous, won't you?'

'I doubt that will be necessary.'

'I just have this feeling that I can't explain … that Marianne's death was not quite …' She hesitated, trying to find the best word.

'Right?' suggested Janet.

'You feel it too?' Meg was surprised.

At that moment, Lauren interrupted to ask how they were doing, having been told by Brenda to keep a close eye on Meg. 'Are you two ladies okay? Is there anything I can get you?'

'Thank you for asking but we're as fine as can be expected,' replied Janet softly.

'And do you feel better since Dr Baker spoke with you?' Lauren spoke gently to Meg.

'Yes,' Meg hesitated, 'well, actually, no, not really. I was just saying that something about Marianne's death doesn't feel quite right.'

Lauren pulled up a chair and sat beside the two ladies. 'Would you like to talk about it?'

'It's not just the fact that I saw someone drawing up that syringe last night,' Meg began, and then had to recount that episode to Janet. 'It's just ... it seems very strange that Marianne's brooch goes missing, Paul reports it to Frau Flic, and then suddenly Marianne dies.'

'It could just be a coincidence, you know,' said Lauren sceptically.

'Hold your judgement, young lady,' cautioned Janet, who was looking very thoughtful. 'I think you both need to hear something.' Meg and Lauren leant towards Janet, eager to hear what she had to say.

'Bear with me. Before either of you came here, we had a resident called Harold Leadbetter; Harry to his friends.'

'I believe I moved into his old room,' chipped in Meg.

'Indeed, you did,' confirmed Janet.

'And is his death connected with Marianne's?' she said with a frown.

'I'm not entirely sure but let me tell you what I know. About a week before Harry died, a book of his went missing. Now, that might not seem very important, but it was a first edition and very valuable. When it couldn't be found in his room or in any of the residents' areas, Harry demanded that Felicity ask the police to search all the staff lockers. She refused point-blank.'

'Really?' Lauren sounded surprised.

'When Harry died the following week, I didn't think too much of it. He had a long history of heart disease, and his death was not really that unexpected. I'd forgotten all about the book until it came to mind just now. Can you see the similarity?'

'Yes, I see.' Meg was nodding. 'Harry had a valuable book stolen and a week later, after Frau Flic refused to call in the police, he died. Marianne's brooch, which was very precious to her, went missing on Tuesday. It was reported to Frau Flic yesterday, and today, she's passed away quite unexpectedly too.'

'Wait a moment,' exclaimed Lauren, looking at Meg and then Janet incredulously. 'Are you suggesting that Frau Flic has something to do with these deaths?'

Meg repeated her suspicions that Ms Felicity Trainer might be the same person as Mrs March to Lauren. 'So, if she is the same person, you think she's killed two people in some other care home and now two people here?' Lauren's voice almost squeaked with excitement.

Meg hastily looked around the room to ensure no one else had overheard. Luckily, only Muriel was still present in the day room, and she was as deaf as a post. 'Hush,' she urged, 'let's keep this just between the three of us, for now.' Janet and Lauren both nodded solemnly.

'Janet, when we spoke about your missing ten-pound note the other week, you said that you had been watching Ms Trainer for some time, I think?'

Janet nodded in reply. 'Yes. That wasn't the first time that money has gone missing recently, or the last. And I already had my suspicions about Felicity.'

'You think she might be a thief as well as a murderer?' gasped Lauren.

'I thought she might have been a thief, yes. But then, watching her carefully over some time, I realised that something altogether different was going on.' Janet paused and Meg stepped in.

'You found out that Felicity and Brian are having an affair.'

Lauren gasped. She thought something had been going on between those two!

'You know?' Janet raised her eyebrows.

Meg told the two of them what she'd seen on the landing, and what she and Marianne had been discussing just yesterday. Lauren chipped in with the couple of small things she'd noticed. Janet nodded sagely. 'That seems to confirm what I suspected.'

'But is she also a thief?' enquired Meg.

'Actually, I was beginning to suspect that Brian was the thief, not Felicity,' said Janet.

'Brian!' Meg and Lauren glanced at each other in astonishment.

'Yes, indeed. He's been behaving ... oddly. But I haven't got any proof. And then you told me your story about Mrs March and that made me think again.'

'You mean, it could be Felicity or Brian?' Lauren asked.

'Or maybe someone else altogether,' pointed out Meg. 'We mustn't jump to conclusions.'

'Exactly,' agreed Janet, 'it's important we don't say a word about any of this to anyone until we have some kind of proof.'

'But if one of them is a thief, and maybe also a murderer, surely we should tell the police?' urged Lauren.

'No, my dear,' cautioned Meg. 'We only have suspicions, without any evidence. And you saw how neither Brenda nor Dr Phil believed me when I told them about the syringe.'

Lauren nodded. 'So we investigate?' she asked, her eyes shining brightly.

'No, we watch, and we listen,' urged Meg. 'That's all.'

Lauren nodded reluctantly.

'There is another thing,' Meg spoke thoughtfully, 'although I don't know what, if any, relevance it has to Marianne's death.' She glanced at Janet, only to realise that Janet's head had drooped and she was on the verge of falling asleep. 'You look exhausted, my dear. Why don't you have a rest.' Much to Lauren's disappointment, she added, 'We can continue this conversation later.'

※

Lunch was a very subdued affair, with everyone sombre and quiet. Even Jack refrained from trying to needle Albert. Sally was supervising the dining room, pouring water for the residents, and so on, and as she looked from one resident to another, she noticed that several of them were just picking at their food. Janet, in particular, had eaten very little and was looking rather pale.

'Aren't you feeling very well, Janet?'

'It's nothing much, love, I'm just tired.'

'That's okay. Shall I get Lauren to take you up to your room for a rest?'

'Yes, please.'

Meg watched, concern etched on her face, as Lauren wheeled Janet out. Perhaps she was being a little unfair involving Janet in all of this. She was a hundred and one, after all.

# Chapter Fourteen

That afternoon, Meg took a short walk outside so that she could clear her head. It seemed as if either Felicity or Brian was a thief. And therefore, one of them could also be a murderer. If indeed there had been a murder. And, if history was anything to go by, she would have placed her bet on Felicity. From what her friend Pat had said, Felicity must have done this before in that other care home. With a flash of inspiration, she came indoors, took the lift to her room and rummaged through her address book.

'Pat,' she muttered, 'Patricia Wilton. There we are.'

She carefully copied the number down onto a piece of paper. Now what? She didn't want to use the public phone downstairs in the hall where anyone could overhear what she had to say. And she had, unfortunately, never seen the need for a mobile phone since her retirement. She made her way downstairs to the office and tapped on the door. Sally was in there alone. 'Can I help you, Meg?'

'I was wondering if you would allow me to use the office phone. You see, I want to phone a friend of mine who's been ill.'

'There's a pay phone in the hall, you know.'

'Yes, I know, dear. But, unfortunately, I don't have any change at all, and I'm so worried about my friend.'

'Come on in,' Sally smiled. 'It's not usually allowed, but just this once won't hurt.'

'Oh, thank you so much.'

'You can take my seat, if you like. I'll just go and check up on Janet while you make your call.'

'Thank you.' She sat down and dialled the number she'd written down. It took quite a time for someone in the care home to answer the phone, and even longer for them to bring Pat to the phone. She kept glancing at the door, hoping and praying that none of the staff would return. At last, she heard a familiar voice.

'Is that you, Meg?'

'Pat! How lovely to hear your voice again.'

'And yours too, dear. Tell me how you are and all about your new home.'

'Pat, I can't talk for long and I've something very important to ask you, so I'm afraid our catch-up will have to wait.'

'Oh dear, that sounds a bit worrying.'

'Do you remember telling me about a man called Tony who died in the same care home as your sister?'

'Yes, I do. That senior care assistant, Mrs March she was called, walked into the tearoom just as I was telling you about her, do you remember? I had ever such a shock seeing her like that.'

'Yes, I remember. And am I correct in thinking that this Mrs March stole a watch from Tony shortly before he died?'

'Not quite. He caught her trying to steal his watch.'

'So, his watch wasn't actually stolen?'

'Not then, no. But here's the odd thing. I remember Mary said his son made quite a fuss about the fact it had gone missing after his death!'

'Pat, do you happen to know what Tony's full name was?'

'Oh dear, let me think ... Tony was short for Anthony, of course. And his surname ... was it Fairfield, possibly? Or Fairfax? Oh dear, I'm not really sure.'

'Never mind. Another question: what was the name of the care home Mary and Tony were in?'

'It was The Cadnum Lodge Residential Care Home.'

'The Cadnum Lodge,' she repeated, as she carefully noted it on her piece of paper.

'And this Mrs March, you didn't mention a first name at the time. Can you remember it?'

'Yes, of course, it was Felicity. Felicity March.'

Meg felt her breath catch in her throat.

'This sounds very mysterious, Meg. Are you going to tell me what this is all about?'

'I will, Pat, but one last question first. Did you ever hear back about the inquiry into your sister's death?'

'Yes, it took months and months before they came to a decision but eventually—'

Meg blanched as she had to slam the phone down on her friend: someone was pushing the door open.

Luckily, it was Sally and not, as she'd feared, Frau Flic. Nevertheless, she had nearly been caught and it had given her a terrible shock.

'Oh dear,' said Sally, 'you look like you've just had bad news.'

'No,' replied Meg.

'But you're shaking!'

'I must be a little chilly, I think.'

'I do hope you're not going down with something. Poor Janet's not feeling at all well, either.'

'No, no, I'll be fine.' She thanked Sally again for the use of the phone and came out of the office breathing a sigh of relief. As she walked to the lift, Frau Flic came out of the kitchen, marched towards her and nodded as she passed.

'Margaret.'

'Good afternoon, Ms Trainer.'

Felicity went straight into the office and Meg realised that she really had had a very close escape. She went upstairs and lay on her bed for the rest of the afternoon, turning everything over and over in her mind.

✿

While Meg was resting in her bedroom, Marianne's daughter and son-in-law arrived at The Cedars, having travelled from Birmingham, stopping for lunch on the way. It was Lauren who responded to the front doorbell. When the couple explained who they were, Lauren's stomach lurched as she struggled for words. 'Oh, I'm so sorry—'

'Mr and Mrs Birchdale,' intervened Brenda, hurrying from the office. 'I am so very sorry for your loss. Please, come in. Can I offer you tea or coffee?' She led the solemn couple into the office and dispatched Lauren to make three coffees. When Lauren returned, they were going through an official-looking document. She set the coffees down on the desk and was about to leave when Brenda called her back. 'Lauren, if you could wait a couple of minutes while we finish the paperwork, then you can take Mrs Birchdale and her husband up to her mother's room and help them pack up her belongings.'

Lauren observed as the various formalities were completed. Marianne's daughter was sitting bolt upright, clutching a damp tissue, which she occasionally dabbed under her eyes. With her petite figure and greying auburn hair, Lauren thought she looked very much like a younger version of her mother, although somewhat more smartly dressed. Her husband simply looked grey: grey hair, grey suit, grey tie; even his face looked grey. She wondered if this was grief or if, perhaps, he wasn't well.

'That's everything, thank you,' Brenda concluded. 'Lauren will take you upstairs now.'

Lauren led the couple to the bottom of the stairs and was about to go up when the man interrupted. 'We usually take the lift, if you don't mind.'

'No problem, Mr Birchdale.' She pressed the button to open the lift doors.

'Please, call us Mike and Jenny,' he replied with a slight smile.

Once in Marianne's room, Jenny gave a sudden sob as she looked at the empty bed. Mike comforted her and Lauren stood awkwardly by the door. Eventually, Jenny pulled herself together. 'Right, I'll sort through Mum's dressing table, if you'll go down to the car, love, and fetch the suitcase and bags.' Mike disappeared back to the lift.

'Can I help, please, Jenny?' Lauren asked. She spent the next half hour folding Marianne's clothes into the suitcase while Mike and Jenny sorted other items into black plastic bags, for disposal, or a large green holdall.

'That's odd!' exclaimed Jenny, breaking the silence that had shrouded their work. 'I've been through all of Mum's jewellery, and I can't find her favourite brooch anywhere.'

'Didn't Mrs Wollstonecraft tell you?' queried Lauren.

'Tell me what?'

'I'm very sorry, but your mother's brooch was reported missing yesterday.'

'Missing? What does that mean? She was wearing it on Sunday when we came down.' She looked at her husband with fresh tears in her eyes. 'Mum especially wanted me to have that brooch. It's been in the family for three generations, you know.'

'Yes, darling, I know.' Her husband put a comforting arm around her shoulder. 'Who was it reported to?' he asked Lauren.

'Paul reported it to Ms Trainer, the care manager.'

'And were the police called?'

'I ... I don't know.' Lauren gulped. 'I'll go and get Mrs Wollstonecraft for you. I'm sure she can help.'

Brenda came but it transpired that she had no answers, having not heard anything about a missing brooch. That struck Lauren as particularly odd. Surely Frau Flic would have reported it to Brenda?

'I'll look into it,' Brenda promised.

'Please do,' Mike instructed crossly. 'Not only was that brooch of great sentimental value, being a family heirloom, but I believe it was also quite valuable financially.'

# Chapter Fifteen

*Friday 9th September 2022*

Friday started with a biting wind and squally showers, one of which soaked Lauren on her way to work. She was sitting in the pantry drying her hair with a hairdryer Brenda had kindly found for her, when Paul walked in.

'Ooh,' he teased, 'we have a drowned Pixie this morning.'

She scowled at him. 'Do you have to call me Pixie?'

'Touchy this morning, aren't we?'

'Perhaps I should call you a fairy,' she retaliated, 'see how you like that.'

'Ouch! That was below the belt!'

'Sorry,' she muttered, cross with herself for her stupid comment. Paul walked away without speaking.

※

To her great relief, Lauren was working alongside Brenda in the dining room, leaving Paul to head upstairs with Frau Flic. But breakfast that morning was a disgruntled affair. For a start, there were only six residents at the table, and a heavy cloud seemed to hover over them. Meg was worrying why Janet hadn't come down to breakfast. Muriel ate in stony silence, and Sylvia simply picked at her food listlessly. Albert and Jack sniped at each other constantly until Annie felt compelled to tell them to behave.

'Oh, do stop squabbling like spoiled children, you two.'

An uneasy silence settled over the residents; you could almost reach out and touch the tension. Then Brenda burned the toast.

'I say, old gal, this toast is a bit cremated, isn't it?' Albert complained.

To everyone's surprise, Brenda, known for her patience and calm compassion, snapped back at him. 'It was only an accident. It's not like I did it on purpose!'

Looking close to tears, she hurried from the dining room, leaving Lauren speechless.

'Look what you've done now!' Jack accused Albert, never one to miss an opportunity.

'What? Never did a thing!' returned Albert indignantly.

'You've properly upset our lovely Mrs W, hasn't he, girls?' He winked at Sylvia and Annie.

'You should stop stirring trouble, Jack,' cautioned Annie.

'Bloomin' Jack-the-lad,' spluttered Albert.

'Old fart,' retorted Jack.

Albert turned an ugly puce, and the veins in his temples visibly pulsed as he slowly raised himself to his feet. Lauren hastily intervened. 'Shall I make some fresh toast?' To her relief, Albert sank back down into his chair.

※

As soon as Meg could, she left the others in the dining room and went to look for Brenda. She hesitated outside the office door, hearing voices. Glancing round to check she was alone, she moved closer to the door, which was slightly ajar.

'You've been acting all moody for the last two days now, and I think the residents are beginning to notice,' she heard Brian say. There was a faint sob in response, before Brian blithely continued. 'You've really got to pull yourself together. Maintain your professionalism in front of the clients.'

'You dare talk to me about professionalism?' she heard Brenda gasp.

'You shouldn't let Marianne's death get to you so easily,' Brian lectured. 'I thought you nurses were taught to never get emotionally involved.'

'That's rich, that is!' Brenda retorted. 'You accuse me of being unprofessional! When you're ... you're ...' She sobbed and ran out of the office, pushing past Meg without appearing to see her. Meg watched in concern as Brenda disappeared into her personal quarters. She was debating whether to knock on the door marked private, when she heard footsteps on the main staircase, so she turned away and headed towards the day room. The footsteps got louder then entered the office, and whoever it was shut the door behind them. Meg tiptoed back, unable to resist a little spying. Despite the closed door, she could just make out the voices by pressing her ear to the gap.

'Felicity, darling ...' Brian sounded as if he was trying to placate her.

'No, Brian, you listen to me. I think it's obvious that Brenda is suspicious about us.' Frau Flic sounded cross.

'Really?'

'Yes, really. And I think we should stop seeing each other for a while ...'

'But we work together!'

'Outside of work,' she snarled.

'You don't mean that!'

'Oh yes, I do! And you had better smooth things over with Brenda or else!'

Felicity stormed out of the office, nearly bumping into Meg. 'And you, Margaret, should know better than to sneak around eavesdropping at doors,' she spat furiously. She marched upstairs past a surprised Paul, on his way down.

Paul jogged lightly down to a speechless Meg, keen to pour oil on troubled waters.

'Have you finished that jigsaw puzzle yet, Meg?'

'Er, no, I haven't,' she managed.

'C'mon, let's go and see if we can't finish it together.' He linked his arm through hers and gently led her into the day room, fussing around her like an overanxious hen.

※

Once breakfast was finished and the dining room tidied, Lauren looked around the hall and treatment room for Brenda or one of the others. Where was everyone? She tapped on the office door.

'Come in.'

Wolly sounded cross so she peered around the door cautiously. 'Um, Mr Wollstonecraft,' she began.

'What is it?' he barked impatiently.

'I've finished in the dining room. What do you want me to do next?'

'Oh really, you need to learn to use your initiative, Lauren. We expect our carers to get on with their work without having to be told what to do every five minutes.' He returned to the forms he was filling in and she took that as a dismissal.

Once outside the office, she muttered angrily to herself, 'Am I supposed to be psychic now, or what?'

She wandered into the day room, where she spied Paul sitting at the table with Meg, chatting cosily over a puzzle together. 'Paul, if you're not too busy playing games, perhaps you can tell me what I should be doing?' she grumbled at him.

'Ooh, who's got out of bed on the wrong side this morning then, Pixie?'

'Probably you, you fairy,' she retorted, then immediately regretted it. Paul coloured furiously, got up from the chair and pulled her to one side.

'Don't you dare mention my sexuality in front of the residents,' he hissed.

'Oh God, I'm sorry,' she began. But the damage was done.

Albert was hovering rather too close for comfort and had evidently overheard her, from the look of astonished disgust on his face.

'Are you one of them?' he demanded. Paul flushed even redder.

'One of what?' teased Jack idly from the sofa, where he'd been amusing Sylvia with anecdotes from the various building sites he'd worked on in his life.

'A bloomin' woofter!' accused Albert loudly. Lauren cringed.

'And just think, he's probably helped you change your underpants a few times,' said Jack provocatively.

'And what do you mean by that?' spluttered Albert, turning round to face him.

'One of what?' puzzled Sylvia, anxiously.

'Never mind.' Jack patted her arm reassuringly, before standing up and squaring off to Albert.

Meg, sensing the tension in the room, struggled to her feet as quickly as she could, whilst the two men, one eighty-six and the other seventy-nine, tried to outstare each other like gunfighters at the O.K. Corral.

'Now then, boys,' she scolded in her best school-teacher's voice. 'Let's just keep this civil, shall we?'

Jack was the first to respond. 'It's none of our damn business what Paul chooses to do in his private life,' he jabbed a finger towards Albert's face with each carefully emphasised word, 'and don't you forget it, old man.'

Albert spluttered furiously. 'What? What?'

'In any case,' interjected Lauren, 'what does it matter if Paul's gay or I'm a flippin' lesbian?'

There was a collective gasp and everyone held their breath, watching Albert's face as it contorted impressively.

'Sorry,' he finally muttered, to no one in particular, 'no offence meant.'

He turned with a stiffly held back, his shoulders tense as he walked back to his armchair, sat down and deliberately opened his paper to study the cricket scores.

'Sorry, lad,' Jack apologised to Paul, 'you shouldn't have had to go through that.' He sat down with Sylvia, who had a look of absolute bemusement on her face.

'What did Albert mean just now? Is Paul a Jehovah's whatnot or something?' Jack struggled to keep a straight face as he hedged around the truth.

'I'm sorry too,' Lauren apologised to Paul, 'I didn't mean to out you.'

'You made a very valid point, my dear, even if the language was bordering on unacceptable,' put in Meg, causing Lauren to flush.

'And I think you'd do best to try and rise above that kind of prejudiced outburst, Paul,' Meg advised. 'You must remember that back in Albert's youth, being gay was still

illegal. Thankfully, we live in more enlightened times now.'
She sat down carefully and scanned her jigsaw pieces.

'Truce?' pleaded Lauren, looking anxiously at Paul.

'Truce,' he said. 'C'mon, let's go and get the coffees.'

As they walked down the hall, he turned to her and grinned.

'Do tell, are you really a lesbian?'

'Like hell I am!'

They both laughed and Paul linked his arm through hers as they headed towards the kitchen.

# Chapter Sixteen

Janet didn't appear at lunch, either, much to Meg's concern. Leaving the dining room, she saw Lauren coming down the stairs, a tray in her hands.

'Is it all right if I go up and sit with Janet for a while?' she asked.

'I don't see why not. She's eaten a little lunch and is feeling much better now.' Lauren smiled reassuringly.

'Thank you so much.' Meg took the lift upstairs and was reassured to hear Janet's voice when she tapped lightly on her door. 'How are you?' she asked as she went in.

'Oh, mustn't grumble,' replied Janet, sitting up in bed surrounded by cushions and cuddly toys. 'Just move those off that chair and come and sit beside me,' she instructed. Meg carefully repositioned a teddy bear, a small circular cushion and two rather impossibly coloured penguins before drawing the chair closer to the bed and settling herself down.

'From my great-grandchildren,' commented Janet, nodding at the penguins.

'I didn't know you had great-grandchildren.'

'Annie Featherstone's not the only one,' she chuckled.

'Well, I'm not going to stay too long and tire you out again,' began Meg.

'Oh, please don't hurry away. I enjoy the company. The others don't often think to stop and chat the way you do. It's like you become invisible once you're consigned to a wheelchair.'

She started coughing, so Meg found a glass of water and passed it to her.

'Not so much chatting, my dear. I'll do the talking and you can lie back and listen.'

Janet nodded and relaxed thankfully against her pillows.

Meg settled herself again, thought for a minute and then began.

'We all know when we get to our great age that life isn't going to last forever.'

'You've got twenty years to catch me up,' wheezed Janet, to Meg's discomfort.

'We get used to the idea that our friends and family are going to disappear one by one,' she continued. 'We get used to death.'

Janet nodded.

'So, I keep asking myself, why did Marianne's death upset me so much? It wasn't as though I'd known her for long. And the only conclusion I can come to is that her death wasn't natural, whatever Brenda and Dr Baker might say.'

Janet was nodding again, when someone tapped on the door. Meg jumped but was relieved when it was Lauren's head that appeared round the door.

'I wondered if I could join you two ladies?' Lauren came in and quietly closed the door behind her. 'I mean, do tell me to go away if I'm interrupting, but I thought you might be continuing what we were discussing yesterday,' she looked at them expectantly, 'and I'd really like to help!'

Meg suppressed a grin and glanced at Janet, who answered Lauren with a twinkle in her eye. 'I think that's an excellent idea.'

Lauren hurried into the ensuite bathroom and reappeared with the bathroom stool, setting it down on the opposite side of Janet's bed to Meg.

'As you so rightly supposed, we were just discussing Marianne's untimely death,' Meg explained. 'Assuming foul play, I feel sure I know the "how". It's something to do with the syringe that I saw being prepared the night before Marianne's death. An overdose of morphine or something, perhaps? But I can't work out the "who" and the "why".'

'What have you got so far?' enthused Lauren.

'Well, my first thought was, it had to have been Felicity. I told you about the thing with my friend Pat. Well, I phoned up and spoke to her yesterday.'

'And?'

'She confirmed that Tony had caught Mrs March trying to

steal his watch. But what's interesting is, she told me that the watch really did go missing after his death!'

'She killed him in order to steal it?' gasped Lauren.

'Yes, possibly. And there's more. I asked Pat what Mrs March's first name was ...'

'Let me guess, it was Felicity,' suggested Janet.

'Yes, indeed,' corroborated Meg. 'So, if Felicity March and Felicity Trainer are one and the same person, then it must make her the most likely suspect for stealing Marianne's brooch and subsequent death, don't you agree?'

'Not forgetting Harry,' interjected Janet.

'Yes, if he was also murdered,' agreed Meg.

'Didn't you say something about an investigation into the deaths of Tony and Mary?' asked Janet.

'Yes, but I still haven't managed to learn the outcome of that.' Meg sighed ruefully.

'Perhaps I could try to look that up,' suggested Lauren. 'It must be on record somewhere if it was an official investigation,' she explained, as both Meg and Janet looked at her sceptically.

'But how will you do that?' Meg asked.

'Easy. You can find out the answer to most things on the internet.'

'I must admit, I'm not very up to date with using the internet,' Meg said thoughtfully. 'I had to adapt to using a computer in my job, of course, when they infiltrated every area of the curriculum. I'm afraid I hated them then, and I've not bothered with one since I retired.'

'That's okay, just leave it to me,' Lauren beamed.

'I'm sure you're busy enough without having to do that. Now then, there are a couple of other things I need to tell you.' She told her eager listeners how Marianne had confided in her after she'd overheard Brian and Felicity arguing in the office. 'According to Marianne, Brian told Felicity about me seeing him on the landing three weeks ago and she was absolutely furious. He was trying to smooth things over, kept saying how much he loved her! And Felicity said that she didn't want to risk losing this job, as well.'

'I heard that last bit too,' chipped in Lauren, excitedly.

'I admit that, at first, I thought this only strengthened our suspicions about Felicity,' Meg continued, undeterred, 'but then it occurred to me that it could also give Brian a motive.'

'How?' demanded Lauren.

'You see, if Brian was aware that Marianne had overheard at least a part of their conversation ...'

'Which he was; I was there when he came out of the office and shouted at her,' Lauren confirmed.

'Yes, my dear. Don't you see? That means Brian might have wanted to kill Marianne to stop her telling Brenda what she'd overheard.'

'Oh golly, yes,' gulped Lauren.

'And, Janet, you said you thought Brian was the thief, not Felicity. If he stole Marianne's brooch ...'

'Then maybe he killed to stop her pursuing it,' finished Janet.

'But if that's the case, he's not going to get away with it,' cried Lauren. She told them about her conversation with Marianne's daughter and son-in-law. 'Although I did think it very odd that Brenda knew nothing about the missing brooch,' she concluded. 'You'd have thought Frau Flic would've passed it on after Paul reported it missing.'

'Which brings us back to Felicity,' groaned Meg.

'Janet, why did you think Brian was the thief? Surely, after everything Meg's said, it had to be Frau Flic, right?' asked Lauren, puzzled.

'That was before Meg told me about Mrs March. At that point, I was just trying to work out who was stealing money from the residents.'

'I'd forgotten about your ten-pound note!' cried Lauren.

'Yes. Well, you see, I've seen Brian giving Felicity gifts that I'm sure he couldn't afford,' replied Janet. 'On one occasion, last month, I think, I saw him give her a necklace when they were out in the garden and quite unaware that I could see them.'

'Oh, I see. That does cast him in rather a dubious light,' said Meg.

'So do you think it was Brian or Felicity who murdered Marianne?' demanded Lauren.

'I don't know. Of course, it might not be either of them,' pondered Janet.

'What?' exclaimed Lauren.

'It's all very well us looking at the motives those two had, but we don't know if anyone else had a motive as well!' Janet pointed out.

'Yes, but who else would want to murder Marianne?' Meg never found out what the others thought because the door suddenly opened and in walked Felicity.

'What are you doing in here, Mrs Thornton?' she tutted. 'And you too, Lauren! Poor Mrs Smith isn't very well and you're chatting away, disturbing her rest.' She ushered them both out of the room despite Janet's protests.

Meg spent the rest of that day worrying how much of their conversation Frau Flic might have overheard. Meanwhile, Lauren was watching each of the residents and other staff members in turn, in case any of them looked like a possible murderer. Neither of them slept particularly well that night.

# Chapter Seventeen

They weren't the only ones having a sleepless night. Brenda was lying awake in the dark, her brain working overtime. She had really lost it today. She had snapped at a client, something she had never done in her working life. She would have to apologise to Albert tomorrow. And then she had nearly accused Brian of having an affair with Felicity!

*So what? He is having an affair, and you know it*, one part of her brain taunted. Yes, but what would've happened if she had challenged him? Would he have denied it? What proof did she have? Worse still, what if she was wrong?

*But you know he's having an affair*, her brain insisted. What if he had admitted it, what then? Would he have walked out on her? That wouldn't have been so bad, surely. But how would the residents have reacted to that? And what about Felicity, would she have gone with him? Would people have looked at her and thought that she was a failure?

Supposing she left Brian; perhaps that would be better. No, don't go there. Where would she live? How would she manage? She had no savings to speak of, and she'd have no job and no home. And what about Dominic? How would Dominic feel if his parents got divorced? Tears sprang to her eyes just thinking of her only son. *I can't do that to him. I just can't.*

'Are you awake?' asked Brian suddenly, breaking into the arguments that whirled in ever-increasing circles inside her head.

'Yes,' she whispered.

He sat up and turned on his bedside lamp. She blinked at him in the unexpected light.

'I've got something I need to tell you,' he said determinedly, staring at the foot of the bed. Her heart sank to her feet and her stomach churned.

'I don't want to know,' she said obstinately.

'That means you already know, then,' he said flatly.

'Please don't,' she implored, sitting up and grasping his arm. He shook her hand off and swivelled his legs over the side of the bed, facing away from her now.

'I've been having an affair,' he said roughly. 'I don't love you anymore. In fact, I'm not sure that I ever loved you.'

She cried out as if in pain.

'Well don't sound so bloody surprised,' he flung at her. 'What kind of a wife are you? You follow me around in the dead of night, like you don't trust me or something. And when did we last have sex, eh? Answer me that!'

She looked at his back, amazed that even now he could try to make out that it was all her fault.

'But it's you that's having an affair,' she said, a little tremulously.

'Only because you drove me to it,' he grumbled.

'You can't blame me!' she argued defensively.

'Why not? Haven't I paid for everything in this marriage? Haven't I given you the home you wanted and the job doing what you always wanted to do? Whose money paid for all of that, eh? My dad's, that's whose. And what thanks do I get?'

'How dare you!' she shrieked. He twisted his head, startled.

'What d'you mean by that then?'

'When we were first married, who paid the rent then? Who propped you up every time you got sacked or made redundant? Who stood by you every time another one of your not-so-great business ideas failed? Answer me that.'

'My dear woman,' he said coldly, 'I have no idea what on earth you are talking about.'

'And who did all the work?' she continued. 'I did all the housework. I did all the gardening. I raised Dominic. What did you do?'

'Oh, do stop being so hysterical.'

She couldn't believe her ears. She picked up the nearest thing on her bedside locker, a rather heavy book, and threw it at him with a frustrated scream. It caught him a glancing blow on his shoulder, causing him to swear. He leapt up, sprang onto the bed beside her and grabbed her two wrists harshly.

'Stop it! You're hurting me.' She wriggled but he simply tightened his grip. She could feel her arms burning hot beneath his hands and fear flooded her body.

'Listen to me.' He shook her angrily. 'I want a divorce so that I can marry Felicity. And I want you gone from this house.'

'You can't do that! What about the residents?'

'What about them?'

'The care home is registered in my name. I have a legal obligation to look after them. Are you going to throw them out, too?'

He grunted and let her go. She sobbed until she thought her heart would break, while he sat there impassively, thinking.

'Okay. I've got a proposition.'

'What?' She wiped her tears in an effort to see his face.

'You agree to a divorce, and we'll do it all nice and quietly. Get Felicity's name put on the register in your place. Then the residents won't be your responsibility any longer, and there won't be any need for you to be here.'

'But ...'

'Hear me out, please. Let's do all this civilly, without any fuss. The residents don't need to know what's happening. If you agree to that, I'll let you stay on here until we can get things sorted.'

'You think the residents won't know something's wrong?'

He looked at her in contempt. 'Not if you don't tell 'em.'

She stared at him in disbelief. This couldn't be happening. He was mad! He couldn't seriously think that she could behave as though nothing had changed.

'Think about it,' he said, standing up and putting on his dressing gown and slippers.

'Where are you going?' she wailed.

'To sleep in the lounge, of course. I won't get any sleep here if you're going to snivel like that all night.'

He slammed the bedroom door and she was alone. She threw herself onto the bed and sobbed into her pillow until she finally fell asleep.

# Chapter Eighteen

*Saturday 10th September 2022*

The next day, the weather had improved dramatically. Gone was the grey, replaced by a rich blue sky with cottonwool clouds. The wind had dropped and the air had that lovely fresh just-washed smell. Frau Flic was in the office when Lauren and Paul arrived, but there was no sign of either Wolly, also known as Stone-face, or Mrs W.

'You two work together upstairs,' she ordered. 'We're short-staffed, again, so I'll oversee breakfast. But after that, I've got lots to keep me busy in the office so try not to disturb me.'

'Okay, Ms Trainer. Will do!' Paul replied cheerfully.

'Oh, and don't bother going into Janet's room. I've been in to see her already.'

'Shall I take her some breakfast?' asked Lauren.

'No need, I've already taken her some cereal.'

'Well, I'll collect her bowl and bring it down,' said Paul helpfully.

'No,' said Felicity firmly, 'there's no need for either of you to disturb Janet at all today. She's not feeling well and would like to rest.'

Paul shrugged his shoulders and pulled a face at Lauren.

On their way upstairs, Lauren asked, 'Is it just me or is Frau Flic in a really grumpy mood this morning?'

'She most definitely is,' he retorted, 'but it's her weekend in charge so we'd better look lively, or else.'

❁

The cloud seemed to have lifted from the dining room too, but Meg was disappointed to see that Janet had once again not come down.

Jack demolished a huge bowl of cornflakes before gleefully collecting his full English from the chef at the hotplate.

'You doing anything nice this afternoon, Andy?'

'Going down to St Mary's later,' the broad-shouldered chef replied with a grin.

'Oh, very nice. I wish I could come with you.'

'You should come along to a game one Saturday. I'm sure Mrs Wollstonecraft would be okay with that.'

'Thanks for that, I haven't been to a match in years.'

'You used to go, then?'

'Yeah, had a season ticket for a long time, went to all the Saints' home games with my boys when they were still living at home.'

Albert rolled his eyes at the table and muttered, 'I might have known you were a football hooligan.'

'Football is a gentleman's game,' retorted Jack.

'Played by a load of overpaid, namby-pamby whiners!' scorned Albert.

'But what do they call cricket? Eh? I mean, it's all balls and stumps!' insinuated Jack. He left Albert searching furiously for a response.

'I don't know where you put it all!' Muriel remarked disapprovingly as Jack sat back beside her and tucked into his breakfast.

Jack patted his stomach. 'Flat as a pancake, even now.'

'Pardon?'

'Flat as a pancake,' he repeated more clearly.

'Yes, I'd be fat too if I ate as much as you,' she replied, at which Albert spluttered and nearly choked on his coffee.

'You be careful there, old man,' warned Jack.

'Less of the old!' snapped Albert.

Felicity slammed a freshly filled toast rack on the table and glared first at Jack, who bit back the retort on the tip of his tongue, and then Albert. 'Now then, you two,' she cautioned. 'Right, has everyone had all the hot food they want?' she continued, barely waiting for their replies before turning to Andy, saying, 'You can clear the hotplate now, Andy.'

He looked surprised. 'Won't Janet be coming down?'

'She's already had her breakfast.'

'But she often likes a boiled egg at the weekend ...' he began.

'I said, you can clear the hotplate.'

He was about to argue but thought better of it.

Meg glanced up anxiously.

'Is Janet still unwell?' she asked.

'She's tired and she needs to rest today. And she doesn't want any visitors.'

Meg frowned. 'Is something wrong?' asked Sylvia.

'Janet's still unwell,' replied Meg.

'Oh dear, is that nice doctor going to come again?'

'Good question. Have you called Dr Baker?' Meg asked Felicity.

'No need for that.'

Meg didn't like the way she said that.

No one lingered over breakfast with Felicity in charge, so by the time Paul and Lauren came down to the day room, all the residents there were either reading or dozing.

'Mrs W not up and about yet?' enquired Paul.

'I haven't seen her today,' replied Meg thoughtfully.

'It's her weekend off, isn't it?' Lauren supplied, surprised Paul didn't know that.

'But she's usually in the day room at this time of day, working or not,' explained Paul.

'It's very odd,' interrupted Albert, looking up from his paper. 'Very odd, indeed.'

※

Lauren fetched the coffees from the kitchen at ten-thirty and noticed that Frau Flic was on her own in the office as she walked past the open door.

'Have you seen either Brenda or Brian yet this morning?' Paul asked a few minutes later, handing her Albert's mug of very milky coffee.

'Now you come to mention it, no.'

'Perhaps they've gone out for the day,' he suggested.

'Ooh, have they gone somewhere nice?' Annie asked.

'Who's that, dear?' enquired Sylvia.
'Brian and Brenda, they've gone out for the day.'
'Oh, how lovely. Have they gone somewhere nice?'
'I don't know.'
'No, I don't know that they actually have gone out somewhere,' explained Paul, but Annie and Sylvia were already speculating as to where they might have gone, so he left them to it.

# Chapter Nineteen

By lunchtime, Meg was beginning to feel more than a little anxious.

'Paul, where did you say Mr and Mrs Wollstonecraft have gone?'

'I don't know that they have gone out, I just haven't seen either of them around this morning,' he replied.

'Mr Wollstonecraft left in his car quite early this morning,' chipped in Andy from the hotplate.

'Really?' asked Paul. 'On his own?'

'Well, he was definitely on his own when he came through the kitchen.'

'Did he say where he was going?'

'No. And before you ask, he had a face like thunder, so I didn't ask.'

'So, where's Brenda, then?'

'In bed with a migraine,' replied Felicity, coming in. 'Not that it's any of your business.'

Paul looked at her in surprise. 'Is she okay?'

'Shall I take her some lunch?' offered Lauren.

'Absolutely not! Brian said she didn't want to be disturbed, and I think we should respect that.'

There was a momentary pause and then Meg pushed herself up from the table.

'And how is Janet?' she asked.

'She's resting,' Felicity answered curtly, and left as quickly as she'd come.

Paul nodded at Lauren to stay and supervise, before quietly following Felicity to the office.

'Ms Trainer,' he began, gently closing the door.

'What now?'

'What is actually wrong with Janet?'

'As I said, she's very tired today.'

'Have you contacted Dr Baker?'

'It's the weekend, and, in any case, the doctor saw her only three days ago.'

'But I'm sure Mrs W would've called him, just to be on the safe side.'

'Are you criticising my judgement now?'

'Of course not,' he said, trying to placate his manager. 'It's just that a lot of strange things seem to be happening today. The residents are still unsettled after Marianne's death, and Brenda would usually be comforting and counselling.'

'I told you, she has a migraine,' snapped Felicity.

'Well, that's also odd. I've been here quite a few years and never known her to have so much as a headache. And why would Brian go out and leave her for so long, when she's ill? It doesn't make sense!'

'Mr Cropper, you would be better spending more time doing your job and less time being nosy about the whereabouts of your employers.'

Paul was shaken by both the unusual formality and the ferocity in Felicity's voice.

'Very well, Ms Trainer,' he replied, before leaving the office.

✽

The atmosphere in the day room was oppressive that afternoon, so Meg pottered out into the gardens. The sunshine was as pleasant now as it had been all summer, so she made her way carefully down to the fishpond. A twinge of sadness overtook her as she sat on the bench gazing at the spot where Marianne had been sitting with her just a few days previously. *Whatever is happening at The Cedars?* she wondered. She hadn't been here long, but she sensed that the atmosphere had recently changed.

She looked up across the lawn and, to her surprise, she saw Brian and Felicity emerge from the kitchen side of the house. Brian led the way, not by the main path that would've taken them past the day-room doors, but along a perimeter path that meandered in and out of the shrubs.

How peculiar! Without really knowing why she did it, she moved with surprising agility and quietness to conceal herself behind a clump of very dense bamboo.

The couple arrived at the bench and sat down. Felicity sounded cross.

'But why did you have to tell her?' she insisted.

'She already knew,' pouted Brian.

'Knew? Or suspected?'

'The same thing.'

'No, it's not. You should have denied it, smoothed things over.'

'I'm just so fed up with us creeping around over this. I want us to be together, as a couple.'

'It was never meant to come to this.' Felicity sounded agitated.

'Maybe not in the beginning, but you must know that I've fallen in love with you ...'

'Don't say that!'

'Let me finish. I love you and ...' he hesitated then withdrew a small box from his jacket pocket '... and I would very much like it if you would agree to marry me, Felicity,' he finished, gazing lovingly into her eyes.

She jumped up, appalled.

'You can't do this! You'll ruin everything!' she cried, and hastened back along the path.

'Felicity,' called Brian, hurrying after her.

Meg stepped out from the bamboo and sank gratefully onto the bench, her hips and knees aching dreadfully from standing still. She sat there for a very long time, thinking about what she'd overheard. Finally, giving a little shiver from the drop in temperature as the afternoon faded, and stiff from being inactive for too long, she struggled to her feet. Leaning heavily on her stick, she made her way shakily back to the house. She needed to talk to Janet, whether Felicity liked it or not.

❁

'Meg, whatever's wrong?' exclaimed Lauren as Meg let herself in through the French doors that had been closed against the late afternoon chill.

'You missed afternoon tea, and you look half frozen!'

She hurried to support Meg, who gently declined her attempts to help her into an armchair. 'Thank you very much, Lauren, but I'm perfectly all right.'

'I'd have come out to find you, if I'd realised. Albert thought you'd probably gone up to sit with Janet.'

'I would very much like to see Janet,' she replied carefully, 'but Felicity made it clear to me this morning that I wasn't to disturb her.'

Lauren looked sympathetic. 'Why don't I take you up to her now? I'm sure it'll be okay.'

She offered an arm to Meg, who took hold of it with gratitude. With Lauren on one side and still leaning heavily on her stick, she made it across the day room. The lift doors were open so they were able to walk straight in.

'I'm worried about Janet,' began Meg.

'Me too,' Lauren sighed. They looked at each other and Meg felt that an understanding had passed between them.

On the landing, they made their way to Janet's door and were just about to knock when Felicity came out of the staffroom.

'Where are you two going?'

Lauren was surprised to see that Felicity's eyes were slightly red-rimmed, and she had lost some of her usual composure. 'We're just going to check that Janet's okay.'

'There's no need, I've already been in,' Felicity said abruptly.

'But Meg here is worried about her friend.'

'There's nothing to worry about, Margaret. You can trust me to look after her.'

*Unfortunately*, thought Meg, *I'm not sure that I can*.

'Oh well, I'll just go and have a little lie-down myself then,' sighed Meg.

Lauren helped Meg into her room and was about to help her onto her bed when Meg gently resisted. 'I've no intention of letting that woman stop me from seeing my friend,' she confided to Lauren.

'You go, girl!' encouraged Lauren with a grin.

Meg eased open her door and looked around cautiously, before tiptoeing to Janet's door, closely followed by Lauren. Meg tapped but there was no reply. Thinking that Janet might be asleep, she tried to open the door. To her amazement, it appeared to be locked. No, that couldn't be right. She tried again but it wouldn't budge. She peered into the lock and saw there was no key. Panic crept up from her stomach, tightening her chest and gripping her throat. She shook the door vigorously, but still it stubbornly refused to open.

'Something is very wrong here,' she exclaimed to Lauren in a frantic whisper. 'This door is locked.'

# Chapter Twenty

'Maybe Janet locked herself in,' Lauren suggested. 'She couldn't have, and, in any case, the key's not in the lock.'

'Could someone else have locked it?'

'But residents are never locked in their rooms. It's in the fire regulations, I believe.'

'Yeah, I think I read that,' agreed Lauren thoughtfully. 'So, what do we do now?'

'Come with me.' Meg led Lauren to the lift, keeping her fingers crossed that Felicity wouldn't hear them. Back in the hall, she quietly edged towards the public phone. But it was so exposed here in the hall, and she really didn't want anyone to overhear this call. Lauren saw Meg hesitate and immediately pulled her mobile out of her pocket.

'You can use my phone, if you like,' she whispered.

Meg shook her head slowly and whispered back, 'I wouldn't know where to begin!' She changed direction and shuffled towards the office. She listened but couldn't hear anyone inside, so she cautiously peeked around the door. Empty.

'You stand guard here,' she whispered to Lauren, 'while I use the office phone!'

She went in and carefully closed the door. She quickly found what she was looking for, a BT phone book on a shelf above the computer. She sat down at the desk and searched for Salisbury Police Station, but it didn't appear to be listed! After a moment's panic, she thought to look at the front of the book. Emergency services; that's what she was looking for. Her worried eyes scanned the page. Police: there were three numbers but none of them for the local police station. She hesitated. Was this a real emergency that required a 999? She wasn't sure.

Thinking about it, she could be overreacting, couldn't

she? After all, Dr Baker hadn't been overly concerned about Janet on Wednesday. And she didn't actually know if anything had happened to Janet, did she? Not wanting to look a fool, she moved on.

There was a number for Crimestoppers, but she couldn't be certain there had actually been a crime. What proof did she have?

In the end, she dialled 101 and waited interminably for someone to answer. That was the problem with centralising everything, she thought. Eventually, a friendly voice responded. 'Wiltshire Police, Helen speaking. How can I help you?'

'I'm worried about my friend,' began Meg.

'If this is a medical emergency, you should dial 999 and ask for an ambulance, ma'am.'

'Oh! I was rather hoping to get some advice before I waste anyone's time.'

'Where are you?'

'I'm at The Cedars on Harnham Road.'

'And where is that?'

'Salisbury.'

'And your friend?'

'She's in her room upstairs.'

'Is she injured?'

'Well, I don't think so, but I'm concerned she might be in danger.'

'The Cedars ... that's a care home, isn't it?'

'Yes, that's right.'

'Are you a member of staff?'

'Oh no, I'm a resident.' Meg bit her lip; she could see where this was going.

'Do you think you can pass the phone over to a member of staff, please, my love?'

'I'm not senile, you know!' she said indignantly.

'I didn't mean to imply that, but I do need to speak to a member of staff.'

Meg dithered but just at that moment the office door was pushed open.

'Well, thank you very much, goodbye.' Meg put the

phone down and looked up as Paul came in, followed by an apologetic-looking Lauren.

'Meg?' asked Paul softly, grabbing the computer chair and pulling it over to sit face to face with her. 'Who were you calling?'

'Oh dear, you're going to think me a dreadful old fool,' she began.

Paul took hold of Meg's hands and squeezed them gently.

'No, I won't. Just tell me what that was all about, please.'

'I'm so worried about Janet. I think Felicity has locked her in her room and may have done something to her.'

'Janet's door can't be locked. And what on earth do you think Felicity might have done?' Meg hesitantly shared some of her theories about Felicity as Paul's eyes grew bigger with each supposition.

'Did you try Janet's door yourself?' Paul eventually asked Lauren.

'Sorry, I didn't think of that,' she groaned, kicking herself mentally. 'Hang on a minute.' Lauren hurried quietly up the stairs, looking anxiously for any sign of Felicity but not seeing her. She knocked on Janet's door and then tried the handle. It was certainly locked, no doubt about it. And there was no sound from within. She went swiftly back down to the office and confirmed Meg's findings.

'Thank you for sharing your concerns, Meg. I should tell Wolly or Mrs W, but I haven't seen either of them at all today.' Meg bit her tongue to stop herself from blurting out that Brian was back from wherever he'd been. Paul continued. 'I think I'll phone Dr Baker and ask him to come and have a look.'

They shared a concerned look and then he made the phone call, talking quietly and professionally to the doctor, before returning the phone to its stand.

'Come back to the day room, now, and let me deal with this,' Paul insisted.

'Is he coming?' asked Meg.

'Yes, he'll be here as soon as he can.'

Meg heaved a sigh of relief that at least something was going to be done. She just hoped that Janet was still alive.

※

By the time Dr Baker arrived, the residents were having dinner. Paul had asked Lauren to supervise the dining room before hovering anxiously in the hall, hoping Frau Flic wouldn't appear and ask him what he was doing. Lauren felt a little put out at being sidelined. After all, it was she and Meg who'd discovered that Janet's door was locked.

'Right, Paul,' the doctor said, coming through the door, slipping his coat off and hanging it on the visitor pegs. 'What's the problem?'

Paul explained as best he could as they went upstairs together. The doctor made several loud exclamations, which alerted Felicity to their approach. She hurried from the staffroom to Janet's door and quickly unlocked it, slipping the key back into her pocket as the pair rounded the corner.

'Dr Baker!' She put just the right amount of surprise into her voice. 'To what do we owe the pleasure?'

'Paul called me with a concern over Mrs Smith,' he replied cautiously.

'Really, Paul, I told you there was no need to bother Dr Baker at the weekend.'

Paul quailed under Frau Flic's furious glare. 'I'm sorry, Dr Baker, but there's really no need for concern,' continued Felicity smoothly. 'I've just been in to check on Janet and she's sleeping peacefully. I really wouldn't like you to disturb her.'

'I'd rather check for myself, now that I'm here.' He stepped towards the door and Felicity stepped back with a smile.

'Of course, Doctor.'

Paul was astounded when the door opened easily. Felicity smiled at him smugly.

The three of them cautiously entered Janet's room, and

sure enough, she was in bed, asleep and breathing evenly. Dr Baker went to her side and gently felt for a pulse. Then he counted her respirations. He nodded at the two carers and they all withdrew from the room without speaking. He pulled them into the staffroom.

'Her vital signs are normal,' he said, 'although she does seem to be sleeping very deeply. I'm surprised she didn't stir at all.'

'I told you there was nothing to worry about. She was just tired and this sleep is doing her the world of good,' said Felicity calmly. Somehow, it didn't ring true to Paul.

'I'm so sorry you had a wasted journey,' she added, glaring at Paul again.

'Not to worry,' the doctor reassured her, 'better to be safe than sorry.'

'I'll see you out, Doctor.' Felicity led the doctor downstairs and Paul followed them.

'Please tell Brenda that I'll call in on Monday morning to check on Janet,' he said as he put his coat on.

'She's in bed with a migraine,' blurted out Paul.

'What?' The doctor looked instantly concerned and Paul was acutely aware that if looks could kill, Felicity would most certainly have murdered him. Phil strode across to the Wollstonecrafts' door, opened it and called down,

'Only me, Brenda. Just wanted to check if you're okay.'

Paul heard a faint reply and saw the doctor hesitate, when he'd thought he was about to go charging down. Footsteps followed and Brenda appeared in the doorway, looking pale and drawn.

'Are you ill?' exclaimed the doctor, searching her face with concern. She avoided his gaze and stared at Felicity.

'How's your migraine, Brenda?' enquired Felicity with frosted politeness.

'Oh, it wasn't a migraine, just a headache,' said Brenda carefully. 'I take it my husband's been exaggerating again?'

'We've all been so concerned about you,' put in Paul.

'That's so kind of you, but there's really no need to worry.'

She came fully into the hallway, gathered herself together

and said, with great dignity, 'I'll just go and say hello to the residents.'

Phil watched her retreating back with concern. Something was definitely not right. He heard Felicity go into the office then looked at Paul.

'Don't worry, I'll keep an eye on her,' Paul reassured him. Phil nodded and left.

# Chapter Twenty-one

*Sunday 11th September 2022*

Sunday dawned as beautiful as Saturday, but no one in the home seemed to notice.

Once again, Lauren and Paul were on long day shifts with only agency help, which Paul explained was not uncommon at weekends. As they made the beds together, Lauren asked, 'What do you think about yesterday?'

'What about it?' Paul looked awkward.

'You know. All those things Meg said about Felicity.'

'Do you know, I'm inclined to think Meg must have made a mistake. I mean, I don't particularly like Frau Flic, but I can't believe some of the things Meg said about her.'

'I can,' said Lauren.

'Well, please don't go about repeating it. It'll only cause trouble.'

'Aren't you worried that Frau Flic might be a mass murderer?'

'Of course she isn't, you ghoul.'

'But what about the mystery of the locked door?'

'That wasn't even locked,' pointed out Paul.

'It certainly was!' she retorted hotly.

'I expect Meg was a little overanxious and simply didn't turn the handle properly.'

'But I tried it too!'

'Oh yeah,' Paul admitted ruefully.

'Suppose Frau Flic did murder both Harry and Marianne and is even now plotting to bump Janet off?'

'Don't be so silly!' he said, rather more roughly than he had meant to. 'I mean, Dr Phil signed both Harry's and Marianne's death certificates as natural causes, didn't he?'

'That's true enough,' she conceded.

'And he wouldn't have made a mistake!' Paul insisted. Lauren wasn't so certain.

They finished the bed and went round tidying the room. Lauren sorted out some dirty washing for the laundry bag outside the door whilst Paul emptied the litter bin and restocked the toilet paper.

'All done?' checked Paul.

'Yep. Five down, two to go,' said Lauren.

'Don't forget, Frau Flic said to leave Janet's room again today.'

'Don't you find that rather suspicious?'

Paul shook his head stubbornly and frowned. He didn't want to believe Meg. To think that they might have a murderer in the home ... it was incredible!

Lauren didn't like to push Paul, so she changed the subject by asking him about a gig he was going to at the Bournemouth International Centre the following weekend, and he chatted quite happily about it. It was better than arguing.

❀

Brenda was doing her best to behave normally but was acutely aware that she hadn't fooled anyone last night. She'd just have to do better today. She tidied and dusted the day room to keep herself busy until the residents started to drift through from breakfast.

'Good morning, Mrs Wollstonecraft. Feeling better today?' asked Albert.

'Much better, thank you,' she said, smiling as brightly as she could.

Albert tottered across to his armchair and opened his *Sunday Telegraph*, scattering several flyers and supplements onto the floor. Brenda went to pick them up.

'Oh, Brenda! How nice to see you up this morning,' gushed Annie, coming in with Sylvia. 'Are you feeling better?'

'Yes, thank you.'

'You had a migraine, I think Felicity said?'

'Just a bad headache.'

'Oh, I think it was probably a migraine,' insisted Annie, 'you looked very pale and sickly yesterday evening.'

'Perhaps you're right,' Brenda said, trying to keep it light.

'Did you say Brenda was sick yesterday?' Sylvia asked Annie.

'I said I thought she looked sickly. Didn't you think so?'

'Oh yes. It's probably because she's pregnant,' nodded Sylvia.

Brenda stood up and looked aghast at her. Albert startled and nearly dropped his paper. 'What? What?' he spluttered.

Annie laughed at their stunned faces. 'Not Brenda, Sylvia! How many times do I need to tell you, it's my granddaughter, Mandy, who's pregnant,' she reminded her friend.

Brenda shakily put the pile of supplements onto the coffee table whilst Albert recovered his aplomb.

The front doorbell chimed, providing a welcome distraction. Wondering who on earth it could be, Brenda crossed the day room quickly, happy to escape. Impatiently, she waved away Felicity, who was coming from the dining room.

'I can deal with this,' she said curtly. *After all, I'm still in charge in my care home for the moment*, she thought.

She opened the door to see an older policeman standing on the doorstep, with thinning hair and a slightly rotund paunch straining his uniform buttons. For a wild moment, she wondered if Brian had called the police to throw her out, and she could only gape speechlessly at him.

'Mrs Wollstonecraft?' he asked politely.

'Yes,' she managed to say, pulling herself together.

'My sergeant asked me to drop by this morning just to check that everything's all right.'

'Really?' Brenda was puzzled as to why the police would be here at all, let alone asking her if she was all right.

'May I come in?'

'Oh yes, perhaps you'd better.' She held the door open and gestured towards the office.

'Thank you.' The policeman carefully wiped his rather

large boots and walked ponderously across to the office. Felicity stood in the dining-room doorway watching him, fear etched into her face.

'What does he want?' she hissed at Brenda as soon as he was out of sight.

'I don't know yet,' replied Brenda tartly.

'Shall I come in with you?'

'No need.'

Brenda followed the policeman into the office and firmly shut the door.

✿

Brenda settled herself and the policeman into the two chairs in the office and offered him tea or coffee, which he politely declined.

'What's this all about?' she asked, a little nervously.

'There was a phone call to our 101 number yesterday,' he began. Brenda looked at him uncomprehendingly.

'I take it from your expression that you don't know anything about that?' he asked.

'I'm sorry, no.'

He flicked open a little black notebook and squinted at something jotted there.

'A call came in at ... erm ... 17.21 yesterday afternoon. It was an elderly lady who said that she was concerned about a friend. She said she wanted some advice, so the operator took an address – this address – and the caller said that she thought her friend was in danger.'

Brenda shook her head disbelievingly.

'How do you know the call actually came from here?' she asked.

'We back traced the number.'

'Oh.'

'Just routine, you know. We have to check nothing's actually wrong, you see.'

'I see,' she said, not really seeing at all.

'The operator established that the lady was a resident, so she asked to speak to a member of staff.'

'And?'

'Well, that was the peculiar part, ma'am. The caller quite suddenly said goodbye and hung up.'

Brenda frowned.

'Would the same staff be on duty today as were here at that time yesterday?' he asked politely.

'Yes', she replied, getting up and going to the office door. To her relief, Paul was within hailing distance, and there was no sign of Felicity.

'Can you come in, Paul?' she asked quietly.

She shut the door carefully after her and waved at Paul to sit in the only vacant chair. The policeman stood up courteously and offered her his chair, before going to stand where he could lean against a large grey filing cabinet.

'PC Daly, sir,' he informed Paul, realising that he hadn't introduced himself earlier.

'What's this about?' Paul looked at Brenda.

'Do you happen to know if any of the residents made a phone call from this phone yesterday afternoon, about half-past five?' she asked him, studying his face and surprised to see him flush slightly.

'Um, yes, that was Meg,' he replied uneasily.

'Meg?' asked PC Daly.

'That's Margaret Thornton, one of our residents,' Brenda explained to him. 'But, Paul, why didn't you tell me about this?'

'You weren't very well at the time, and I didn't want to bother you.'

'Yes, of course. But whatever was Meg doing phoning the police?'

'She ... um ... she was concerned about Janet.'

'Janet Smith, another resident,' explained Brenda, as PC Daly diligently scribbled in his notebook.

'Why was she concerned about Janet?' she puzzled, unaware that she was asking the very questions the policeman wanted to ask.

'She ... um ... you see, Janet was resting in her room all day because she was feeling tired. And Meg went up to visit her and thought the door was locked,' continued Paul.

'Do you make a habit of locking residents in their rooms?' interrupted the constable.

'Oh no,' said Paul, 'it wasn't really locked, you see.'

'Of course we don't lock residents in their rooms,' put in Brenda indignantly. 'That would be a breach of fire regulations.'

'Quite so,' agreed PC Daly, slightly amused at her defensiveness.

'But why on earth would Meg think that someone had locked Janet in her room?' Brenda demanded.

Paul swallowed awkwardly. He didn't want to repeat what Meg had said about Felicity.

'It's better to tell the truth, young man,' encouraged the policeman.

Paul reluctantly tried to explain, glossing over some of the detail, but it was clear that neither Brenda nor the policeman could follow what he was saying.

'Excuse me asking this, but is this Meg ... um ... suffering from some kind of delusions ... or dementia?' he asked, beginning to think that this was the waste of time he'd told his sergeant it would be.

'Absolutely not!' insisted Brenda hotly.

'Very well,' he sighed, 'I'd better speak to the lady herself then.'

❁

Meg was in the day room doing her jigsaw puzzle. Paul brought her into the office and went out again immediately. Brenda was about to sit down when PC Daly coughed.

'I'd rather speak to Mrs Thornton on her own,' he said.

'Oh!' exclaimed Brenda.

'Yes, I think that would be best,' agreed Meg, much to Brenda's surprise.

'Very well, I'll leave you to it.' She left the office and shut the door behind her.

'Now then, Mrs Thornton, in your own time, please.' PC Daly smiled reassuringly. Meg was only too happy to oblige.

Half an hour later, Meg saw PC Daly to the front door and wished him goodbye, before taking the lift upstairs. *The old lady has probably got hold of the wrong end of the stick*, he thought. But it wouldn't hurt to check up on one or two of the facts later in the week, if he had the time. Just to make sure there was nothing in it.

# Chapter Twenty-two

Meg spent the remainder of the morning reading in her room, unwilling to face the other residents. Doubtless they would want to hear every detail, and she had just promised PC Daly not to spread any rumours until they could be substantiated, which was quite right and proper.

Paul brought her a cup of coffee, asked if she felt all right, and left without further questions, for which Meg was thankful.

Brenda looked in just before lunch to ask if she would like to take her meal in her room 'just this once'.

'I would be very grateful for that, please,' she accepted with alacrity.

'I expect you don't feel up to talking about this with the other residents yet?' Brenda suggested.

'It's not just that,' she explained a little awkwardly, 'but the constable did ask me to keep the details to myself.'

'Of course,' Brenda sounded disappointed, 'but if you do want someone to confide in, you can rest assured that it won't go any further than me.'

'I know,' she nodded. 'And I hope you know that you can always confide in me?'

Brenda hesitated.

'Are you quite recovered from your migraine, my dear? Only you still look dreadfully pale,' Meg remarked casually, watching Brenda like a hawk.

Tears sprang into the corners of Brenda's eyes. 'You know, I'm not sure I am completely over it.' She sank onto the edge of Meg's bed. 'Do you promise not to tell any of the others?'

Meg offered a hand to Brenda. 'You can rely on me,' she said reassuringly.

Brenda reached out as though to take Meg's hand but then quickly withdrew her own, pulling the sleeves of her tunic top down to cover her wrists. But not before Meg had noticed some bruising in the area.

'Are you quite sure it was a migraine and not something else?' she probed gently.

Brenda gulped. 'Is it that obvious?' she whispered.

'Only to me. I don't think any of the other residents have noticed.'

'Brian's having an affair.' She almost choked on the words.

'I know,' Meg replied calmly.

'You do? Oh Lord, does everyone know?'

'Not everyone. But it's a pretty big thing to try and hide, don't you think?'

'I just keep hoping this whole nightmare is going to go away.'

'Do you really think it will blow over that easily?'

'Not really.'

'Is there something else?'

'Brian ...' Brenda broke off, biting back the words she'd been about to say. No, it was too much to say the divorce word out loud. 'No, you're wrong, Meg. I'm absolutely sure Brian and I can work this out. Please, don't say a word of this to anyone. Promise me?'

'I told you. You can trust me,' Meg said carefully.

Brenda stood up and carefully dabbed her eyes, took a couple of deep breaths and smoothed down her tunic top.

'Could you possibly just confirm one thing for me, please?' Brenda asked.

'If I can,' Meg promised.

'Was Janet's door really locked when you tried it yesterday?'

'Yes, it was.'

'You're absolutely sure?'

'I'm certain.'

'And you think it was Felicity who locked it?'

'I have good reason to think so.'

Brenda sighed as she left the room.

Moments later, Lauren knocked lightly on the door. 'It's only me,' she grinned at Meg. 'I've brought your lunch up.'

'Thank you, my dear, that's really kind of you.'

'Well, Mrs W told me to bring it up to you, so not really my idea, I'm afraid. Do you feel like a bit of company while you're eating?'

Meg smiled. 'Take a seat, if you like.' Lauren chatted away happily to Meg as she ate, avoiding asking her any questions until she had put her knife and fork down. 'Now then, what happened this morning with that policeman who came?' she demanded, eager to know if their concerns about Frau Flic were being taken seriously. Meg happily shared with Lauren, who already knew the details anyway. So, she wasn't really breaking her promise to PC Daly, was she?

Lauren was pleased to hear that PC Daly was going to investigate Meg's concerns about Frau Flic; she just hoped he'd do it quickly before anyone else got murdered.

✿

Later that afternoon, Lauren was in the treatment room preparing a tray to go and change Janet's leg dressing. She wanted an excuse to ask Janet whether, despite being virtually unable to walk, she had somehow locked her door herself yesterday. Because that would explain it all, wouldn't it?

She was startled to hear raised voices from the office and stuck her head out into the hallway. It sounded like Brian and Frau Flic were arguing. She crept across to the closed office door, aware that most of the residents were occupied with their visitors. Frustratingly, the voices were now only murmuring, and she couldn't make out the words. After a quick glance around, she pressed her ear to the door. Frau Flic was speaking in a sickeningly sweet tone of voice. 'Do you promise me?'

Brian replied earnestly, 'I promise.'

'Swear to God and hope to die?' Lauren couldn't believe what she was hearing. This was totally unlike the Frau Flic she knew!

'I absolutely swear,' Brian replied.

'Good!' Frau Flic snapped loudly, all traces of saccharine sweetness gone from her voice. 'Because if you try to wriggle out of this, I promise I WILL KILL YOU!' Lauren sprang back from the door, startled by the vehemence of those final words.

'Of course, darling, haven't I just promised?' Brian was saying as he opened the door and backed out of the office. Lauren ducked back into the treatment room and hid behind the door as Brian headed into the basement flat. *Oh my God*, she thought, *maybe Meg was right!* For a while, she could think of nothing else but those four ferociously spoken words. She dithered for several more minutes before finally deciding to carry on with what she'd been planning. Taking the tray, she checked the hall before stepping out of the treatment room. She had just started up the stairs when the office door flew open.

'Lauren?' Felicity's voice sent a chill down her spine.

She froze. 'Yes?' she called, without turning round.

'What are you doing?'

'Just going to change Janet's dressing.'

'For one thing, I've already done it. And for another, I told you yesterday, you are not to change dressings without supervision for the moment.'

Lauren turned round and faced Felicity.

'What on earth's wrong, girl? You look like you've seen a ghost.'

'I'm fine, Ms Trainer. Just fine.'

'Pop that tray back into the treatment room then come to the office, I'd like a chat.'

Felicity stood back and watched Lauren as she did as instructed. Once the door was closed, Felicity turned on the charm and tried to persuade a truculent Lauren to tell her about the events of the day before. Lauren fudged as best she could, but eventually conceded that Meg had found Janet's door to be locked.

'Surely, you don't believe that, you're an intelligent girl,' Felicity purred.

'Of course not, Ms Trainer,' Lauren lied convincingly.

'I think Marianne's death has upset quite a few of the

residents. Janet is still not feeling well, and Meg, well ... I can only say that she is behaving completely out of character. She isn't usually prone to such fanciful flights of fantasy.'

'If you say so, Ms Trainer.'

'So, Lauren, it's important that the staff work together to try to calm things down and help the residents get back to normal. You do see that, don't you?'

'Yes, Ms Trainer.'

That night, Lauren wasn't the only person from The Cedars who didn't get much sleep for worrying about the day's extraordinary events.

# Chapter Twenty-three

*Monday 12th September 2022*

As usual, it was the chef, Andy, who arrived first the next morning. At six foot one, his physical presence was imposing, with a thatch of unruly blond hair, broad shoulders and bulging biceps. He whistled tunelessly as he changed into his whites and then turned on the radio on the kitchen windowsill to listen to Spire FM as he prepared breakfast. He greeted Sally as she came through the kitchen, thinking that she looked as though she'd had a very rough night. 'Partying on a Sunday?' he asked her.

She explained she'd been to a wedding over the weekend, and he chuckled. Then he saw Lauren and Paul arrive about five minutes later and noted that she looked like she'd had a rough night too. Even Paul seemed unusually taciturn. 'Typical Monday morning,' he muttered to himself.

*Right, time to get the cod fillets out of the freezer for lunch.* He went into the large pantry that was part utility room and part staff locker room. He lifted the lid on the larger of the two chest freezers. That was odd; it was full to the brim with boxes, bags and packets rammed in chaotically. Those desserts should be in the other freezer, for a start. He lifted the lid on the second freezer. Now he knew why all the contents had been transferred. The only thing occupying this freezer was a very – dead – body. He paled slightly and reached for his mobile phone.

✻

The operator who took his 999 call asked him to stop anyone from entering or leaving the property until the police arrived, and to keep everyone away from the crime scene.

He locked the back door and went through to the office, where Sonia and Jan were chatting to Sally before going off shift.

'Sally, who's in charge this morning?'

''Fraid it's me this morning, why?'

'You might want to sit down for this.'

'Oh well, we'll be on our way then, leave you to it,' said Jan, laughing.

'No, I'm sorry but you won't be able to go home just yet,' Andy insisted firmly.

All three looked at him with curiosity that turned to horror when he explained why.

Sally burst into tears.

The next hour was something of a blur. After her initial outburst, Sally had pulled herself together. As senior care assistant, they were all looking to her to lead. She asked Andy if he would be able to prepare some kind of a breakfast in the dining room. 'The residents will still need to eat.'

'No problem, I can do hot drinks and toast without going to the kitchen, but I won't have enough milk to offer cereals,' he warned. 'The question is, do we tell the residents what's happened?'

'Not until we have to. Sonia, would you mind staying near the front door to make sure no one enters or leaves, please? And, Jan, do you feel up to going downstairs to inform Brenda and Brian, please? I'll go and break the news to Paul and Lauren and then help them bring the residents down to the dining room.'

When the others had all gone, she sat down for a moment, stunned. She couldn't get her head around this. Bad enough that there was a dead body in one of their freezers, but who on earth would want to murder Felicity?

✿

Two very young constables in uniform were the first on the scene, pulling into the driveway with a screech of tyres that sent the gravel scattering. One, PC Doughty, asked where the body was and rushed off to confirm that it really was a dead person, and not just a pile of rags or a dummy or something. He returned a minute or two later to fetch what he needed from the car to start taping off the crime scene. The other, PC Tomlinson, stayed and took some details from Sonia before taking over her front-door duties.

From then on, there was a steady stream of vehicles arriving. The drive was soon full up, and cars lined the pavement for some distance either side of the home. PC Tomlinson sent each arrival round the outside of the building to the back door, where they signed in with PC Doughty and put protective clothing on before entering the scene to carry out their various tasks.

❂

Meg woke up that morning after a very restless night, wondering what today might bring. As soon as she came downstairs, she began to suspect that something new was wrong. Andy was in the dining room looking very apologetic about the limited breakfast. 'The kitchen is temporarily out of bounds,' he explained. She didn't mind just having toast but was frustrated that Andy wouldn't explain further. When Jack arrived, he was particularly put out to find neither cereals nor cooked breakfast on offer. But still Andy stayed tight-lipped. In fact, Meg thought, he looked decidedly worried. What on earth could be bothering him?

Breakfast was eaten with much mumbling and grumbling and was nearly over when Brenda came into the dining room, looking pale and upset. She studied the six residents around the table then called for their attention.

'What? What?' spluttered Albert. 'What's going on?'

'I have something I need to tell everyone, so I trust you will excuse the staff joining you in here,' Brenda began. She stepped outside the dining room and called in the rest of the staff as Meg pondered if perhaps Brenda was going to announce her and Brian's divorce. The staff filed in and spread themselves out around the table close to the residents. Meg was surprised to see that the night staff hadn't gone home, and she noticed that Sally had been crying.

Brian sidled in and joined Andy in the hotplate area, keeping his eyes on the floor. Meg's heart sank. She had a queasy feeling that this could only be bad news, and she prayed that it did not concern Janet, who was conspicuous by her absence.

'I'm sorry to have to tell you all that something truly awful has happened during the night,' Brenda announced, in a slightly wobbly voice. Meg's stomach lurched and she pushed her plate away, wishing she hadn't eaten anything.

'And I need to introduce Detective Inspector Bywater and, um, Sergeant . . . ?'

Sergeant Williams, ma'am,' he filled in for her, as he and another man came into the room.

*Oh, dear God, no*, thought Meg. *Please tell me that Janet hasn't been murdered!*

'Good morning, everyone.' The sergeant spoke quietly but firmly in impeccable English, with just a hint of a West Indian lilt. 'I'm sorry to have to inform you all that Ms Felicity Trainer was found dead this morning.'

There were lots of gasps and cries, but the staff members were on hand to comfort those residents who needed it. Sally bent down beside Muriel to explain to her what had been said. Meg sat very still, her heart racing and her mind in a whirl. She felt very relieved that it wasn't Janet, but shocked to learn that Felicity was dead. If Felicity was the murderer, how could she be dead? Was it suicide?

Meg studied the two men who had entered the room. The inspector was perhaps mid-thirties, she guessed, and the only description that came to mind was 'medium'. He was medium height, not more than five foot nine, of medium build, with medium brown hair that was neither too long nor too short, and a face that was clean-shaven and remarkably undistinguished. A veritable Mr Average! He was wearing a grey suit with a white shirt and a tie that was so nondescript it could have been any colour or none. She felt slightly disappointed. The sergeant, on the other hand, was much more interesting. He had to be at least six foot, maybe taller, with a closely shaved head and skin that shone like polished ebony. He was sufficiently muscular to be appealing but not overweight. About late twenties, she guessed. He looked incredibly smart in a tailored dark blue suit and pale blue shirt. She realised that she was staring at him and looked away quickly, hoping that he hadn't got the wrong impression.

The inspector spoke and Meg was relieved to hear that his voice had an air of quiet authority. 'I've only just arrived, so I need a little time to acquaint myself with what's happened, but we appear to be looking at a suspicious death.'

Several people gasped, and Meg studied his face closely. A suspicious death, what did that mean? She ran through the alternatives: accident, suicide or murder. But it made no sense for Felicity to be the victim of murder!

'Why is it suspicious?' demanded Jack, echoing her thoughts.

'All in good time, sir. I will tell you more in due course. Now, it's standard procedure that we need to ask everyone present in the house a few questions, nothing to worry about. But until we are able to talk to each of you individually, I'd be very grateful if you could avoid speculating among yourselves. It rarely helps. And, I'm afraid, no one is to leave the house this morning until we have given you permission to do so.'

He looked round to see if anyone would challenge him. Sylvia started crying quietly and Albert looked thunderous, but no one spoke. The DI turned to Brenda.

'Can you confirm that this is all the staff and residents, please?'

'Everyone except those staff not on duty today, and Janet, our eldest resident, who is still in her room.'

'Will you go up and fetch her to join the rest, please?'

'She hasn't been very well recently,' explained Brenda.

'Perhaps you would go and assess whether she can be brought down or not.'

'Of course, Lauren and I will go together.'

'Good.' He looked around the room again. 'Now, Mrs Wollstonecraft has kindly agreed to let us take over her office, so we'll do the interviews in there. I would prefer it if you would all wait in one room together. It makes it easier for us to find you.' He smiled and raised an eyebrow at Brenda.

'Yes, I suggest we all go into the day room together. Would it be possible for our chef to go to the kitchen to bring a trolley of refreshments down, please, Inspector?'

'Not immediately, I'm afraid, but I will inform him as soon as it's possible.'

'What about lunch?' Jack demanded.

'Don't worry, sir, we'll make provision for that in due course. Perhaps I can have a few words with the chef while you all move through to the day room.'

While the remaining staff assisted the shocked residents, Brenda and Lauren went upstairs.

# Chapter Twenty-four

They knocked on Janet's door and went straight in, expecting to find her reading in bed as she often was at that time in the morning. They were surprised to find the curtains closed, the lights out and Janet fast asleep. Surprise turned to concern as they tried to wake her. Despite her pulse being steady, her breathing was shallow, and she was unresponsive.

'Sit with Janet and if her condition worsens, ring the bell immediately. I'm going down to the office to call Dr Baker,' said Brenda.

✿

Detective Inspector Bywater was not particularly happy to see Brenda return on her own. 'Where's the other carer?' he demanded. But when Brenda explained, he was full of sympathy and signalled to her to use the phone.

'Dr Baker's on his way,' she soon informed him, replacing the phone in its stand. 'I need to send our senior care assistant up to monitor Janet. Lauren, who's up there now, has only been here a few weeks and doesn't have the necessary experience.'

He considered for a moment. 'Could you go back up and join Lauren yourself,' he suggested. 'You can both stay with your resident. What room number is she in?'

Brenda told him and went back upstairs. As soon as she was out of sight, he strode across the hall to PC Tomlinson on the door, where he set in motion various arrangements to keep an eye on all the staff and residents of The Cedars. He didn't like potential suspects roaming around and comparing notes. He returned to the office where Viv, his sergeant, had just finished rearranging the furniture with the male carer.

'Thank you, sir. Will you go and wait with the others in the day room now, please.'

Paul hesitated.

'Is there a problem?'

'Just that two of our carers have been at work all night. They really need to get some sleep because they're back on duty again tonight.'

'Thank you, I am aware of that. We'll interview them first then send them off home.'

'That's great. And there's another thing.'

'Yes?'

'One of our residents wants me to inform you that you need to interview her as soon as possible. She says she has important information you'll want to hear.'

'Really?' The inspector looked mildly amused.

'She's a pretty sharp lady, sir. A retired schoolteacher.'

'Thank you, we'll get round to her in due course.'

'One final thing, sir.'

'Yes,' the inspector sighed.

'I assume it's okay for people to use the downstairs toilets.' He nodded to the two doors down the corridor towards the kitchen. 'Some of our residents need to go a little more frequently than others.'

The inspector smiled wryly. 'Very well.'

He requested another uniform to stand guard outside the toilets, which were a bit too close to the kitchen door for his liking.

'Right, Viv,' he said, striding back into the office. 'Shall we go to the crime scene first and see if the forensic pathologist has any information for us about the body yet? It would be useful to have an idea of how long she's been deceased before we start the interviews.'

'You think he'll tell you that, sir?' grinned Viv, revealing a set of perfect teeth.

'I can always hope,' sighed the inspector.

The atmosphere in the day room was tense. Meg sat in her armchair studying the faces around the room. Albert, sitting next to her, had buried himself in his *Telegraph* and appeared oblivious to what was going on. But Meg soon realised that he had not once turned the page, so he was probably more perturbed than he wanted people to think.

Sylvia and Annie were on the small settee, whilst Jan had pulled up a chair to sit with them. They were chatting quietly, Annie's face serious for once and Sylvia's even more confused than usual. The poor dear clearly didn't understand what was going on. She didn't cope well with change and the last week had seen all too much of that. Jan had spent some considerable time reassuring Sylvia, but Meg suspected that they were now speculating about what might have happened, despite the inspector's warning. Annie and Jan were speaking in turns, with Sylvia resembling a spectator at a tennis match.

Jack was doing the quick crossword on the back of his *Sun* but was making slower than usual progress as he kept pausing to stare into space, deep in thought.

Sally sat with Muriel; both silent, Muriel wearing her habitual frown.

Sonia had gone to Janet's corner of the day room and was dozing fitfully in a chair. The stress showed in lines etched across her forehead and around her mouth.

Brian was at the opposite end of the day room, seated at the table in the bay window, his head in his hands. His hair was ruffled, his face unshaved and he wore a rumpled sweatshirt and tracksuit bottoms. A few tears had trickled down his pale face, leaving damp traces, and he had blown his nose loudly, several times. He was obviously very distressed at losing his lover. More than that, he also seemed on edge from the way his foot tapped on the floor and his fingers picked at the handkerchief each time he blew his nose.

Andy sat upright and impassive on the other side of the table, clearly lost in his own thoughts. Only the slight pallor of his skin hinted at the awfulness of what he must have seen. He looked up as Paul came in and nodded. Paul sat next to him, eager for information but getting none.

A young WPC – if that's what they were still called – slipped quietly into the day room and stood just inside the door, her eyes roaming round the occupants of the room. Interesting; did the inspector think one of them was going to make a run for it?

As time went on, Meg grew increasingly anxious when neither Brenda nor Lauren returned. Had something happened to Janet?

'I say!' interjected Albert, quite suddenly. 'Are we going to sit around waiting all blasted day? Eh?'

'Keep your hair on,' replied Jack, a sudden twinkle appearing in one eye. 'Or is it a bit too late for that?' he chuckled, looking pointedly at Albert's shiny head.

Brian looked up. 'Can't you show a bit more respect for the dead?' he complained, and Jack had the grace to flush uncomfortably and mutter an apology.

Paul spoke up. 'The inspector said that he would start the interviews as soon as possible, but we'll all have to wait our turn.'

'And how long will that take?' demanded Jan. 'Some of us want to get home to our families and our beds!'

'He did say he would interview you and Sonia first so that you can get off home,' answered Paul sympathetically.

'And did you pass on my message?' Meg asked quietly.

'I did, yes,' replied Paul.

Albert gave her a long hard stare then opened his paper again with a harrumph! Meg turned her mind to the reason they were all there. Very little had been said but Felicity was dead, presumably in or near the kitchen, given that it was now out of bounds. She gathered that Andy had discovered the body and called the police. An accident in the kitchen, possibly? But that seemed unlikely. Felicity had been alive and well after dinner last night, so she would've had no reason to be doing anything in the kitchen. Suicide? Surely it would've made more sense for Felicity to do that in her own room, where she wouldn't have risked being interrupted. So that left – murder! But who on earth would have a reason to murder Felicity?

# Chapter Twenty-five

Detective Inspector Daniel Bywater, Salisbury born and bred, marched ahead of his sergeant, Vivian Williams, a third-generation Jamaican born in Southampton. They made their way around the outside of the house to where a cordon had been erected. Pulling on white suits, overshoes and gloves, they logged in before following the path the CSIs had marked as being cleared of any evidence. At the back door, they hesitated, but the crime scene manager spotted them.

'I guess you want a quick look,' she grumbled, 'as if the scene wasn't contaminated enough already by the chef and that idiot PC Doughty, who didn't have the sense to put on overshoes before trampling his size tens all over the place.'

'I wouldn't intrude but protocol dictates that we see the scene for ourselves,' Dan deferred politely, 'and we'd like a word with the pathologist, if he's still here?'

The crime scene manager waved them through the back door, where they were confronted by a somewhat grumpy Dr Hamnet, pathologist. Only his blue eyes and bushy grey eyebrows were visible over his mask.

'What do you two want?'

'Any ideas yet as to cause and time of death?' the inspector asked.

'You should know better than to ask! I won't have those answers until I've completed my examination, run the necessary investigations and done a full post-mortem. And, before you ask, that could take days, we've such a backlog.'

'Just give me a few clues to be going on with, won't you? It's very hard knowing what questions to ask when we're so much in the dark. I was informed that our victim has been bashed over the head and put in a freezer, is that right?'

'Humph, well, I guess that's close enough for a layman, yes. See for yourselves.' He moved out of their way and the detectives immediately saw their victim, squashed most unnaturally into an open freezer, face as pale as alabaster except for dark patches of dried blood that had apparently come from an ugly head wound.

'She was struck on the occipitotemporal suture with the proverbial blunt instrument – I can't tell you what as we haven't found it yet – and I can't confirm that is the cause of death, yet, either.'

'Would she have seen her attacker coming?' asked Dan.

'Possibly not. Either that or she felt comfortable enough with the perp to turn her back to them.'

'And she was put in the freezer afterwards?'

'Quite definitely, yes. There's no blood spatter to suggest that the blow was delivered in the freezer, and you can see that the ice hasn't been cleaned away.'

'So, we're looking for someone strong enough to have lifted a dead body into the freezer?'

'Or who had help.'

'Yes, of course.'

'But I can't determine yet whether she was unconscious or dead when she was put in the freezer,' the doctor warned. 'She certainly wasn't awake, poor lass. There's no restraints or signs of a struggle.'

'You think she could have frozen to death?'

'More likely suffocated, if she wasn't already dead. But like I said ...'

'You'll know more, later,' chorused the two detectives.

'Exactly.'

'And time of death?'

'Impossible to tell! The body's part frozen, and that makes it very difficult to use the usual indicators such as core temperature and rigor mortis. I can't even hazard a guess yet.'

'Okay, we'll just have to identify when she was last seen and work from there,' Dan said miserably.

The doctor nodded and the detectives turned away, having seen enough.

'Have you confirmed where the primary crime scene is yet?' Dan asked the crime scene manager.

'There's some scrapes and traces of blood in the pantry, but we're still processing in there so I can't say yet whether they were from the blow to the head. She could've been moved from somewhere else.'

'You'd better conduct a search of the house and gardens as soon as possible,' Dan sighed. 'Although I doubt anyone would have wanted to move the body very far. And see if you can find the murder weapon and any clues as to motive, while you're at it.'

'And shall we question the suspects as well?' the crime scene manager retorted sarcastically, ducking out of sight before Dan could get a reply in.

'Cheeky mare,' he muttered, as they moved away from the back door.

'What do you think, Viv?' Dan asked, as he slipped easily out of the protective suit and put it into an evidence bag.

'Needs to be someone fairly strong to give her a hard enough whack to at least knock her out. And to move the body afterwards if they didn't have help. I'd say that rules out most of the residents here,' Viv replied thoughtfully whilst struggling to extricate himself from his suit. They were never quite broad enough across the shoulders for him.

'Right,' sighed Dan, 'let's get these interviews started, then.'

'Anything in particular you want me to do, guv?'

'You can cover all the basics – I'd like a chance to watch them before I start asking the more probing questions.'

'Yes, guv. Start with the staff?'

'Yes, indeed, the residents are less likely to be of much help, and they're not going anywhere.'

'What about this woman who says she has some information for us?'

'It'll be just my luck to have a bloody Miss Marple on my hands!'

They both laughed.

Meg watched from the day-room windows as the two detectives rounded the corner of the house to the driveway, stopping when they saw Dr Baker talking to the PC at the front door, a brown medicine bag in his hand. A conversation ensued and Meg thought the doctor looked unusually perturbed by their news, then more relieved after they had answered his frantic questions. Interesting. She edged towards the day-room door so she could just hear what was being said as the doctor raced upstairs and the policemen came into the hall.

'Guv?' asked Viv.

'The good doctor was very concerned to know that it wasn't Mrs Wollstonecraft, don't you think?'

'Yes, he was. I wonder what that was all about.'

Meg thought she knew. She moved back from the doorway and melted into the room as the DI approached the female constable, before announcing to the room that they were ready to start the interviews.

'About time too!' snorted Albert.

'Can we have one of the night staff first, please?' the inspector asked.

Jan stood up quickly, beating Sonia, who had barely moved. Sonia settled back into her chair with a disgruntled sigh.

'Come with me, please, ma'am.'

Jan followed him out, impatiently.

# Chapter Twenty-six

Upstairs, Dr Baker was somewhat alarmed when PC Adams moved to follow him into Janet's room. 'Can I have a little privacy with my patient, please?' he demanded, barring the doorway to the constable.

'Sir, I just need to check you aren't exchanging information with the others.'

The doctor turned to see Brenda and Lauren by Janet's bed. 'Brenda!'

She stepped towards him hesitantly, before burying her head into his shoulder and shaking with sobs. He put his arms around her and held her close, murmuring reassurances into the top of her head. He waited until she pulled away before asking, 'Whatever's happened here?'

'Oh, Phil! It's been so awful here this morning. Andy found—'

'Ma'am,' interrupted the PC, 'the inspector doesn't want you sharing that information with anyone outside of the house, please.'

She looked at him uncomprehendingly. 'Oh.'

'Just tell me about Janet,' Phil coaxed gently.

'We came to get her washed and dressed but we can't wake her. Her condition's not changed since I phoned you.'

'How long has she been like this?'

'To be honest, Phil, I don't know. Janet hasn't been downstairs for several days and ...' She broke off, unable to say Felicity's name. 'One of the other carers has been looking after her. I haven't been made aware of any problems, so I assumed Janet's been okay since you came out to her on Saturday. Oh God! That sounds awful, doesn't it? But it's been so stressful here this weekend ...' She dissolved into fresh tears as a wave of guilt overtook her.

She was the matron, for goodness' sake. She hadn't a clue what had been happening to her patients, so distracted had she been by her own troubles.

'It's okay,' soothed Phil, catching her as she looked about ready to fall. He signalled for Lauren to pull a chair across and helped Brenda to sit down.

'I'll examine Janet first and we'll take it from there,' he said calmly. She nodded.

'Well,' he said, straightening up after a thorough examination, 'the good news is, there's none of the symptoms I would expect to see with either a stroke or heart attack. But her reflexes are very weak, her blood pressure is quite low, her breathing is shallow and, as you said, it's impossible to rouse her. If I had to hazard a guess, I'd say she's been heavily sedated, possibly with a benzodiazepine.'

'Sedated?' muttered Brenda.

'I can't know that for sure.' He squatted in front of Brenda, taking her hands in his own. 'I think it's best to send her up to the hospital for some tests. I'll call an ambulance and alert A&E that she's on her way in.'

Brenda nodded in a trance-like state.

'Lauren,' continued Phil, looking up, 'perhaps you could go and get a cup of tea for Brenda.'

PC Adams stepped forward. 'I'm sorry, sir, but the two ladies need to remain here together.'

'What the hell is this about?' the doctor said, rounding on the PC angrily.

'It's protocol, sir. With a suspicious death, we can't let any of the potential suspects go wandering around on their own or discussing the case with anyone else.'

'Protocol be damned!' stormed Phil. 'Can't you see how distressed Mrs Wollstonecraft is? And what do you mean, she's a potential suspect?'

'If you would please calm down, sir, I'll see what I can do to ease the situation.'

Just as he was about to really lose his rag, Brenda called out, 'Phil?'

He rushed to her side, immediately concerned.

'It's okay, really, just stay here with me until the ambulance arrives.'

He nodded. 'Okay.'

He made the calls on his mobile standing next to the window and all the time watching Brenda with concern in his eyes.

'They should be here quite soon,' he said. He indicated for Lauren to sit back down in the other chair whilst he went to Brenda's side and put a hand on her shoulder.

They remained pretty much like that until the ambulance finally arrived.

✿

Meg discreetly checked her watch and noted that Jan had been gone nearly thirty minutes and still had not emerged from the office. If the police were going to spend this long with everyone, the interviews would likely take all day. She sighed, pushed herself out of her chair with some difficulty, feeling the stiffness in her hips, and made her way to the bookcase.

'Are you all right, Meg?' asked Paul.

'Just a little stiff, nothing serious. But I think we may as well resign ourselves to a long wait, so I thought I'd see if I can find a book I haven't read yet.'

'If you can't find a book, you could always start another jigsaw puzzle,' he suggested.

Brian, who was sitting in her usual chair at the table, looked up, his face bereft.

'Do you want to sit here to do your puzzle, Meg?' he intoned flatly. 'I can move.'

'Well, if you're sure you don't mind?' She accepted his offer, mainly to get a seat near the window where she could keep a better eye on what was happening outside. 'I must admit, comfortable though the armchair is, I do find it better not to stay there too long. The joints stiffen up, you know.'

Brian nodded and wearily stood up, gazed around the day room and located a free armchair not far from Sonia, by the French doors. He slumped into the chair and dropped his face into his hands. The poor man was clearly distraught.

As she sat down, Paul stood up and made a circuit of the residents, checking that no one needed anything.

'Isn't it coffee time, yet?' demanded Albert tersely.

Paul glanced at his watch. 'Still a bit early for coffee, Albert. And, in any case, Andy can't go to the kitchen until the police allow him to.'

'Damned cheek, I say.'

Paul declined to reply, still wary of Albert since his scathing remarks on Friday.

'I wouldn't say no to a game of draughts, if you've got the time,' offered Jack.

'I think time is something we all have plenty of today,' Paul replied, with a wry smile. He fetched the board and pieces from a cupboard next to the bookcase and set up a small table so that they could play.

Albert stood up and took a couple of steps towards the PC in the doorway.

'Are we going to be confined to this room all day?' he demanded.

'I'm sorry, sir, it really is better if you all stay together until you've been interviewed,' replied PC Moira Gordon, with a warm, friendly smile that was intended to reassure.

'Better for whom?' he grumbled. 'And what about our, erm, needs?'

'Sir?'

'Damn it, woman, I need the bathroom.'

'Oh, of course, sir.' She flushed slightly, turning to direct him down the hallway to another PC who was standing outside the two cloakrooms. She watched until her colleague had opened the gents' door for Albert then returned to her 'at ease' position facing into the day room.

Meg watched with interest, noting how tense Albert's shoulders were and tutting at him when he swore at the WPC. She was only doing her job, poor woman. But then her attention was suddenly drawn to a movement outside the windows. She turned to see two paramedics in green walking towards the house, dragging an ambulance trolley between them. And she could see the yellow of an ambulance and the blue of its still-flashing lights just visible in the road immediately outside the entrance. She gave an involuntary cry of shock, at which Andy turned to also look out of the window, and Sally came hurrying to her side.

'What's wrong, Meg?' she enquired anxiously.

Meg pointed to the two paramedics, now talking earnestly to the policeman outside the front door. 'I'm fine, thank you, Sally, but why are they here?'

Her comment caught the attention of the others. First Paul, then Jack, joined the group in the bay window, and Annie and Sylvia stopped their murmured conversation and looked anxiously across at them.

'What's happening?' called Annie.

'There's an ambulance here!' Jack replied over his shoulder.

'Who's that for?' she asked in a concerned voice.

Jack couldn't answer, but he moved slightly so that he could see out into the hallway as the paramedics made their way indoors and into the lift.

'They're going upstairs,' he announced.

'It must be for Janet!' surmised Meg.

There were gasps all round and anxious conversation bubbled up, speculating as to what could possibly be wrong with Janet.

After what seemed like an interminable wait, the paramedics reappeared from the lift with their patient now on the trolley.

'She doesn't look too good,' said Jack.

There were murmurs of concern and Sylvia began to weep. 'Whatever is happening to our happy little home?' she moaned. Annie patted her arm sympathetically.

'What's going on?' demanded Muriel, upset that something was clearly happening and no one had bothered to tell her. Paul went to explain, whilst Sally put a reassuring hand on Meg's shoulder as they watched Janet's departure through the window.

Everything seemed to happen at once then. Albert returned from the cloakroom. The office door opened, and

Jan finally emerged, closely followed by the two detectives. The inspector spotted Dr Baker and the others coming downstairs and spoke quickly and quietly to the doctor, before escorting Brenda and Lauren into the day room.

# Chapter Twenty-seven

Detective Inspector Bywater cleared his throat, and the day room fell silent as everyone focussed on him. 'As you've probably all gathered, we've had to call an ambulance to transport one of your fellow residents, Mrs Janet Smith, to Salisbury District Hospital.'

Concerned looks passed around the room.

'I understand from the doctor that her condition appears to be stable, and he is strongly of the opinion that she should make a good recovery. I'll leave Mrs Wollstonecraft to fill in all the details, but I also wanted to let you know that I've sent my sergeant to see if we can arrange for chef to have some limited access to the kitchen to get you some refreshments.'

'About time too,' grumbled Jack, whilst Albert muttered something similar.

'Inspector,' broke in Brenda, 'what about arrangements for lunch?'

'Ah yes, I was coming to that. I took the liberty of discussing that with your chef earlier and, with his agreement, I've ordered in sandwiches and cakes for everyone here, as I'm afraid he's not going to be able to have access to the kitchen this morning. Is that acceptable to you, Mrs Wollstonecraft?'

'I'm sure a cold lunch is acceptable, provided our residents get a cooked meal this evening. My main concern is what time lunch will arrive. One of our residents is diabetic, you see, and is used to eating at twelve-thirty sharp.' She looked up at the inspector and he noticed how exhausted she looked.

'Yes, I understand. That's why I was going to ask your chef to bring some snacks with the beverages, just in case. The Rose and Crown said they'd deliver as quickly as possible, but they couldn't promise what time that would be, given the last-minute nature of our order.'

There were quite a few nods of approval at this as the sergeant returned and spoke quietly in the inspector's ear. 'Ah good. Andy, would you go with PC Thomas, and he'll help you sort out the refreshments now.' Andy nodded and promptly left, glad to have something to do.

'Perhaps I could talk to ...' the inspector consulted the list that Jan had helped him draw up '... Sonia next, please.'

Sonia hurried after the two detectives, whilst everyone else in the day room gathered round Brenda, bombarding her with questions.

✿

Sonia came out of the office after about twenty minutes, popped her head into the day room to ask Brian to go into the office next and said goodbye to everyone, relieved to be going home to her bed at last. Brian slouched out of the day room about as eagerly as a man going to the scaffold, thought Meg, watching him shrewdly.

A few minutes later, Albert surprised her by wandering over and asking if he could sit at the table with her. She looked up in surprise.

'I didn't know you were into jigsaws,' she said softly.

He shuffled a little uncomfortably, glanced around the room and then sat down and leant over the table towards her. 'Ah, well, thing is, I'm not really.'

She smiled, having guessed as much.

'You, erm ... you seem to be assessing everyone,' he continued, 'and I couldn't help wondering what your conclusions are.'

'You're asking for my opinion?'

'Don't come all coy with me now. I've been watching you and you're on the ball, right enough. I've seen both Marianne and Janet confiding in you, and if they both trust you ... well, so shall I.'

She was surprised at the touch of deference in his voice. 'You do know we're not supposed to be discussing the case?' she warned, a wary eye on the WPC.

'Poppycock!'

Well, before we discuss this, I'd like to know what you think about Marianne's death.'

'Marianne? Tragic loss, that. Been at the home for a long time, y'know.'

'Yes, but was her death natural, do you think?'

'What? Of course it was! We'd have had the Old Bill here sooner if there'd been anything funny about it. Why?' He frowned at her, and she hesitated.

'If you think otherwise, spit it out, old gal,' he encouraged.

'Janet and I believe that someone stole something valuable from Marianne and then killed her to stop her insisting on the police being called in.'

'Really? That's a bit far-fetched, surely.'

'I can see why you might think that, but we also believe that the exact same thing happened to Harry Leadbetter five months ago.'

'What? What? How would you know? You weren't here when poor old Harry passed on.'

'You're quite right, but Janet was certain those two deaths were connected.'

'Really? And you agree, do you?'

'I do.'

'Do you think Felicity was murdered too?'

'Thinking about it, yes. I suspect she probably was.'

'That's three murders in less than six months!' he exclaimed sharply. Meg put a finger to her lips in warning and looked around, but no one else appeared to have heard.

'So, who do you think the murderer is?' Albert spoke more softly.

'That's an interesting question.' Meg paused thoughtfully. If Felicity killed Harry and Marianne, then someone else must have murdered her. But having two murderers on the loose seemed unlikely. If Brian killed Harry and Marianne then, possibly, he could have murdered Felicity as well. The same might apply to Brenda too, of course. Or was there another suspect she hadn't considered yet? But what about Tony and Pat's sister Mary? If they were indeed murdered, Felicity was the only suspect common to both care homes. That took her back full circle. However unlikely, there had to be two different murderers!

Albert was looking at her thoughtfully. 'There's more to it, isn't there?' he asked.

She nodded but was prevented from saying any more by the arrival of the coffee trolley. Albert tapped the side of his nose and retreated to his own seat.

※

As soon as the coffees were distributed and a tea poured for Meg, who didn't drink coffee, Lauren made a beeline for her.

'Can I ask you something, please?' she asked the older lady quietly.

'Sit down, dear,' suggested Meg, indicating the seat facing away from the WPC. Lauren slid into the seat, glanced furtively around and then spoke in hushed tones to Meg. 'You thought it was Ms Trainer who locked poor Janet in her room, didn't you?'

'I'm almost sure of it,' replied Meg, nodding her head.

'Then it must've been her that also sedated Janet.'

'Janet was sedated?' asked Meg anxiously.

'That's what Dr Phil said. But why would she do that?'

'I think she was trying to prevent Janet from talking to me, you know.'

'And you think she murdered both Marianne and that other resident?'

'I'm afraid so, my dear.'

'So, if she's a murderer, who on earth murdered her?'

'That's a very good question.' Meg eyed Lauren thoughtfully. 'Do you still have your phone with you?'

'Of course,' replied the carer with a grin.

'Am I right in thinking you can look up information on the internet on your phone?'

'Uh – yeah.' Lauren regarded Meg with surprise.

'Well, I would like you to do something for me, discreetly, if you would, please.'

She bent forward to whisper to Lauren, who then nodded.

'One more thing,' added Meg, 'when we are released from our confinement here, would you be able to check all the ground-floor doors and windows for me, please?'

'You're thinking someone broke in, to murder Frau Flic?' asked Lauren in amazement.

'Not really, but it's as well to rule out the possibility,' replied Meg.

Lauren nodded, stood up and sauntered casually to the other side of the room, before covertly commencing a Google search, whilst keeping one eye on the others to make sure no one saw her doing it.

❁

Brian eventually reappeared from the office, looking like a man who'd had a last-minute reprieve, Meg observed thoughtfully.

'It's you next, Brenda.' He nodded towards the office, before going to the trolley and making himself a very strong coffee.

Brenda was followed by Sally, then Paul, then Lauren. It seemed the police were talking to the staff first in order of seniority, although Meg had rather hoped to have been able to talk to them before either Brian or Brenda. Too late for that now.

There were several attempts to discover what questions had been asked and what information given, but each time the reply was a variation on *We've been warned not to talk about it.*

Just as Lauren returned, clearly relieved to have got her ordeal over and done with, a PC came in to announce that lunch had arrived, and they could all go to the dining room to eat. The staff helped the residents through, Sally taking Jack to the treatment room en route for his insulin, under the watchful scrutiny of PC Gordon. To Meg's surprise, the dining-room tables had been pushed together so that staff and residents could all eat together. The tables had been covered in white paper tablecloths and there were delicious-looking platters of sandwiches in white, wholemeal and granary breads with several different fillings, including her favourite cheese and pickle. There were slices of pork pie and sausage rolls, much to Jack's delight, and a mouth-watering selection of cakes. It was like a good old-fashioned party buffet except that they sat and waited for the platters to be passed around by the staff instead of the usual serve-yourself scrummage.

There was an excited hum of conversation, and the event could have been a festive one if only the reason for bringing them all together like this hadn't been so terrible. It was only as the meal drew to a close that Meg realised that neither of the detectives had joined them and nor had Andy. No sooner had she had that thought than Andy appeared in the doorway.

'If you've finished your meal, Meg, the police would like to talk to you next,' he announced. Meg left the room, her stomach suddenly writhing with butterflies, making her wish that she hadn't eaten quite so much!

# Chapter Twenty-eight

Meg took a deep breath, knocked lightly on the office door and entered, looking a great deal more confident than she felt.

'Come in and take a seat,' smiled the inspector, indicating the wingback chair that Paul had brought in from the day room.

As she lowered herself carefully into the chair, leaning her stick against the shelves, she assessed the two detectives. The inspector was leaning back in the swivel chair with his hands together like a steeple, his gaze fixed on her in a slightly disconcerting way. The sergeant was in the office chair, leaning over the table, pen in hand. They had both taken their jackets off and loosened their ties a little, but the sergeant still somehow managed to look the smarter of the two.

'Are you comfortable, ma'am?' the sergeant enquired.

'Yes, thank you,' she replied.

'I'm Detective Sergeant Williams and this is my boss, Detective Inspector Bywater,' he began. 'I just need to start with some basic details, please.'

She responded clearly and calmly to his questions, giving him her full name and myriad other details.

'And can you tell me exactly when and where you last saw Ms Trainer?'

'She came into the day room to say goodnight when she went off duty yesterday, around 8.30pm, I think.'

'Was anyone else there with you?'

'Jack was watching TV, but the others had all retired to their rooms for the night.'

'Did you speak to her at all?'

'Only to say goodnight, that's all.'

'And how did she seem to you? Did you notice anything unusual?'

'There was nothing unusual about her popping in to say

goodnight like that, she often did. But I did think she looked a little pale and drawn around the eyes, as if she had been crying earlier in the day.'

'She'd been crying?' He sounded surprised.

'Well, I can't be certain, but I think so, yes.'

He finished his notes and glanced across at the inspector.

'Thank you for that, Mrs Thornton.' The inspector now leant towards her and smiled, having been watching her intensely during the sergeant's questioning.

'Are you sure you didn't see Ms Trainer at any time after that, perhaps on the first-floor landing later in the evening, or anywhere else?'

'Absolutely sure,' she confirmed.

'Would you have been aware if Ms Trainer had come up or down the staircase to the second floor at any time during the night?'

'I very much doubt it. The stairs are carpeted, these old houses have good thick walls, and once I'm asleep, I doubt I would've heard anything.'

'You didn't hear any unusual noises during the night at all?' he insisted.

'None at all, Inspector.'

'Did you leave your room at any time during the night?'

'No, we have ensuite bathrooms, you see, so I had no need to leave my room.'

'And what time did you leave your room this morning?'

'About half past eight, I think. Lauren should be able to confirm that, Inspector.'

'Thank you. Now, tell me, would it surprise you to hear that Ms Trainer was murdered?'

'Oh, it definitely is murder then, Inspector?'

'Yes, it is,' he smiled. No flies on this one.

'I was very much surprised, Inspector, because I rather thought she would have been the murderer, not the victim.'

'Why on earth would you think that?' he exclaimed, sitting back in surprise.

'I believe she may have murdered at least four times already, you see.'

'And who do you think Ms Trainer murdered?' he asked incredulously.

'Well, there's Tony and Mary, of course, and then Harry and Marianne.'

He exchanged looks with his sergeant.

'Could you start at the beginning and tell me everything you know, please.'

She told them the whole story. The inspector, to his credit, listened impassively, but she could see the look of incredulity pass across the sergeant's face, and she could almost hear him thinking *Batty old woman*.

'Are you convinced that Ms Trainer is one and the same person as Mrs March?'

'Yes, I am.'

'How can you be so sure?'

'I may forget the occasional word now and again, Inspector, but I have a remarkably good memory for names and faces. It goes with the territory when you are a teacher. I could still name every pupil I ever taught, you know.'

'Yes, Mrs Thornton, I believe you could,' he said thoughtfully. 'And you and Janet are both sure that Ms Trainer murdered all these people?'

'That's what we think,' she conceded.

'But none of these deaths were thought to be suspicious.'

'That's true, Inspector. I think Felicity Trainer was a very clever young lady and not a particularly nice one, I'm afraid.'

'Why didn't you say something to the police sooner?'

'I did, Inspector. You'll find PC Daly took a statement from me yesterday morning.'

'Really?'

'I take it you weren't aware?'

'No, but there are a lot of police officers in Salisbury.'

'Of course.'

They both smiled then the inspector asked if there was anything she wanted to tell them, so she filled them in on what she knew about Brian and Felicity. They were startled to hear that Brian had actually proposed to

Felicity and even more astonished to learn that she had apparently rejected him. She then told them of her suspicions about the relationship between Dr Baker and Mrs Wollstonecraft.

'I can't believe there are so many goings-on in such a small place,' Dan remarked.

'No one else you'd care to mention?' asked the sergeant, regarding Meg sceptically.

'Well, I'm certain that Paul has feelings for the doctor, which are clearly not reciprocated. And I strongly suspect that Lauren has taken a shine to Paul. But, you know, Sergeant, I really don't think those relationships are quite so relevant, do you?'

There followed a pause whilst the inspector was clearly trying to make up his mind what to ask next.

'Mrs Thornton, you do realise that if you are right and Ms Trainer did murder these people, then someone different must have murdered her? Do you know just how improbable that is?'

Meg nodded. 'Yes, Inspector. But it's the only conclusion that makes any sense.'

'May I ask who you think killed Ms Trainer?'

'Oh, I really wouldn't like to say, Inspector. I have my suspicions but no proof, you see.'

'Yes, indeed,' he sighed. 'That's all our questions for now, Mrs Thornton, but we may well want to ask you some more questions later.'

He stood up and politely handed her walking stick to her as she struggled out of the chair.

'Aren't you going to warn me not to leave the country, or something?'

'I take it you don't have any plans to travel?' he queried, raising an amused eyebrow.

'No, of course not, Inspector.'

'But I would just like to ask you not to say a word about your interview to anyone else, please. Not one word.'

'Oh, I quite understand. You couldn't have judged my reaction to finding out that Felicity was murdered if someone had already told me that.'

She smiled and left the two detectives looking at each other in amazement.

'What did you make of that, then, guv? Is she as nutty as a fruitcake?' Viv asked.

'I don't know,' replied Dan thoughtfully. 'She's either as batty as they come or she's a very astute woman. I just wish I knew which!'

※

By the end of the afternoon, Meg learnt, the house and gardens had been searched for forensic clues and the door to Felicity's flat sealed with crime scene tape, pending further examination. Furthermore, a number of items had been removed from the kitchen and taken away by the CSIs.

Felicity's body had been taken away, her departure watched by a very subdued group in the bay window. The cars had mostly gone for the day, leaving a very bored-looking PC stationed at the front door. The staff and residents had been released from their containment in the day room, having all been questioned and had their fingerprints taken by a CSI – purely for elimination purposes, the inspector had reassured them. Meg realised that they would all be considered suspects until proven otherwise.

The French doors in the day room had been locked and the key removed by the sergeant 'for added security', he said, although Meg suspected it was a ploy to ensure that no one could enter or leave the building without being logged by the PC on the front door. Her beloved late husband had explained to her the importance of keeping a crime scene log. The carers were busy catching up on their work. And, so, the residents found themselves left to their own devices at last. Muriel and Sylvia had both retired to their bedrooms to lie down before dinner, but the remaining four were sitting around the table in the bay window.

# Chapter Twenty-nine

'Let me see if I've got this clear,' said Jack carefully. 'You and Janet think that Harry and Marianne were murdered.'

'Yes,' nodded Meg.

'And you think that Felicity most likely murdered them, because she used to be this Mrs March and might have done the same thing in some other home.'

'If you're right about Felicity, then who on earth killed her?' demanded Annie.

'The very question we are here to discuss,' replied Albert, asserting his control over the situation. 'Now then, I suppose it is just possible that Felicity murdered Harry and Marianne and someone else murdered her in revenge, but it's much more likely, in my opinion, that someone else murdered all three,' he proclaimed triumphantly. 'Stands to reason there's only going to be one murderer!'

'I'm afraid it's not as simple as that,' interrupted Meg.

'Poppycock!' bristled Albert.

'You're assuming all three murders are linked,' she cautioned.

'Surely it's obvious!' Albert dismissed her objection with a wave of his hand.

'Well, I don't see how we can be certain that either Harry or Marianne were actually murdered,' put in Jack.

'Oh, surely they weren't!' added Annie. 'It's just too awful to think about.'

'And it's very unlikely that there should be three murders in the same home, isn't it?' argued Jack.

'Which just goes to prove, the murders must be linked!' pointed out Albert smugly.

'But that would mean there's a serial killer on the loose!' exclaimed Jack.

'Oh, I hate all this talk of murder!' wailed Annie.

'I know, dear,' soothed Meg, 'but even if I'm wrong about the other two, which I don't think I am, we most certainly have had one murder, I'm afraid. We need to consider who killed Felicity.'

'Can't we just leave all that to the police?' objected Annie.

'Yes,' agreed Jack, 'it is their job after all.'

'Well, I wouldn't trust that sergeant as far as I could throw him!' snorted Albert. 'I just hope the inspector keeps a close eye on him.'

Meg looked at Albert and with deceptive calm asked, 'And why would you think the sergeant can't be trusted?'

'Obvious! The man's a bloomin' nig-nog!'

Jack and Annie squirmed, clearly embarrassed but not brave enough to say anything. Meg, however, was not about to let him get away with that. 'Albert, you are a prejudiced old-fashioned bigot!'

'I beg your pardon!' spluttered Albert.

'And even if you can't be persuaded to bring your opinions into the twenty-first century, the least you can do is to keep them to yourself!'

'How dare you!' he raged, turning a worrying shade of puce.

'I dare because you are in the wrong, and it's high time someone put you right.'

The veins on his forehead were now starting to bulge alarmingly. 'You ... you ... bloody impudent woman!'

'Albert, you need to understand that racial discrimination is, quite rightly, against the law. And so, for that matter, are several other forms of discrimination.' Meg glared darkly at him. 'Including sex discrimination,' she added pointedly.

'And what would you know about the law?' he challenged aggressively.

'Please, just stop all of this!' cried Annie.

'Hear, hear!' agreed Jack.

'Albert, I think it's about time you calmed down and apologised to Meg. You're behaving like a spoilt child!' Annie scolded.

'What the devil?' he growled angrily at her.

'Time to cut it out, old man,' intervened Jack. 'You're in the wrong and you know it!'

'You're all taking her side?' Albert looked shocked.

'It's not about taking sides. It's about what's right and what's wrong. You were bang out of order the way you spoke to Paul the other day, and you're out of order now!'

Albert stared at Jack, his mouth agape with astonishment. Annie held her breath.

'Well, all right then, I ... I might have been a little outspoken, I suppose,' Albert grumbled awkwardly. 'No offence meant.'

Meg held up a hand to Jack to stop him replying to that one. There was a moment's silence as Albert clearly struggled with his emotions.

'Well then, Meg,' Albert sounded deflated, 'just what do you propose we do about Felicity's murder?'

'Why do we have to do anything?' asked Annie.

'Because it's something that should concern us all,' Albert insisted.

'I think Albert has a point.' Meg intervened before Jack could speak. 'The fact that there is quite possibly a murderer either living or working in this home is something that should concern each and every one of us,' she explained gently.

'Oh no!' gasped Annie. 'Surely you don't think one of us could have done it?'

'Personally, I doubt very much that one of the residents is the murderer, but the police won't rule anyone out until they know more, so we are all under suspicion.'

Jack nodded thoughtfully. 'Who are the prime suspects?' he asked.

'Any of the carers, I suppose,' said Annie doubtfully.

'Not forgetting Wolly and Mrs W,' put in Albert.

'Oh no,' gasped Annie, 'surely not Brenda!'

'I'm sorry, Annie, but until we know a lot more, we simply have to include everyone. We know that Felicity was alive until at least 8.30pm, when I last saw her.' Meg looked questioningly at the others, but none of them had seen the care manager any later than that. 'Well then, Lauren, Paul and that agency carer were still on duty until eight-thirty, and the night staff, Sonia and Jan, came in at eight. And Brian and Brenda were on the premises too. And that's assuming no one entered the home that we don't know about yet.'

'Where do we start?' Albert looked at Meg for guidance, and she suddenly realised they were all looking to her to take the lead.

'Well, cause and time of death would be the first facts to ascertain in a murder case.'

'And how do you know that?' wondered Albert.

'My late husband was a detective with Bournemouth Police,' she replied quietly. He looked suitably impressed and nodded for her to continue.

'Then, there are three things the police need to establish: means, motive and opportunity,' she said. 'As we don't know how she was killed or exactly when she was killed, the only thing we can really look at for now is motive. Who had a reason to kill Felicity?'

'Who do you think's the most likely suspect?' demanded Albert.

'Well, I suppose Brian must be, given his affair with Felicity and her rejection of his proposal.' She explained all that she had seen and heard.

'How come I never noticed any of this?' grumbled Albert.

'Because you're always preoccupied with the cricket scores,' retorted Jack.

Before Albert could reply, Lauren spoke suddenly from the doorway, having come to say goodbye to the residents before going offduty and hearing the last part of their conversation. 'If Wolly killed Frau Flic, how do you explain me overhearing her threatening to kill him?'

Amid gasps of astonishment and shrieks of 'Surely not!', Meg looked thoughtfully at Lauren.

'Come and sit down and join us, my dear,' she invited.

Lauren took the chair beside Meg.

'Here, d'you think we should have one of the suspects discussing this with us,' interjected Albert. 'After all, she's on our list!'

Meg replied that as Lauren had only recently joined the staff at The Cedars, she was probably the least likely to have had cause to murder Felicity. 'And,' she added, 'I rather think we might need a younger person to assist us with our enquiries.'

Somewhat reluctantly, the others accepted Meg's reasoning.

'I say,' suggested Jack thoughtfully, 'if Stone-face and Flic were having it off, like you say ...' Albert groaned and pulled a face at the vulgarity '... then surely that makes Brenda a strong suspect. You know, the jealous wife killing her husband's mistress.'

Sylvia and Annie protested loudly, but Meg agreed that was certainly a possibility. 'Like I said, we can't rule anyone out until we have some more facts.'

'Well, how do we go about getting these facts?' demanded Albert.

'I have a few ideas,' replied Meg, 'but you will all need to play your part. We don't want our murderer getting suspicious if just one of us goes around asking lots of questions.'

They spent the next hour carefully devising plans for each of the four residents present. With that settled, Albert, Jack and Annie all made their excuses to leave.

❁

'What about me?' Lauren demanded, once the others were out of sight.

'Did you get a chance to check the doors and windows?' asked Meg.

'Yeah, that bit was easy, no signs of a break-in so far as I could see. But the pantry was still sealed off with police tape, so I couldn't check the back door.'

Meg mentally noted that Felicity's body must have been in the pantry area. 'Never mind, you did your best. How about that information I asked you to look for?' returned Meg.

'It wasn't that easy, with everyone in the same room,' replied Lauren regretfully, 'but I did find Frau Flic's Facebook page. The odd thing is, it was only created in July 2020. And she has very few friends too.'

After Lauren had explained how Facebook worked, Meg agreed that it did indeed seem suspicious that Felicity's profile had only been created after she would have left The Cadnum Lodge as Mrs March.

'Would you be able to do some more research into Ms Trainer and Mrs March?'

'Of course!' cried Lauren enthusiastically.

Meg outlined several lines of enquiry for her. So absorbed were the two of them that it wasn't until another carer came into the day room to call Meg to dinner that Lauren realised just how late it was.

'Ta-ra, then, Meg. I'll be able to do all that during my day off tomorrow,' she said. She winked before scuttling across the hallway in the hope no one would realise that she was still on the premises so long after her shift had ended.

# Chapter Thirty

*Tuesday 13th September 2022*

During an otherwise sombre breakfast, Meg nodded to Jack, who went over to Andy to get his cooked breakfast, as usual. At that same moment, she slopped a small amount of her coffee onto the tablecloth and cried out, 'Oh no! What a clumsy fool I am!'

As planned, that drew Paul's attention. He fussed around, reassuring her that she didn't need to worry, making sure she hadn't scalded her hand. With Albert and Annie joining in a conversation about having accidents with hot drinks, no one was paying any attention to Jack.

'Morning, Andy, how are you feeling today?'

'Morning, Jack, not so bad, thank you. And yourself?'

'Still a bit shaken up after yesterday, to be honest. But probably not half so shaken as you must have been, finding Frau Flic's body like that.'

'It was pretty gruesome, I must admit.'

'So I gathered,' Jack nodded, trying to look as though he already knew exactly what had happened.

'I can't offer you the full works this morning,' Andy apologised. 'Wasn't allowed into the pantry last night, so I couldn't get any more sausages out of the freezer.'

'No problem, I quite understand. The police had to seal off the scene, didn't they?'

'Yeah, I get that. But there's two of them back again this morning in their white suits,' the chef grumbled.

'That must be pretty inconvenient when you're busy preparing the meals.'

'Luckily, I don't have to put up with them in the kitchen. They're just in the pantry today.'

'Ah yes ... that's where ...?'

'Yes, in the smaller freezer.'

'Aye, that's what I'd heard,' Jack nodded, hiding his excitement.

Andy leant forward. 'Between you and me, mate, it gave me a right nasty shock when I opened the freezer and saw her stuffed in there, her head all bloody and bashed in.'

'I bet it did!'

'And as for the mess those crime scene bods have made of my kitchen; grey fingerprint powder over everything and all my stuff moved about.'

'Did they take many things away for testing?'

'Strange, that. Now you come to mention it, I couldn't find the cast iron skillet this morning. They must have taken that.'

'Could be the murder weapon.'

Andy straightened up and studied Jack thoughtfully.

'Don't know as I should be telling you all of this,' he said a little stiffly.

'No problem, Andy, it's just between the two of us,' Jack said with a wink, and Andy relaxed. He popped an extra egg on Jack's plate.

'Go and eat your breakfast, and stop pestering me,' he grinned.

※

After breakfast, Meg took the lift to go back to her room, where she had deliberately left her reading glasses. As she had hoped, Brenda was on the landing with the laundry trolley and a very young and clueless-looking agency carer, clearly in the middle of doing the rooms.

'No Sally this morning?' she said sympathetically to the weary-looking Brenda.

'No,' she sighed. 'Sally's on a late shift today. And I'm having to use agency staff to fill the gaps; what with Lauren on a day off, Tanya on holiday, Sandra leaving us last month and now ...' She gulped.

'Ah yes, poor Ms Trainer. What a nasty shock that was.'

'Yes,' Brenda said awkwardly, looking away.

'You must be devastated. She'd worked here for quite some time, I believe.'

'Just over two years.'

'She was such an efficient manager, wasn't she?' Meg enthused.

'Efficient? Yes, I suppose she was.' Brenda didn't look convinced.

'I expect you're going to miss her?'

Brenda's mouth narrowed to a thin line and she didn't answer. Very telling.

Meg wandered into her room and was delighted to see that Brenda hadn't done it yet. Hers was often the last to be done, being furthest from the linen cupboard, where the carers invariably started. She fiddled about until Brenda eventually came in.

'Oh, sorry, Meg, I can come back later, if you like?' Brenda turned to leave.

'No, come in, Brenda, carry on. I'm just looking for my reading glasses. I can't seem to find them anywhere. As soon as I've got them, I'll be out of your way.'

'Do you need some help?' Brenda came in and smiled weakly.

'Oh, thank you, my dear.'

'When did you last have them?' she asked.

'Just last night when I was reading my book in bed.'

Brenda started searching in and around the bedside locker. Meg waited a few moments before triumphantly "finding" the red optician's case under her dressing table. 'Ah, there they are! I wonder how on earth they got there.'

Brenda looked up and smiled.

'At least you've got them now ... oh, are you feeling okay?' Meg had wobbled a little after bending down to pick up the case, and she allowed Brenda to help her shakily into the chair beside the bed.

'Oh, I must have stood up too quickly,' she quavered, 'I came over quite dizzy then.'

'You just sit here and rest a moment and I'll be right back.' Brenda left the room and returned a minute later to check Meg's blood pressure. 'Good, that's normal,' she said.

Meg nodded feebly. 'Just a touch of vertigo, I'll be right as rain in a minute.'

Brenda patted her hand reassuringly. 'No rush, take your time.'

'I expect it's just the shock of the last few days,' she said, carefully watching Brenda's face out of the corner of her eye. 'What with Marianne dying so suddenly and Janet's illness and now Felicity ...'

'Yes, poor Janet,' murmured Brenda distractedly.

'Do you think she'll be in hospital for long? Oh! She will be back, won't she?'

'No need to worry, she's going to be fine. I rang the hospital this morning and they told me she's woken up at last and is feeling quite perky this morning.'

'I expect it was her heart, wasn't it?'

'No, the hospital said her heart's fine ...'

Brenda hesitated, so Meg squeezed her hand comfortingly. 'It might help you to talk about it. You look so stressed and you know I don't gossip.'

'Thank you, my dear,' Brenda smiled, 'but I thought I was looking after you?'

'And you're doing an excellent job of it.'

'Well,' Brenda started, as Meg held her breath, 'I must admit, it was all very strange.'

'Yes?' she encouraged.

'You see, I was under the impression that Janet had been ill since last Thursday, but she told the nurses this morning that there was nothing wrong with her, certainly up to Saturday afternoon. She seems a bit hazy after that.'

'Perhaps it was the shock of Marianne's death?'

'Maybe but ... Dr Baker was convinced yesterday that Janet had taken an overdose of sleeping tablets.'

'Oh no! She wouldn't!' Meg gasped, truly shocked.

'Oh no, dear, I don't think for one second she chose to take them, not like that.' Brenda looked at Meg thoughtfully. 'You were worried about Janet, too, weren't you?'

'Yes, my dear. I am absolutely sure that her room was locked when I tried it on Saturday. And so was Lauren.'

'You think someone had been keeping Janet there against her will? But why?'

'I hate to say this, but Felicity was quite rude to me on

Friday when she found me visiting Janet, and I got the distinct impression that she was trying to keep us apart over the weekend.'

Brenda frowned. 'That makes sense of something else Janet said to the nurses. Apparently, Felicity insisted she stay in bed on Saturday even when she asked to get up and be taken downstairs. And Janet was quite upset that Felicity wouldn't even allow her any visitors. That's when Felicity gave her "something to help with the stress", and after that, she remembers very little.'

'You think she was drugged?'

'Sedated, yes. The hospital confirmed this morning that Janet had an extremely high level of temazepam in her blood. But Janet's never been prescribed that.'

'Do you think Felicity ...?'

'Who else could it have been?' sighed Brenda. 'But now we'll never know, will we?'

'Will Janet be okay?'

'Yes. The sister I spoke to thought she might be able to come home later today.'

'Thank goodness it was no worse!' Meg was genuinely relieved.

'Oh God,' Brenda groaned and sank her face into her hands. 'I should've taken more notice of you on Sunday. You said then you thought something was wrong.'

'You were rather distracted on Sunday. I expect you had other things on your mind.'

'Oh dear, was it that obvious?'

'Yes, my dear, we all noticed something had seriously upset you. You were nothing like your normal self.'

'And I tried so hard not to show it!'

'Would you like to talk about it?'

Brenda suddenly sat up straight and visibly pulled herself together.

'Oh, it was nothing that serious,' she tried to sound convincing, 'just a silly argument I had with Brian. It's all blown over now.' She gave a slightly choked laugh and stood up.

'You don't need to mention my little outburst to anyone, do you?' she appealed.

'Don't worry, Brenda, you know you can count on me to do the right thing.' Meg carefully avoided making a promise she had no intention of keeping.

'Of course. And you do feel quite all right yourself, now?'

'Much better, thank you.'

Brenda went into the bathroom and started furiously cleaning the toilet as Meg picked up her glasses case and quietly took herself down to the day room, deep in thought.

# Chapter Thirty-one

Albert had eaten his breakfast as slowly as possible, listening for Brian to come up from his flat, as agreed with the others yesterday. But it didn't seem as though he was going to emerge. Sensing that Paul wanted to get on, he finished off his long-since cold toast and stood up. 'Righty-oh! Time to find my paper.' He stretched and watched as Paul began clearing the table. Albert strolled out into the hall and spent an inordinately long time studying the notice board. He'd never realised there was so much rubbish on it; he didn't usually bother to look. Just as he was beginning to think he was going to be out of luck – not that he would've abandoned his post, of course – Brian finally opened the basement door and squinted at him in the sunlight that flooded the hallway.

'Good morning, Mr Wollstonecraft,' he said respectfully.

Brian glanced at him suspiciously. 'Morning, Albert,' he mumbled, as he headed for the office. He looked the picture of a broken man, but Albert steeled himself to do as they'd agreed.

'I say, Brian, I've got a bit of a problem.'

'Yes?' muttered Brian disinterestedly.

'Mind if I come in and talk to you about it?' he said, as he followed Brian into the office and shut the door.

'I am quite busy today, Albert. Can't it wait?' Brian was studiously checking through a small pile of freshly delivered letters on the desk.

'Sorry, but I really am in a bit of a bother.'

Brian slumped at the desk and looked at him wearily. 'Go on, then.'

'Well,' he warmed to his part, 'my watch has gone missing. Had it yesterday, can't find it anywhere this morning.'

'I expect it'll turn up,' Brian said, trying to brush him off.

'Thing is, I'm a bit anxious it might have been stolen, after all these other things that have mysteriously gone missing.'

'What?' Brian pricked his ears up warily. 'Why? What other things?'

'You know, Janet was missing some money from her purse last month, and then Marianne mentioned that her favourite brooch had been stolen.'

'Really?' Brian feigned disinterest but Albert could spot the tension in his shoulders, just as Meg had described for him to look out for.

'A couple of other people reported cash going missing, too. And I seem to remember Harry losing a book, so it's been going on for some time. Do you suppose we've got a thief among the staff, eh?'

'Absolutely not!' Brian blustered. 'All our staff have been thoroughly checked before coming to us! I'm sure this is all a lot of fuss over nothing!'

'You think Marianne and Janet were mistaken?'

'Bound to be. It happens, I'm afraid, at their age. Residents forget where they've put something and then they can't find it. Or they forget they've already spent some of their cash. Nothing mysterious about it at all!'

'Really?' mused Albert. 'That's just what Ms Trainer said to Marianne.'

Brian sagged down in his chair, looking distraught again.

'Still feeling pretty torn-up over her murder, aren't you?' Albert suggested.

'What's that supposed to mean?'

'Couldn't help noticing how upset you were yesterday. Reckon she must have meant something quite special to you, eh?' He winked at Brian, who almost recoiled in horror.

'Absolutely not! I-I-I don't know what on earth you're talking about!' he stammered.

'Well, you two always worked together very closely, didn't you?'

'That was our jobs!' snapped Brian.

'Of course, of course!' Albert chuckled as Brian flushed quite pink with indignation.

'Now, about my missing watch ...'

'I'll get one of the staff to search your room for you. I expect it slipped down the back of something.'

'Most kind, thank you. Well, better leave you to get on with your work.' Albert sauntered out of the office feeling quite pleased with himself. He patted his blazer pocket to check that his watch was still safe where he'd put it earlier.

Brian stared at the door for a long time after Albert had gone. Just how much had the old busybody guessed? He couldn't actually know anything, surely?

✿

Annie had to wait until after lunch before she could perform her task. Sally, Paul and an older agency carer came on duty at one o'clock, and Annie then waited impatiently for Brian and Brenda to go downstairs for their lunch before making her way to the office.

She tapped hesitantly, hoping she could go through with this.

'Come in,' called Sally.

Annie popped her head around the door. 'Do you mind if I ask you something?' she asked, not needing to pretend to sound upset, because she really was.

'Of course not, come in.' Sally looked at her sympathetically. 'Come and sit down.'

Annie obeyed, pulling a hankie out of her pocket and dabbing her eyes as she sat.

'I know I'm being an old fool ...' she began.

'I'm sure you're not,' soothed Sally.

'You see, it's all these deaths. It's really worrying me.'

'Whatever do you mean?' Sally frowned.

'Well, first Marianne, then Felicity. And now Janet. It's like someone is picking us off one by one,' she sobbed convincingly.

'Whoa! Just a minute there, Annie, it's not like you to get yourself so muddled up. Marianne died of natural causes and Janet's not dead.'

'Isn't she?'

'No, I don't know where you got that idea from. Janet

was taken to hospital yesterday because she was unwell. But Mrs Wollstonecraft informed me at handover that she's a lot better this morning. In fact, she's coming back here later this afternoon.'

'Oh, that is good news.' Annie clapped her hands. Then her face fell. 'But someone definitely murdered Felicity, didn't they?'

'Well, yes, that is what the police said,' Sally agreed, reluctantly.

'I suppose it must be someone who broke into the house,' she suggested, watching Sally's reaction. 'Perhaps they got in through the back door?'

'I don't think anyone broke in. Andy would've seen something when he arrived yesterday morning, if they had, and he never said anything. And the police never mentioned any broken windows or anything like that.'

'But that means someone in this house murdered Felicity!' gasped Annie. Sally paled slightly and furrowed her brow in thought.

'I suppose that's why the police were asking so many questions about who last saw Felicity on Sunday evening. Not that I could help; I had the weekend off to go to my cousin's wedding. I only got back home from Reading late Sunday night.'

'Yes, of course, you weren't even here. I wonder who did see Felicity last?'

'I think it was one of the night carers, from what Brenda said,' replied Sally.

'Do you think one of them murdered her?'

'Oh no!' Sally cried, then paused. Annie waited patiently.

'I know I shouldn't speak ill of the dead, but she was a very difficult manager to get on with sometimes. I don't think any of the staff really liked her. And it is true that Jan had fallen out with her on several occasions . . .'

'Oh, why's that?'

'Jan was always moaning that Ms Trainer was on her back all the time, pulling her up over silly little things and giving her orders when Jan was in charge and Felicity wasn't even on duty.'

'Well, I suppose Ms Trainer did live on the premises. It must have been difficult for her to be properly off duty.'

'Yes, exactly. And I'm sure Jan wouldn't have murdered her just for being so bossy! You know, the more I think about it, the more I think it was Sonia, not Jan, who was the last to see her alive. So, Jan can't have murdered her, can she?'

'Maybe not,' agreed Annie, not mentioning that the murderer was unlikely to be telling the truth. 'And what about Sonia?'

'What about Sonia?' asked Sally, looking at Annie suspiciously.

'Well, you know, I just wondered if she also had a reason to want Ms Trainer dead.'

'Isn't that something for the police, rather than us?'

'Oh, I didn't mean ... I was just worried ...' Annie flustered, realising that she had maybe pushed her questioning a little too far.

'Don't worry,' reassured Sally, 'I'm sure you're quite safe. I really can't believe any one of us here would've murdered Ms Trainer.'

*But someone must have*, thought Annie, *if there were no signs of a break-in. Unless Felicity had let the murderer into the home herself.*

'I wonder if Ms Trainer ever had any visitors, you know, friends who came here to visit her, that sort of thing?'

'Not that I know of,' replied Sally. 'She went out occasionally, but I never saw her bring any friends back here. In fact, the only person I ever saw her spend time with was Mr Wollstonecraft. Oh! Not that I meant anything by that ...' Her voice trailed off.

Annie couldn't wait to report back to the others, but she had to spend another five minutes or so with Sally chatting about other things, as instructed by Meg, so that Sally didn't get too suspicious. 'Tell me all about the wedding you went to,' she urged. Sally was happy to oblige and by the time Annie left the office, Sally had forgotten their earlier conversation.

Annie made straight for the day room, where Meg, Albert

and Jack were waiting for her. They'd agreed to play whist together at the table so the others wouldn't think it too odd that the four of them were chatting. It would also keep the staff at a distance, thinking they were busy.

Meg carefully shuffled the cards. 'Right,' she said, 'who's going to report back first?'

# Chapter Thirty-two

The four friends had barely finished sharing their findings when a dark blue Vauxhall Astra pulled into the gravel drive. They recognised the two detectives from yesterday as they got out and stretched. 'Ooh, I wonder why they're back again,' pondered Annie.

'Bound to have more questions, now they've started gathering information, reading through everyone's statements and checking the evidence they collected yesterday,' Jack asserted, earning a begrudging nod from Albert.

'Right, time for some action then,' announced Meg. She stood up and moved with surprising speed so that she was in the hall innocently perusing the notice board by the time the detectives rang the doorbell.

Paul came out of the office to open the door and greeted the men.

'Sorry to disturb you again, sir,' began the sergeant.

'No problem. And do call me Paul. Come on in!'

'Thank you, Paul,' the sergeant smiled. 'Can we possibly use your office to conduct some more interviews, like yesterday?'

'Of course! I'll grab that extra chair again for you.'

The detectives came into the hall, greeting Meg politely when they saw her.

'Good afternoon, Inspector and Sergeant,' she beamed. 'Are you here to interview everyone, again?'

'Well, maybe not everyone,' smiled the DI.

'No, of course,' agreed Meg. 'I suppose it will depend on whose statements require further clarification.'

'Something like that.'

'Well, would you mind starting with me, seeing as I'm here already?'

'Thank you, Mrs Thornton, but your statement yesterday was quite clear.'

'That may be, but I wish to pass on some more information that I think you'll find useful.'

'Oh really?' sighed Dan, looking slightly less than impressed. He forced a smile onto his face. 'Well, in that case, you'd better come straight in.'

His sergeant suppressed a chuckle. Undeterred, she made herself comfortable on the wingback chair whilst the detectives took up their positions behind the desk. Paul offered drinks and Viv asked for two coffees, one black, no sugar, and the other white with one. 'Okay then, Mrs Thornton, what can you tell us?' asked Viv, pen at the ready.

'I informed you yesterday that I suspected that Felicity Trainer was also Mrs March.'

'Yes, you told us that.'

'I presume you have already spoken to PC Daly. Has he found anything yet?'

'Unfortunately, PC Daly is out of the station today, but we will be contacting him as soon as he's available.'

'Oh, I see. Well, I wanted to tell you that I think Brian must have known that Felicity was a thief and was colluding with her.'

'Why is that?'

'Because, if he wasn't involved, he would have done something about it, wouldn't he?'

Neither Dan nor Viv could fault that logic, so they simply nodded for her to continue.

'So, it follows that Brian was at least aware of the murders of Harry and Marianne, although I rather think Felicity is more likely to have actually carried them out.'

'Why?' enquired Dan.

'Because she was a trained nurse, and they were both killed in such a way that made the deaths appear natural. I doubt Brian would have known how to do that. Don't you agree? He isn't a trained healthcare professional. In fact, to be rather blunt about it, he isn't even that efficient a manager. And, of course, I am certain that it was Felicity who gave Janet the sedative. An overdose of temazepam, wasn't it?'

Viv looked up in surprise as Dan drew in a sharp breath and leant forward.

'And how do you know that, Mrs Thornton?' he asked.

'I believe one of the staff may have mentioned it,' she replied airily.

'I won't deny that Janet was, accidentally or otherwise, given temazepam,' began Dan.

'Oh, I'm sure it wasn't an accident,' insisted Meg. 'Felicity was trying to stop Janet and I communicating after she'd walked in on us discussing the murders last Friday.'

'But the point is,' Dan argued, 'we have no evidence to suggest that either Harry or Marianne was murdered. We've examined their death certificates and Dr Baker was satisfied both deaths were natural. So how exactly do you propose they were murdered?'

'I think they were given an injection of something—' Meg began.

'No, stop!' Dan interrupted. 'We are here to investigate the confirmed murder of Felicity Trainer, not the imagined murders of former residents.'

'But don't you think you should investigate the allegations? After all, if I am correct, it will have a bearing on your current case.'

'We have already initiated a line of enquiry to establish whether Felicity Trainer was formerly Mrs March and, if so, what were the facts of any former investigation.'

'Oh good, then you will have discovered that Felicity Trainer did not exist before July 2020?' Meg metaphorically crossed her fingers but, to her pleasure, the look that passed between the two detectives confirmed her suspicions.

'And how on earth do you know that?' demanded Dan.

'There is a lot of information available on the internet these days.'

Dan regarded her thoughtfully; she was obviously more resourceful than he gave her credit for. 'Well, yes, there does appear to be a coincidence between Mrs March disappearing and Ms Trainer appearing,' he began cautiously.

'I'm guessing Trainer was her maiden name?' suggested Meg.

'It was her mother's maiden name,' supplied Viv, before being quelled by a thunderous look from Dan.

'Ah, I see!' exclaimed Meg triumphantly.

Luckily, Dan's retort was bitten off by the interruption of Paul delivering their coffees. He took a tentative sip at his drink whilst composing himself, before addressing Meg again. 'Mrs Thornton, we will investigate Felicity's background, as we would for any murder victim. And I promise you, we'll look into your allegations concerning various thefts from residents. As a matter of fact, we have a team on their way here this afternoon to search for any possible stolen items and other evidence.'

Meg nodded her approval.

'And if I can find any evidence that either Harry or Marianne might have been murdered, we will pursue that too. But for the time being, I have a really pressing need to investigate the murder of Ms Trainer. Surely you can understand that?'

'Indeed,' nodded Meg, slightly mollified.

'If you don't have any new information relating to this enquiry, we really do need to push on with the other interviews we have planned for today.' Dan stood as though to bid her farewell, but Meg wasn't ready to move yet.

'Well, Inspector, I do have some other thoughts to share with you.'

'Thoughts? With the greatest of respect, Mrs Thornton, we need solid facts and evidence, not your thoughts.' Dan was beginning to sound exasperated. He sat down and exchanged knowing glances with his sergeant, who pulled a face.

'Fact one, Felicity was murdered sometime between 9pm Sunday and 7am Monday, which gives us a window for the time of death,' Meg responded firmly.

Dan nodded. He could place the time of death more accurately based on the preliminary findings from the pathologist, but he wasn't about to tell Meg that.

'Fact two.' Meg crossed her fingers again. 'Cause of death was possibly blunt force trauma. She was struck on the head, probably with the cast iron skillet you removed for analysis.' The look on Dan's face confirmed that for her.

'Fact three, her body was then moved into one of the freezers, where Andy discovered it on Monday morning.'

Dan groaned, inwardly cursing the chef, who had no doubt told all and sundry.

'Of course, if the blow to the head wasn't the cause of death, she might have either suffocated or frozen to death. I'm sure your pathologist will have been able to determine that at the post-mortem.'

'You seem awfully familiar with some of the terminology used around murder cases,' said Dan, suspiciously.

'My late husband was a DCI with Bournemouth CID,' she admitted. The two policemen looked completely taken aback.

'Was he DCI Grant Thornton?' ventured Dan, incredulously.

'Yes! How ever did you know?' It was Meg's turn to look incredulous.

'My father was a DC in Bournemouth, and I can remember him singing the praises of the DCI he worked under at that time. He had something of a reputation when it came to solving murder cases.'

'Yes, I see,' Meg smiled. 'It's a small world sometimes, isn't it?'

Dan agreed that it was. 'Was there anything else you wanted to add?' he asked weakly, rapidly revising his opinion of this witness.

'Where was I? Oh yes, fact four, you suspect that someone inside the house during those hours must have murdered Felicity as there were no signs of a break-in. Which leads me to fact five. It is most unlikely to have been any of the residents as none of us has the physical strength, or mobility, to hit someone hard enough to knock them out, let alone move the body.'

'And how do you know she was knocked out?' asked Viv, now curious.

'That's a reasonable assumption, I think. If she had been conscious, she would have struggled and fought back, in which case Andy would've noticed something wrong as soon as he arrived.'

'Mrs Thornton, listen to me. I'm not going to dispute any of the facts you've just enumerated. But you know that we need to gather solid evidence before we can arrest anyone. And, if you are right and one of the staff members murdered Ms Trainer, surely you can see that you could be putting yourself in danger if you start discussing what you think you know with anyone else inside the home.'

Meg could hear the genuine concern in his voice and warmed a little to him. At least he hadn't ridiculed her suppositions. 'Very well,' she nodded.

'Now,' he continued with a kindly smile,' do you have any other insights for us?'

'Well, we know that Brian and Felicity were having an affair. I'm sure that he was rather more in love with her than she was with him, and we know that she rejected his proposal. I'm sure Brian doesn't deal well with rejection, and that must give him a strong motive for murder. But I don't want you to overlook Brenda. I feel sure she knew about her husband's affair.'

'And how on earth do you know that?' demanded Viv.

Meg explained how upset Brenda had been on Saturday evening, having been absent for most of the day with a supposed migraine. How distracted and pale she had been all day Sunday. And she told him about the comments Brenda had made about her 'silly argument' with Brian. 'I suspect the truth is that Brian told Brenda about his affair with Felicity on Friday evening and asked for a divorce. That would explain Brenda's behaviour over the weekend. And it would explain why Brian then felt free to propose to Felicity on Saturday.'

Dan shook his head in amazement at her deductive powers.

'Moreover, Inspector, I was watching everyone's behaviour in the day room yesterday, and not once did Brenda or Brian speak or try to reassure each other. Don't you think that's a little strange, if their marriage had been good?'

Dan had to concede the point.

'Furthermore, I was chatting with Brenda just this morning and happened to comment that she must miss having Ms Trainer around. She didn't reply, and the expression on her face was very telling.'

'Well, thank you for that, Mrs Thornton.' Dan tried again to end their conversation, but Meg hadn't finished.

'One final thing. I don't know if Lauren has told you yet, but she heard Felicity threatening to kill Brian just hours before she was killed.'

'What!' Viv and Dan exchanged looks again.

'She didn't mention that yesterday,' confirmed Dan, 'so we'll need to hear that directly from her. Perhaps you could send her in, when we've finished.'

'I only mentioned it because Lauren is off duty today; otherwise, I would've asked her to tell you herself.'

'Are you sure you aren't confusing what Lauren told you?' interjected Viv. 'Surely it was Brian who threatened Felicity, not the other way round?'

'I don't get confused, Sergeant,' replied Meg frostily, 'but I expected that you would need to confirm it with Lauren, in any case.'

Dan thanked Meg warmly for her cooperation, before helping her up from her chair and opening the door. When he closed the door behind her, Viv looked up. 'I think I put my foot in it there,' he admitted ruefully.

'Yes,' said Dan, 'she really is the most observant old dear, and her brain is clearly razor sharp.'

'So, not a batty old woman then?' joked Viv.

'Definitely not,' mused Dan, thoughtfully. He'd have to ask his dad a bit more about DCI Thornton.

# Chapter Thirty-three

Almost against his better judgement, Dan charged out of the office and called after Meg. 'Mrs Thornton, wait a moment.' He caught up with her and said quietly, 'I don't suppose you could help us with our next interview?' So it was that Meg fetched Brenda and brought her into the office. Brenda sat on the very edge of the swivel chair, which Dan had repositioned beside the wingback chair that Meg once again occupied. He sat casually on the edge of the desk.

'How can I help, Officers?' Brenda asked, licking her dry lips and looking from one to the other suspiciously.

'Mrs Wollstonecraft, how long have you and Brian been married?' asked Dan gently.

'Thirty-three years,' she replied.

'Would you say that your marriage has been a good one?'

'Well ... yes ... mostly.' She hesitated, not liking where this might be going.

'You must know your husband well after that length of time together.'

She nodded, not trusting herself to speak.

'So, if your husband had been having an affair behind your back, I think you'd know about it.'

She swallowed hard and thought for a moment. They appeared to know, so was there any point in denying it?

'Yes, Inspector, you're right.' She fiddled with the gold band on her ring finger and stared at the floor. 'I suspected my husband was having an affair. But I didn't know for sure, you understand?'

'Oh, I think you did, didn't you?'

She looked wildly around the room, as if searching for an answer. Meg spoke gently to her. 'Why else did you spend all day Saturday hiding away with a migraine?'

'I wasn't hiding!' Brenda protested.

'Brenda, I'm sorry, my dear, but your behaviour on Saturday was completely out of character, and we could all see you'd been crying.' Meg reached out a comforting hand. 'And you were distracted and out of sorts on Sunday too. You can't deny it.'

Brenda stared at the floor again. 'You're right, of course,' she whispered.

'Would you now tell us what you knew and when, please?' Dan persisted.

Brenda broke down into pitiful heaving sobs. Meg gave her arm a reassuring squeeze and the inspector passed her a clean handkerchief, before going to the kitchen to get a glass of water. He waited until she had pulled herself together. 'Mrs Wollstonecraft,' he said softly, 'how much did you know?'

'I've thought for a while that Brian was having an affair with Felicity Trainer. Little things at first, you know, the way he looked at her, the way they spent more and more time together, the way she behaved around him. Then, last month, I caught him coming down from her room late at night. And, on several occasions, I was sure I'd seen him giving her presents. I wondered where he could be getting the money from. I even checked our bank statements, so that I would have some proof, but there were no unusual transactions.' She paused and took a deep breath.

'Go on,' encouraged Meg, squeezing her hand.

'On Friday night, Brian told me about the affair. He said he wanted a divorce. I was devastated, obviously. That's why I was too upset to see anyone on Saturday. I only came upstairs because Phil called out to me, and I knew he'd come down if I didn't go up.'

'Phil?' Dan asked.

'Dr Baker. He's very caring.' She bit her lip.

'Were you having a relationship with Dr Baker?'

'No!' she said forcefully. 'He was just a friend.'

'A good friend whom I saw you embracing,' Meg said gently. Brenda shook her head vehemently. 'Yes,' persisted Meg, 'I saw you in the staffroom upstairs, on Thursday, after

Marianne had died. I didn't think you'd seen me.'

'We weren't having an affair, I promise you.' Brenda looked from Meg to Dan and back again. 'Really, we weren't.'

'No, I don't think you were,' Meg reassured her, 'but the two of you do have feelings for each other.' Brenda couldn't dispute that.

'Now then, Mrs Wollstonecraft,' Dan was eager to push the questioning forward, 'I want you to think very carefully about this: when did you last see Felicity Trainer?'

'Like I told you, on Sunday afternoon, after lunch.'

Dan looked at Viv, who flicked back in his notebook.

'You said you saw Ms Trainer go into the office after the residents' lunch. You went out for a short walk in the garden to try to clear your head, then you came in and went straight downstairs to your flat,' he recited.

'Yes, that's right,' she confirmed.

'You didn't see her again after that?' insisted Dan.

'No. I had a lie-down on my bed and I must have fallen asleep because the next thing I knew, Brian was coming downstairs asking about dinner.'

'You didn't arrange to meet Ms Trainer later?'

'No, why would I?'

'You stayed in your flat all evening and all night?'

'Yes. Look, I've already told you all this.'

'I just find it a little strange that you would spend so long cooped up in a small flat with your husband, given the strain on your relationship. It must have been very awkward.'

'Not really. I shut myself in the bedroom with my Kindle. Brian watched some TV and then slept on the sofa.'

'Let me get that clear, you didn't actually see your husband at all during the night?'

'No, Inspector, I didn't.'

'But you vouched that he hadn't left the flat at all during the night? How could you possibly know that, if you were shut in your bedroom?'

She gasped, suddenly catching his drift. 'Oh!' she cried.

*Very interesting*, thought Meg. *Brian could easily have*

*slipped out without Brenda noticing.* She waited for Dan to continue with that line of questioning but, to her surprise, he changed tack quite unexpectedly.

'One final thing before you go, Mrs Wollstonecraft. Do you always use your own private kitchen, or do you ever have occasion to use the main kitchen at all?'

'I mostly use my own kitchen for preparing our private meals, but of course I use the big kitchen a couple of times a week, when Andy is off duty.'

'You cook for the residents?' He was surprised.

'It's a small care home, we can't afford two chefs. Andy has two afternoons off a week. On those days, either Brian or I cook the evening meal, which Andy has usually left prepared for us. He also has alternate Sundays off, so we do all the meals then.'

'I see. So, you are both likely to have handled a lot of the equipment in the kitchen?'

'Yes, of course.' She looked a bit puzzled, but Dan declined to say anything more.

*Ah*, thought Meg. *He's establishing whether either Brenda or Brian could have left prints on the cast iron skillet. And, of course, they both could have done so quite innocently.*

# Chapter Thirty-four

After he had dismissed Brenda, and Viv had finished writing up his notes, Dan thanked Meg for sitting in. 'But I don't want you present in this next interview,' he explained. 'Brian is an entirely different kettle of fish to Brenda, and I don't think he'd respond well to you being present.' Reluctantly, Meg agreed. She left the office and went across the hall to look at the notice board. As soon as Brian had entered the office and shut the door behind him, she tiptoed nearer, trying desperately to hear their words.

Brian crossed the office full of confidence and sat squarely on the chair, staring at them defiantly. 'Inspector?' he asked, a little impatiently.

'Mr Wollstonecraft, I just wanted to check a couple of things you said in your statement yesterday,' Dan said, deliberately sounding as officious as possible.

'I don't know what else I could possibly tell you,' he said belligerently.

'For a start, you could have told us that you were having an affair with Felicity Trainer.' Dan stared right into Brian's face and saw the fear in his eyes.

'Don't know what you mean!' Brian blustered.

'Sir, several witnesses have reported that you were having an affair with her.'

'Stuff and nonsense, what witnesses?'

'Do you deny going up to Ms Trainer's flat late one evening last month?'

'Too bloody right, I do!'

'Even though you were seen?'

'It's all nonsense!' Brian waved a hand impatiently.

'You deny having an affair with Ms Trainer?'

'Yes, I've just told you that!'

Dan delivered the *coup de grâce*; 'In that case, why would you have told your wife that you were?'

Brian opened and closed his mouth several times, the colour draining out of his face. He subconsciously touched the wedding band on his left hand.

'She told you that, I suppose?' he said at last.

'Yes, and I understand you asked her for a divorce, Mr Wollstonecraft.'

'Very well, yes, I did. So what?'

'You lied to us, sir, and we detectives tend to take that sort of thing very seriously. You see, it could make us have serious doubts about other parts of your statement.'

'I don't know what relevance the state of my marriage is to your inquiry,' challenged Brian. 'I told you, I didn't murder Felicity.' He broke off, sounding genuinely distressed. 'I couldn't have murdered her. I loved her so much.'

The tears rolled down his face, and Dan discreetly ignored them.

'I believe you did love her, sir. But she rejected your proposal, didn't she?'

'My ... my what!' He looked shocked.

'You proposed marriage to Ms Trainer on Saturday afternoon.'

'What proposal? You're being ridiculous now!' Brian's face was suffused with anger.

'You deny having proposed to her?'

'Of course I do. I was still married, for goodness' sake!'

'But you had already asked your wife for a divorce,' Dan quietly reminded him.

Brian fell silent, only his eyes giving away the fact that he was desperately trying to think of a way out of this mess.

Dan calmly changed subject, as though the other matter was finished with.

'Remind me, Mr Wollstonecraft. Where were you between eight-thirty Sunday evening and seven-thirty Monday morning?'

'I was in my flat downstairs.'

'And can anyone confirm that?'

'I've already told you; I was with my wife all night.'

'Ah yes, but you didn't tell us that she was shut in the

bedroom, while you were sleeping in the lounge.'

'What?' Brian looked shaken to the core.

'So, you see, she can't really confirm anything, can she? How would she have known if you had gone upstairs during the night?'

'I don't know what you mean. I didn't go upstairs, I promise you. That's the truth.'

Dan switched direction again, a sure way of throwing a suspect off track.

'What little presents did you give to your lover, Mr Wollstonecraft?'

'What! What presents?'

'You were seen giving presents to Felicity. Your wife wondered where you might have got the money from, and I'd say that's a pretty good question, wouldn't you?'

'No!' Brian looked around frantically.'I don't know what you mean!' He licked his lips nervously and looked up at the ceiling.

'Well, okay, I did give her a necklace on one occasion, a gold sweetheart locket on a chain,' he conceded. 'I had money in my personal account, so why shouldn't I spend it how I choose?'

'Thank you, Mr Wollstonecraft.'

'That's it?' He seemed surprised.

'Yes, you can go.'

Brian gulped and leapt up from his chair, almost racing for the door.

'But, Mr Wollstonecraft,' Dan said, as Brian wrenched open the handle, 'don't leave Salisbury, please. I'm sure we will have some more questions for you in the very near future.'

❀

Meg had to remove herself pretty smartly from her listening post outside the office door as Brian charged out. Despite the door being closed, she'd heard almost everything Brian had said, as he'd been shouting for most of the time. Not to mention telling a whole pack of lies! Now that she'd heard the interviews with both Wollstonecrafts, there was a lot of thinking to be done. She headed to the day room to find the others.

'I say, old gal,' exclaimed Albert, 'where have you been hiding out? I thought we were, um, y'know,' he lowered his voice, 'going to discuss the case.'

Meg sank down gratefully in the chair opposite Albert, her knees aching from standing too long again. But before she could fill them in on what had happened, she heard voices in the hall. Was that the sergeant and Brian?

'Albert, we do indeed need to discuss the case. But, right now, I need you to find a way of listening in on what's being said in the hall. I'd go myself, but I think they've seen too much of me already today.'

'Not a problem, m'dear. You sit there and rest and I'll go a-spying.' Meg couldn't help but smile at the astonished Jack and Annie. Albert sauntered casually into the hall and along to the cloakrooms, noticing on his way that Wolly and that sergeant seemed to be examining the security system by the front door.

※

Dan emerged from the office to find Brian still discussing the security system with Viv. He didn't see Albert emerge from the gents' and sidle along the corridor, out of sight but able to listen in.

'Does the alarm system cover all the windows and the back door?' Viv was asking.

'Yes, that's right. But not the front door. You see, Brenda and I live in, and we need to be able to come and go as we please. The front door is solid oak, secured with a top-of-the-range five-lever mortice deadlock with a rim automatic deadlatch. Of course, we only use the mortice lock at night.'

'And who is responsible for locking the mortice and turning the security system on and off, please?'

'The night staff do that. They lock up and set the alarm usually between about ten and 11pm, and then they unlock the mortice and deactivate the alarm between about six and six-thirty, when the newspapers are delivered.'

'So, after 6am, the doors are open?'

'They are a little less secure, Sergeant, but they are all still locked. Only someone with a key could gain entry. Andy has a key to the back door, as do Brenda and I. We also have both keys to the front door, as did Felicity. It really is very unlikely that someone could have got into the house at night without either setting an alarm off or having had the keys.'

'Well, thank you for showing me that.' Viv looked across to Dan, who was hovering in the background. 'Seems pretty unlikely an outsider could have got in, guv, unless he or she had inside help.'

'Yes, I heard! You seem to know a lot about household security, Mr Wollstonecraft?'

'Yes, indeed. I worked for a locksmith for a while in my youth,' he said proudly.

'Really? You also worked for a logistics firm at some point too, I heard.'

'Yes, that's right.'

'And now you run a care home?'

'That's me, Inspector. What can I say? Versatile is my middle name.'

'Yes. Well, I'm sorry to be a nuisance, but I had a thought while I was in the office waiting for my sergeant to come back. Presumably, you have the personnel records for all the staff somewhere on site. You know, CVs, references, DBS checks, and so on.'

'Yes, Inspector, they're all in the office.'

'Would it be possible to look at them now, while we're here?'

'Of course. I'll unlock the filing cabinet and show you where they are.'

Albert ducked into the treatment room as Brian headed for the office, and Viv raised a questioning eyebrow at Dan.

'We have to stall for time until the warrants have been issued,' he muttered, *sotto voce.* 'The superintendent said she'll try to hurry the warrants up, but we need to keep

Brian under observation until she rings back with the go-ahead.'

Viv nodded his understanding, and they followed Brian into the office.

'There you are, Inspector, all the personnel records are in that bottom drawer, which I've unlocked for you. Now, if you don't need me around ...' Brian's voice trailed off as he edged towards the open door.

'It would really help, sir, if you could stay and give us your impression of each of the members of staff as we look through their records. Help us to get a more balanced overview.'

'Oh, right, I do have a few things to do this afternoon ... but ... oh well, I'm sure I can spare half an hour to help you.' Viv closed the office door.

Albert slipped stealthily past the office and returned to his waiting friends to pass on everything he'd learnt. He couldn't resist adding that it seemed as though Brian's arrest was imminent and it had been obvious all along to him that Brian had killed Harry, Marianne and Felicity. 'Stands to reason there's only one murderer,' he proclaimed triumphantly.

# Chapter Thirty-five

About half an hour later, a minibus pulled into the drive. Four pairs of eyes watched with curiosity from the day-room window as a dozen or so police officers got out and stretched their legs, before standing around in small groups chatting, apparently waiting for someone.

'Why are all those policemen here?' moaned Annie, her voice trembling slightly.

'That must be the police search team,' nodded Meg thoughtfully.

'Whatever are they searching for?' Annie asked tremulously.

'Clues!' declared Albert resolutely.

'Evidence such as stolen goods,' suggested Meg.

A few minutes later, another car arrived, delivering a bespectacled ginger-headed youth carrying a metallic silver box, who joined the others in the drive.

'What's he got there?' asked Albert.

'He must be one of the CSIs,' said Jack, knowledgeably.

'Oh really, an expert now, are you?' challenged Albert.

'No, he just watches too much TV,' said Meg dryly, causing Jack to grin and Albert to chuckle.

Eventually, a marked police car arrived, with two occupants. The driver, a uniformed PC, stayed in the car while a plain-clothes detective got out of the car clutching a sheaf of papers. He marched, full of self-importance, up to the PC on the front door.

The PC signed the newcomer in and a minute or so later he reappeared with the inspector, who gathered the men and women in the drive around him and spoke urgently, explaining what he wanted them to do and dividing them into two teams. As he spoke, they all pulled on forensic gloves. A moment later, they headed for the front door.

'Why are they wearing gloves?' wondered Annie.

'So that they don't contaminate any evidence they find,' supplied Jack. Albert looked at him thoughtfully.

※

Dan returned to the office after briefing the search teams. Because the office door was left open, Jack could hear most of what was being said from just inside the day-room door, where he'd positioned himself after a nod from Meg.

'Mr Wollstonecraft, the search team has arrived, and they have a warrant to search Ms Trainer's flat and seize any possible evidence relating to her murder. I also have a warrant to search your flat ...'

'No!' shouted Brian. 'What right do you have? You can't do that!'

'This warrant gives me the right, sir.'

'This is harassment!' blustered Brian. 'I want a solicitor!'

'You're not currently under arrest, Mr Wollstonecraft, but if you want to consult a solicitor, that's your prerogative. Feel free.'

Jack returned to their table when Dan came into the hall, and reported to the others that the police were searching both Frau Flic's and the Wollstonecrafts' flats.

※

Dan gave the search teams the go-ahead, and the first team leader immediately headed upstairs, whilst the second knocked on the door to the basement flat, opened the door and called out in a loud voice, 'Anyone at home in the basement, police search team entering now!' He paused and listened, before standing back slightly as a frightened Brenda crept up the stairs and clung to the door-frame.

'W-w-whatever's happening?' she stammered, a worried expression creasing her forehead as she looked at Dan.

'We have warrants to search both Ms Trainer's flat and your flat, in relation to Ms Trainer's murder.'

'What, right now?' she asked. It was the team leader who

politely asked her to move aside, and she looked stunned as six police officers descended into their flat.

'Would you mind coming into the office for a moment?' Dan pushed the door open and she walked through, in something of a daze.

Dan beckoned to the bespectacled CSI standing patiently next to Viv.

'Mr and Mrs Wollstonecraft, I have another warrant here that relates to the seizure of personal mobile phones.' He showed it to Brian, who looked shocked, and to Brenda, who seemed resigned.

'Can you give this technician your phones, please?' Dan commanded.

Brenda pulled hers from her cardigan pocket without comment, and the CSI took it gingerly from her in his gloved hands, dropping it into a clear evidence bag, which he then duly labelled.

The CSI turned to Brian, who looked up sullenly. 'Do I have to?' he demanded. 'I use this phone a lot for both personal and business matters. It has all my contacts in it.'

'I'm sorry, sir, you must hand it over. However, I will give you a receipt and promise to return the phone as soon as possible.'

Brian extracted his phone from a jacket pocket and watched anxiously as the CSI repeated the procedure of bagging and tagging.

'Do either of you possess a second mobile phone?' Dan asked.

Brenda shook her head and Brian muttered, 'Fat chance.'

'You do realise that if we discover another mobile in your flat, it will look very bad for one or both of you,' he warned.

'I told you, I haven't got another phone!' Brian snapped back at him.

Dan nodded at the CSI, who replied, 'I'll get these to the lab now, sir, and we should be in a position to return them tomorrow morning, if that's okay with you?'

'Yes', Dan acknowledged, 'I take it I'll have the report on my desk by then too?'

'I'll do my best, sir.' The young man hurried to his car and set off immediately.

The two detectives withdrew from the office, closing the door on Brian and Brenda, so that they could chat quietly in the dining room whilst waiting for the search teams to do their job.

※

At the whist table, where a game of whist was yet to be played, the four friends were again arguing about what the search teams were looking for. 'It's obvious,' insisted Albert, 'they're looking for evidence to convict Brian.'

'But you're assuming that Brian is guilty,' objected Meg.

'Surely they're just looking for whatever evidence they can find, and then they'll determine who that evidence points to,' supplied Jack.

At that moment, Brenda wandered into the day room, so their conversation was cut short. She looked around and noticed the four residents seated at the table playing cards. She was bemused to see Jack and Albert playing as partners. Meg looked up and smiled reassuringly at her, and she attempted to smile back.

Sylvia was on the settee removing the perfectly good purple nail varnish that had been applied the previous Wednesday. She looked lost in her own little world.

Muriel was fast asleep and looked relaxed and peaceful. How Brenda envied her. There was no sign of Sally, who should have come on duty by now, nor any of the other carers. Brenda wondered for a moment where they could be. Then she wandered over to the French windows and sank into a chair, gazing unseeingly at the garden.

Annie whispered to the others, 'Poor thing, she looks completely worn out with worry. I wonder if we should do something to try to cheer her up.'

'I think the best thing we can do is to solve the murders. If Brenda is innocent, that will be the best tonic we can give her. If not ...' Meg grimaced.

'Surely you don't think Brenda killed Felicity?' hissed Annie.

'Poppycock!' muttered Albert, under his breath.

'We need to keep our eyes and ears open,' Meg insisted quietly.

'Talking of eyes open,' interrupted Jack, 'an ambulance has just pulled up outside.'

Oh no,' groaned Annie, 'who can it be for this time?'

Meg looked up and felt a sudden lifting of her heart as she saw two paramedics manoeuvring someone out of the ambulance.

'It's Janet!' she exclaimed.

'Did someone say Janet?' called out Sylvia.

'It's an ambulance bringing Janet back,' explained Jack.

'Why, where's she been?' asked Sylvia.

Brenda hauled herself out of the chair to go to welcome Janet and was surprised to discover Sally in the hall, ready and waiting with Janet's wheelchair and a warm blanket.

The paramedics helped transfer Janet from their stretcher chair to her own, fussing over her like she was the Queen of England. Brenda was relieved to see Janet looking wide awake and with it.

'Where would you like to go, Janet?' asked Sally. 'Up to your bed or into the day room?' Brenda felt as though she might just as well not be there.

'Oh, I've had enough of bed for a while,' chuckled Janet, 'I want to live a little!'

Sally was about to wheel Janet to the day room when the detectives appeared from the dining room.

'Mrs Smith,' said Dan warmly, 'we're so pleased to see you looking well. I'm Detective Inspector Bywater and this is Detective Sergeant Williams.'

'Ah yes. That nice young constable who took my statement at the hospital told me all about our terrible tragedy.'

'On that subject, could you spare us a couple of minutes in the dining room, please?' asked Dan. 'But only if you feel up to it,' he added, catching the expression on Sally's face.

'There you are, I've been asked on a date by a nice young man already!' chuckled Janet. 'You can tell my friends they'll just have to wait,' she informed Sally, as she was being wheeled into the dining room. 'I'll be perfectly all right with two men to look after me.' Sally smiled as she withdrew, so pleased to have the doyen of their home back safely.

# Chapter Thirty-six

'Mrs Smith,' Dan sat down and leant towards her so that she didn't have to strain, 'I know my DC took a statement from you earlier regarding the sleeping tablets you were given, so I won't make you go over the same ground again. But I do want you to tell me exactly what you've seen over recent weeks that made you suspect that Brian might have been stealing from the residents.'

'I see Meg's kept you well informed,' nodded Janet.

'Yes, she's shared a lot of information with us which we are obviously cross-checking. But she had marked Felicity as the thief . . .'

'And murderer,' added Janet.

'Yes, if any former residents were indeed murdered.'

'Oh, I'm sure of that,' insisted Janet.

'But you told her you suspected it was Brian and not Felicity.'

'Inspector, I'm a hundred and one years old. I am confined to this wheelchair all the time when I'm not in bed. I can barely stand, and I can't walk more than a couple of steps. When people look at me, they see a broken-down old biddy. So, they mistakenly assume my mind must be in the same state as my body. They push me next to the French doors so that I can see the garden and then they forget I am there. I've seen Brian taking money from the other residents on more than one occasion. And I've watched him and Felicity flirting and canoodling in the garden. And I saw him giving her presents; most recently, a necklace.'

'Thank you, that very clearly suggests that Brian is a thief. Do you have any evidence that he is also a murderer?'

'None at all, Inspector. I wish I did.' Janet's head dropped and Dan realised with a twinge of guilt that she was tired.

'Thank you very much, Mrs Smith.' He took hold of her hand and was surprised at the strength of her grip.

※

Meg was delighted to see Janet return to the day room. She watched as the sergeant wheeled her over to the French doors under Sally's instruction. Everyone called out a warm 'Hello' or 'Welcome back!' as she processed through the room, and Janet acknowledged each greeting with a royal wave and a beautiful smile. Once Janet was settled and Sally had gone to fetch the tea trolley, Meg spoke quietly to the others.

'I don't think we should crowd Janet just now. She's probably had enough questions from the police and the staff already today.'

'Quite so!' agreed Albert.

'One good thing,' commented Jack, 'at least we know that it was Felicity doping her, so Janet's quite safe being back home.'

'Yes, indeed,' enthused Annie.

'But we still have to prove who killed Felicity,' Meg reminded them.

'What? I thought we'd agreed it was Brian,' Albert insisted. 'I say we leave it up to the police now. Though they're certainly taking their time arresting him, aren't they?'

'They have to gather a lot of evidence before they can arrest someone,' she said.

'And forensic tests take time to produce results,' added Jack.

'What? Oh yes, of course! I understand that,' Albert replied, although he hadn't until they'd pointed it out.

'I'm sure the police are working hard to find evidence against whoever killed Felicity,' Meg said pensively. 'My concern is whether or not they are also looking into Marianne's and Harry's deaths.'

At that point, Sally and another carer entered with the tea trolley, and the four friends abandoned their pretence at whist and occupied themselves with tea and normal activities. Albert and Jack left the table and seated themselves in adjacent armchairs, where Albert quizzed Jack about the forensic and police programmes he loved to watch. Annie drifted over to the settee and pulled her knitting from her bag, attempting to answer Sylvia's questions without giving anything away. *Not that Sylvia is likely to remember anything if I had told her*, she thought, as Sylvia asked for the tenth time where Felicity was. Brenda wandered in again and returned to her isolated chair, on the opposite side of the French doors from Janet.

Meg alone remained seated at the table, absent-mindedly shuffling the cards before starting a game of patience. Halfway through, she heard the police team trample down the stairs from Felicity's flat and watched them congregate in the hallway. The inspector came out of the dining room and examined the various evidence bags their leader showed him. Unfortunately, whatever the items were, they were too small for her to see from that distance. Shortly afterwards, the team from the basement returned and the hall was crowded with so many police officers in such a small space that she couldn't see what, if anything, they had found. The search teams eventually filed out of the front door, laughing and joking now their task was completed. Meg watched through the window as they divested themselves of their gloves and seated themselves back in the minibus.

✦

In the office, Dan was showing an evidence bag containing a jeweller's ring box to Brian. 'Is this the engagement ring you purchased for Felicity?'

Brian looked at it morosely. 'Yes,' he conceded.

Dan pointed to the writing on the box. 'Is that where you purchased this?'

'Yes.'

'And how did you pay for this, Mr Wollstonecraft?'

'How? I told you. Money from my private account.'

'No, I meant did you pay by cheque or use a debit or credit card?'

Brian looked down at the floor. 'Can't remember,' he mumbled.

'Really? You must have purchased this recently and you can't remember?'

'I told you. I can't remember. So much has happened since then ... I ... I can't think straight at the moment.'

'So, when did you purchase it?' tried Dan.

Brian stayed silent.

'You do realise, we're going to go to the jeweller's and find out everything for ourselves, don't you? You could save us all a lot of time and trouble.'

Brian looked up, fear in his eyes. 'Saturday morning,' he mumbled reluctantly.

'Thank you. Now, what about these other pieces of jewellery?' Dan asked, showing him several other items in evidence bags. Brian dismissed them nervously, saying they must all belong to Felicity.

'But some of these were found in your flat, Mr Wollstonecraft.'

Brian looked around helplessly, shrugged his shoulders and denied knowing anything about them. Dan wasn't convinced but for now he'd get forensics to do their job. He carried the bags out to the minibus, which immediately departed, going via the lab to drop off all the evidence before returning the officers to the station. He then looked into the office to inform Brian that they were leaving, before accompanying Viv to his car. He glanced at his watch as they left the house, and sighed. It was unfortunate that they would probably still catch the tail end of rush hour.

# Chapter Thirty-seven

Meg watched the vehicles leave then resumed her game of patience, forehead furrowed as she pondered the events of that afternoon. What seemed like barely five minutes later, Andy popped his head into the day room to ask if it would be all right to serve dinner in fifteen minutes. Sally hurried off to prepare Jack's insulin. Meg took the opportunity to slip across the room to tell Janet how pleased she was to see her back safe and sound. Janet grasped her hand in gratitude, tears in her eyes. 'Have you solved the case yet, my dear?' she asked.

'We've been working on it,' Meg replied, a wary eye on Brenda, who seemed not to be listening. 'Albert is certain that Brian is the murderer, but I'm not so sure.'

'Then you'd better keep at it,' advised Janet. 'And talking of Albert,' she nodded towards the armchairs where Jack and Albert were just rising, still deep in conversation, 'just what is going on with those two?'

'I think Albert's been knocked off his high horse and has realised that Jack's not so bad after all,' Meg laughed.

'I'm pleased,' said Janet, nodding. 'Albert's been quite lonely since Harry died.'

Before Meg could speak again, Sally arrived to take Janet to the dining room, so Meg followed on.

❁

By mid-evening, a disgruntled Meg was back in the day room. Jack was watching TV, engrossed in a *CSI* programme, but she really couldn't get into the somewhat convoluted American plot. Nor could she read, with the TV distracting her, and she preferred natural light to do a puzzle. Brenda had shut herself in the office after Brian disappeared downstairs, and Sally and the other carers were busy helping some of the residents to bed. As there was no one around to talk to, she turned her mind to the murders. She racked her brains trying to recall that elusive something that she felt sure was an important clue. It was as if she'd had it in her hand earlier and it had somehow wriggled out and flown away.

A new scene flickered onto the TV screen, of a scientist drawing up liquid with a needle and syringe, and suddenly it snapped back into her mind. The night before Marianne's murder! The hands in the treatment room drawing up a syringe! How could she possibly have forgotten! Meg got up slowly and painfully with some vague idea of checking the treatment room out but, as she entered the hallway, one of the night carers, Milana, was just arriving for the night shift. Of course, Sonia and Jan must have completed their week of nights by now. She said a brief hello and asked Milana how she was. Then Brenda came out from the office, so she decided she may as well go to bed as this was obviously not a good time to poke around.

✦

Meg got undressed and into bed and tried to read her book to pass the time, but the bedside light was not quite sufficient for her eyes. Impatiently, she waited for midnight to approach, before carefully swinging her legs to the floor and putting on slippers and dressing gown and quietly crossing to her door. She cracked it open an inch or two and stood looking and listening. There was no sound from the staffroom, just a rather stentorian snoring coming from Albert's room. She crept out, her stick clasped firmly in one hand. She knew she daren't use the lift; the door's pinging could alert anyone downstairs to her presence. Regrettably, it would have to be the stairs. She stepped down the top step. Not so bad, really. She descended another three steps before the pain in her hip started to increase. Determinedly, she gritted her teeth and continued down, one step at a time then two deep breaths, in and out, in and out. Eventually, she reached the bottom with no sign of anyone having heard her.

The night light on the first-floor landing barely reached down here; the hall was in almost total darkness. At least the absence of light from the office indicated that it was unoccupied, which was a relief. Brenda must have gone to bed eventually. She felt her way along the wall until she reached the lift doors then crossed the corridor, knowing that the treatment room was opposite. Once inside, she closed the door as quietly as she could, held her breath and turned on the light. Once she was able to stop squinting in the harsh glare of the fluorescent tube, she looked around.

There was one of those step stool things for the staff to use to reach the higher shelves and she perched her bottom on it, grateful to take the weight off her hip. She allowed her eyes to travel around the shelves and worktops, trying to take in everything she could see. What could she remember seeing the night before Marianne died? A pair of hands, taking something out of the small under-the-counter fridge. She looked at the fridge and saw the padlock. Presumably, only the staff had a key to access it. She continued her visual search and then spotted a small key on a hook under the shelf above the worktop. She opened the fridge and studied the contents. She discovered that the only container that looked even vaguely like the one she could remember was Jack's insulin. *Would insulin kill as easily as morphine?* she wondered. Okay, so they took the insulin out onto the worktop and closed the fridge. She mimed that part, not wanting to risk leaving her prints on something that might turn out to be vital evidence. Then they had reached for a needle and syringe. Sure enough, blue plastic tubs on the worktop contained a supply of packaged needles in one and syringes in the other. They had started to draw up the liquid, but that was all she had seen.

She thought hard, desperately trying to recall any other details. The hands, were they male or female? She couldn't be sure, but something was niggling her mind. Then she spotted the boxes of sterile surgical gloves on the shelf above the blue tubs. Of course, they had been wearing gloves! They must have put the gloves on before touching anything, so as not to leave fingerprints. That's when her eyes alighted on a yellow box with red writing on it. Danger! Sharps! She peered in through the opening on the top and could see lots of discarded needles. She knew that Jack had insulin injections three times a day, so this was obviously for the safe disposal of his needles. And where better to discard the needle after killing Marianne than in here with all the others!

She looked around the room and found a swing-top bin. A careful inspection revealed that the bin was three-quarters full of discarded gloves, syringes, dressing packets, sterile wipes, and so on. Her heart raced ... supposing the killer's gloves were still in there? She sat down on the step stool again to think. She needed to tell the inspector as soon as possible so that someone could come and collect the evidence. It would have to be the phone in the office, she realised, as she hadn't thought to bring any money down with her. She scanned the room once more to make sure she hadn't disturbed anything, then turned out the light and stood patiently in the dark, waiting for her night vision to recover.

She cautiously opened the treatment-room door and listened. All quiet. She started towards where she knew the office to be, walking slowly because of her painful hip and leaning heavily on her stick. Taking the stairs instead of the lift had been a mistake.

Then Meg groaned. How could she possibly phone the inspector? She didn't have a number for him! She would have no choice but to wait until the inspector himself reappeared. Cross with herself, she turned a little more sharply than was wise and her painful hip gave way under her. With a startled cry, she lost her balance and tumbled to the floor. A light appeared at the top of the stairs and a voice called softly, 'Who is it?' Tempted for a brief moment to stay quiet in the hope they might not find her, she then gave in to the inevitability of discovery. She had no hope of getting up off the floor without help. She called out in reply and two sets of feet ran lightly down the stairs, the hall light snapped on and she looked up into the concerned faces of Milana and Bridget.

There was much fussing as to what on earth she was doing downstairs at this time of the night, so Meg told them she had come down to retrieve her book from the day room because she couldn't sleep. Then, after a careful but gentle examination of the leg that was twisted awkwardly beneath her, Bridget informed her that she was not to move until help had been summoned. Meg sank her head in shame; so much for being discreet!

Milana went to wake Brenda whilst Bridget settled herself on the floor next to Meg, squeezed her hand reassuringly and phoned for an ambulance.

# Chapter Thirty-eight

*Wednesday 14th September 2022*

When Meg woke the next morning, she couldn't for a moment work out why the light in her room was so different. Then she heard the rustling of bed covers, the swish of curtains and quiet voices murmuring nearby. *I'm in hospital*, she thought. She tried to move but the pain in her hip caused her to cry out, and the memory of the previous night came flooding back.

'Ah, you're awake now.' A smiling nurse appeared at the bottom of her bed. 'Do you need something for the pain?'

Meg nodded and rested back against her pillows. The nurse returned and helped her to sit up and take two tablets, before checking temperature, pulse and blood pressure. 'All back to normal,' she declared. 'I expect you'll be able to go home later this afternoon, after the doctors have been round.'

'Nothing broken, then?' Meg asked.

'No, you were very lucky,' the nurse replied cheerfully. 'You will have a little pain and inflammation from the soft-tissue damage, I'm afraid. But some bed rest, painkillers and physiotherapy will soon sort you out.'

The nurse bustled away efficiently, leaving Meg to wonder if it might not have been better if she had broken her hip. At least then, they would've had to replace it. Then she remembered that she had a murder to solve and that she'd better get a move on and do it before the police arrested the wrong person.

After a somewhat mediocre breakfast and an extremely uncomfortable trip to the bathroom in a wheelchair, Meg asked if she could make a phone call. The nurse pulled down the rather daunting contraption hovering above the head of the bed and showed her how to make a call.

'The only problem is, 'Meg confessed, 'I don't actually know the number of the person I need to call.'

'No problem,' answered the nursing assistant who was helping her. 'You can look it up online ...' she caught sight of the look on Meg's face '... or I can get the phone book from the office for you.'

Meg kept her fingers crossed as the nurse scanned the book for her, as she didn't have her glasses with her. She was delighted to learn that only one Peachy was listed, and the address was, as she'd hoped, in Downton. The nurse dialled the number for her then hurried off. Meg waited.

'Hello?' asked a rather sleepy voice.

'Is that Lauren?' Meg said doubtfully.

'Yes, who's that?'

'It's Meg ... Mrs Thornton.' Meg succinctly explained why she was in hospital. 'I do hate to bother you because I know you've another day off today. I wondered, if you've nothing else planned, whether you might be able to visit me?'

'No probs!' Lauren replied instantly. 'I'll just get dressed and grab a quick coffee. I should be able to make the nine-forty bus, with any luck.'

'My dear, you had better do more than just grab a coffee! Breakfast is the most important meal of the day.'

'If you say so,' Lauren replied non-committally, 'but I can't wait to tell you what I found out yesterday when I did that research you asked me to do.'

'Excellent news, thank you, Lauren. I look forward to seeing you later.'

Meg leant back against her pillow and wondered if she was right to involve the young carer. But the truth was, she could no longer do much sleuthing on her own, and she doubted if the others would be inclined to help, now that they had made up their minds that Brian was the murderer.

✿

Meg dozed on and off during the morning, disturbed only by the hot drinks trolley making its rounds. After drinking the tepid liquid served to her as tea, although it tasted vaguely of coffee, which she detested, she was forced to request the toilet and was very relieved when they brought a commode to the bedside rather than inflicting the wheelchair on her again. Not that the commode was any more comfortable, but at least she didn't have to be wheeled anywhere on it. The nursing assistant settled her back into bed and drew open the curtains to reveal a visitor waiting.

'I'm sorry but visiting time isn't until 1pm,' the nurse said sternly.

Meg's face fell but Lauren replied without hesitation, 'Oh, but I was just bringing my granny a book she wanted. I won't be stopping long.' She held up a carrier bag and smiled beseechingly at the nurse, who muttered something about five minutes and bustled off to answer another ringing bell.

Meg gazed at Lauren, taking in the fashionably ripped jeans, plain black sweatshirt and rather fetching red headgear, before smiling. 'So, you're my granddaughter now, are you?'

Lauren threw herself into the bedside chair, tugged the beanie from her head and pulled the curtain slightly round her. 'Don't want the staff to see me from the corridor,' she explained. 'Yeah, sorry if that was a bit cheeky, but I didn't want to let on I was from The Cedars in case it gets back to someone there that I've been here.'

Meg nodded. 'That was quick thinking. What have you got for me?'

Lauren delved into the bag she'd brought with her and passed Meg a hardback book. 'I came prepared, just in case anyone checked,' she grinned.

Meg squinted at the book to find it was a *Guide to Places to Visit in the British Isles*. 'And why do I need this?' she mused.

'Open it up,' Lauren advised. Sure enough, inside were a couple of loose printed pages. 'I printed off a summary of everything I found out, for you to study later.'

'Thank you very much, my dear, but you'll have to read it to me. I'm afraid I don't have my reading glasses here.'

'Well, I'll just give you the edited highlights,' grinned

Lauren. 'I started by trying to find that investigation into the murders at The Cadnum Lodge, but had absolutely no luck with that, I'm afraid.'

'Not to worry, my dear,' soothed Meg, albeit she was a little disappointed. 'What did you find?'

'Well, to begin with, I wasn't able to find out much, but then I remembered that my mum uses a couple of those genealogy websites. She's tracing our family tree, or something. Anyway, I logged in to her account and was able to access all sorts of records. It's just as we thought; Felicity Trainer didn't exist before July 2020. But she has the same National Insurance number and date of birth as Felicity March, who mysteriously disappeared in ... July 2020!'

'That supports my belief that Ms Trainer and Mrs March are one and the same,' Meg interrupted.

'Yeah, exactly. Anyway, I did some digging into records of births, deaths and marriages and, to cut a long story short, Felicity Julia Hampton, registered nurse, married Robert Sylvester March, accountant, on the 26th of June 2015. I was a bit disappointed that she wasn't Felicity Trainer, until I found her birth certificate. Felicity Julia Hampton was born on the 27th of April 1985 to Richard Aubrey Hampton and Sarah Margaret Trainer in Liverpool.'

'Yes, the sergeant mentioned that Trainer was her mother's maiden name.'

'Oh,' pouted Lauren, 'you already knew!'

'Oh no, my dear, not all of it. The sergeant let slip that one little fact, much to the inspector's displeasure, I might add. But to hear the full facts, well, that is very interesting.'

'Right. Well, I did some more digging and, as far as I can see, Felicity and Robert March never had any children. Nor have they ever divorced. And ... there's no record that Robert March is dead!'

'Really? So that means ...'

'They were still married!' finished Lauren triumphantly.

'No wonder Felicity was so put out when Brian proposed to her. She was in no position to marry him!'

'Exactly. But the thing I don't get is why did she threaten to kill him?'

'We'll probably never know for sure, but I suspect that while he was genuinely in love with her, she was only using him to get what she wanted. His proposal would have caused all sorts of problems had it become public knowledge, not least of which the risk of him finding out that she was already married.'

'Do you think Brian killed her before she could kill him?' asked Lauren.

Meg shook her head. 'That's what some people might think, but I'm afraid I suspect it's something else altogether. Did you find out anything about Brian and Brenda?'

'I've got their birth records.' Lauren pointed to the second page of notes. 'And they got married on the 15th of May 1989. I also found a birth record for one son, Dominic. He'd be thirty-two now.'

'Good work,' smiled Meg. She then proceeded to tell Lauren all that had happened the day before.

'Wow, you certainly have been busy. I didn't think about personnel records. I'll have to see if I can get a look at those when I'm back on duty tomorrow.'

'Yes, but be very careful, my dear. If someone has murdered once, there's nothing to stop them from murdering again.'

'Don't you worry about me, Mrs T. It's you I'm worried about. Whoever the murderer is, they've probably heard that you've been sneaking around at night and now they'll be keeping an eye on you.'

'I don't think I'll be doing any sneaking around for quite a while, unfortunately,' Meg said ruefully.

'Don't worry, I can be your assistant sleuth!' enthused Lauren.

'On that subject, can you use your magic phone to look up something for me, please?'

Lauren whipped her phone out of her pocket and looked at Meg enquiringly.

'Is it possible to kill someone by injecting insulin?' she asked.

There was a pause as Lauren tapped the question into her phone and studied the answers. 'Yes,' she said at last.

'If you inject insulin into a diabetic when their blood sugar is already low, it will quickly cause something called hypoglycaemic coma, followed by death.'

'What about a non-diabetic person?' Meg asked.

Lauren tapped away again. 'Yes, injecting insulin will cause the person's blood sugar level to fall low and lead to them experiencing symptoms such as hunger, fatigue, shakiness and irritability. If it's not treated, then coma and death can follow.'

'So, if you were to inject someone early in the night, they might not wake up and realise their symptoms until it was too late, so to speak,' Meg mused to herself.

Just then, the nursing assistant returned to their bay of the ward and stopped, frowning at Lauren. 'I thought I said five minutes,' she scolded.

'No worries, I was just leaving.' Lauren jumped up and, to Meg's surprise, dropped an affectionate kiss on her forehead. 'I'll see you later, Granny,' she said with a wink, before sweeping up her things and making a hasty exit.

Meg settled back against her pillows, smiling.

# Chapter Thirty-nine

It was just after lunch when the two detectives arrived back at The Cedars. They were admitted by Sally, who immediately ushered them into the office.

'Can I get you anything to drink? Tea? Coffee?' she asked.

'Yes, please,' accepted a grateful Viv. 'Coffee, please; one black, no sugar, the other white with one. And can you tell us who's in charge this afternoon, please?'

'I am,' replied Sally from the doorway.

'Do you know if Mr and Mrs Wollstonecraft are both in this morning?'

'I think Mr Wollstonecraft is still in their flat, but Mrs Wollstonecraft's gone up to the hospital.'

'Oh, nothing serious, I hope?' Dan enquired.

'One of our residents had a fall during the night. Fortunately, she didn't break anything, so Mrs Wollstonecraft's just gone to take her some clothes so that she can come back to us.'

'Which resident was it?' Dan asked, a worried look on his face.

'Mrs Thornton,' Sally said, confirming his fears. He waited until she'd left the office before speaking.

'I do hope her fall had nothing to do with her investigating the murders,' he said.

'You think someone might have pushed her?' asked Viv. 'Perhaps hoping she'd break a hip or something to get her out of the way for a while.'

'Anything's possible but we'll wait around until she returns, if we can, and ask her for ourselves.'

'I wouldn't like to think of the old dear being in danger,' mused Viv.

'Don't worry, we'll be taking the likely culprit into custody before we leave.'

Sally returned with the two coffees. 'Did you want to talk to me?' she asked, 'or can I get someone else for you?'

'Is it possible to talk to Janet Smith?' Viv said.

'She's in the day room. I can bring her into the office, if that helps?'

'Thank you, yes.'

✿

Janet Smith appeared delighted to see them again, if the broad smile on her wizened face was anything to go by.

'How nice of you to come and see me again,' she said, winking mischievously.

'Wild horses wouldn't stop us,' Dan bantered back, pleased to see she looked wellrecovered from her recent experience.

'Have you come to arrest Brian?' she demanded.

'And why would we do that?' countered Dan, amazed by her sagacity.

'I presume you have uncovered some evidence, if you are back here again and, as you know, I strongly suspect Brian of being both a thief and a murderer.'

'We're still gathering evidence,' said Dan, neither confirming nor denying it was Brian they'd come for, 'and hopefully you can help us with that.'

'Yes, of course.' Janet's bright eyes twinkled with excitement.

Viv pulled out an evidence bag containing a pretty Victorian flower brooch.

'Do you recognise this?' he asked gently, placing the bag in her waiting hands.

'Oh yes, indeed,' Janet confirmed almost immediately, 'that was Marianne's brooch.'

'You're quite sure?'

'Very,' she said firmly.

'Thank you. And what about this ring?' He exchanged evidence bags and watched her face closely as she turned it around, examining the signet ring from every angle.

'I'm fairly certain it was Harry Leadbetter's,' she said,

'but I'll tell you who can confirm that. Ask Albert Grimshaw. He and Harry were good friends.'

'Thank you, that's most helpful,' Dan acknowledged, as Viv took the evidence bag back from her.

'Anything else?' She looked at the two men expectantly.

Viv passed her two more evidence bags, containing an older engagement ring and a plain gold wedding band.

'Where did you find these?' Janet asked.

Viv glanced at Dan before replying. 'They were in the Wollstonecrafts' flat, but we'd like you to keep that to yourself, please.'

Janet nodded. 'And how do you know they don't belong to them?'

'We think that's unlikely. Both the Wollstonecrafts were wearing their wedding rings at the time of the seizure, and records show that neither of them has been married previously.'

As before, Janet examined them carefully before speaking. 'I'm certain the engagement ring was Marianne's,' she announced. 'I'm not so sure about the wedding ring, it's less distinctive, But I notice it's the same size so it could have been hers too.'

'Thank you very much,' said Viv warmly, as he retrieved the bags.

'Have you ever thought of joining the force as a detective?' asked Dan.

'Oh, I don't think they'd have me, Inspector. Not at my age.'

'Oh, I don't know. You're more observant than some of my team,' he remarked. 'Present company excepted,' he added, as Viv shot him an injured look.

'Would you like to go back to the day room?' Viv asked. When she nodded, he manoeuvred the wheelchair out of the office.

✿

Viv returned a moment later with Albert in tow.

'What-ho?' he asked. 'Got some more questions for me, have you?'

'Just one, Mr Grimshaw. Could you just take a look at this ring, please.' Viv passed him the evidence bag as he spoke.

'Good grief!' exclaimed Albert. 'That's Harry's signet ring! How on earth did you get it?'

Dan didn't reply but instead asked, 'Where did you think it was?'

'It should have been given to his daughter.' Albert's face suffused with anger. 'I know for a fact that's what he requested in his will, because he told me.'

'Thank you,' said Dan quietly.

'Well, spit it out, Inspector, how did you get hold of it, eh?'

'I'm sorry, sir, we really can't answer that.'

'Ha! I bet it was in the Wollstonecrafts' flat, wasn't it? That proves Brian is both a thief and a murderer! Just as I thought!'

The detectives declined to comment, simply thanking Albert for his help. They waited until he had left the office before speaking again.

'Right,' said Dan, 'let's see if the uniforms have arrived and we'll go and knock up Mr Wollstonecraft. He's got a lot of explaining to do.'

Viv went out to the car park and returned with PCs Adams and Gordon. They knocked on the door to the flat and waited until Brian came out into the hall. Albert watched, hovering in the doorway to the day room.

'What's up now?' Brian demanded truculently.

'Mr Brian Wollstonecraft, I am arresting you on suspicion of theft and handling stolen goods. You do not have to say anything, but it may harm your defence if you do not mention, when questioned, something that you later rely on in court. Anything you do say may be given in evidence.' Viv recited the caution as the two PCs politely but firmly took Brian's hands behind his back and cuffed him.

'What!' spluttered Brian. 'I didn't steal anything! I can explain!'

Albert, who had been listening, marched up and glared at Brian, barely inches from his face. 'Was it you who stole Harry's signet ring?' he demanded.

'No, no, I promise you. I didn't!'

'You bloody liar!' spat Albert, now furious.

'No, it was Felicity who was stealing things, not me. I merely discovered them in her room one day! I was planning to hand them back to the families.'

'A likely story!'

Before Albert could say any more, Dan and Viv gently steered him away from Brian.

'Sir, we've got this now,' soothed Viv.

'Please, Mr Grimshaw, let us do our jobs,' added Dan.

'Harrumph!' snorted Albert. 'You've taken long enough to get around to arresting him, and now Meg's in hospital! If he had anything to do with that ...' Albert pointed a finger a Brian, who quailed at the ferocity of his look.

'I don't know what you're talking about!' wailed Brian.

'Sir, we'll be questioning Mr Wollstonecraft down at the station and, don't worry, we'll get to the bottom of it all,' Dan explained.

'But you've only charged him with theft!' Albert growled. 'What about the murders, eh? What are you doing about those?'

'Sir, we are waiting for the results of a number of forensic tests. We are working as quickly as we can, I assure you. We have sufficient evidence to charge Mr Wollstonecraft with theft and/or handling stolen property. That will enable us to hold him for twenty-four hours, by which time we may be in a position to add further charges or to charge someone else, according to what we find.'

'Good!' retorted Albert, who watched with angry eyes as Brian was led to the waiting police car and driven away by the two PCs.

# Chapter Forty

Once the patrol car had pulled out onto Harnham Road, Dan turned round to see a cluster of faces at the day-room door, both staff and residents.

'There's nothing more to see, ladies and gentlemen. Would you please all return to whatever you were doing,' Dan requested firmly, in a tone that brooked no argument. 'Sally Reid?' he continued more gently. 'We'd like a word with you in the office, if possible, please.'

Once they were seated, Sally, on the verge of tears, asked, 'Whatever am I going to tell Brenda when she gets back?'

'That's okay,' Dan reassured her, 'we'll talk to Mrs Wollstonecraft.'

Sally sighed, visibly relieved.

'Mrs Reid, we'd like a little bit more background on Felicity Trainer, if you can help us.'

'Oh, well, we worked together for two years, but I wasn't really a close friend or anything,' she replied warily.

'Tell me, did she have an accent when she spoke?'

'An accent? You mean, like Sonia and Milana? No, Ms Trainer was definitely English.'

'No, I'm sorry, I should have explained better. I mean, did she have a regional accent, like Cockney or Geordie, perhaps?'

'Oh, I see what you mean.' Sally looked thoughtful. 'Mostly, I'd say no, she just spoke plain English, if you understand what I mean. But just occasionally, when she lost her temper, there was a bit of an accent there.' She screwed up her face, thinking. 'Scouse, perhaps?' she suggested.

'Thank you,' smiled Dan.

'Can I ask you a question?'

'Go on,' Dan replied cautiously, but was saved by a

knock on the door. 'Come in!' he commanded, and was happy to see Mrs Wollstonecraft's face when the door opened.

'Oh, sorry, Inspector, I didn't mean to interrupt. I was wondering what was happening in here,' she said, with a questioning look at Sally.

'Mrs Wollstonecraft, please come in. I take it you've brought Mrs Thornton back from hospital?' enquired Dan.

'Yes, she's here with me now. Did you want to speak to me or to her?'

'Both of you!' Dan stood up. 'Perhaps you'd like to wait in here with my sergeant.' He gestured to his recently vacated seat. 'Mrs Reid, is there somewhere I can go with Mrs Thornton for a quiet chat?'

Sally slipped out of the office with him, going straight to Meg's wheelchair.

'Meg, are you okay? You had us all really worried, you know!' she exclaimed.

'Oh, it was just a stupid fall, nothing more serious than a few bruises.'

Dan looked at her pale face and realised that she was probably tired and in pain.

'Mrs Thornton, I'd like a private chat but there's no hurry,' he said. 'Would you like to go and have a rest first, perhaps?'

'Thank you, Inspector. I must admit I do need to lie down. If Sally takes me to my room, will you come and visit me there? You'd better give me a few minutes to make myself decent, first.'

Dan promised her that he would, and watched as Sally steered the wheelchair to the lift. Back in the office, he quickly sat down and broke the news to Brenda that her husband had just been arrested.

'What?' she said, looking stunned. 'Arrested? What for?'

'We have reason to believe that he has been stealing from the residents for some months now,' Dan explained.

'Stealing?' There was no mistaking her genuine look of confusion. 'What's he supposed to have stolen?'

Once again, Viv produced the evidence bags, explaining what they were and where they'd been found.

'I can't believe this,' she said, swallowing anxiously. 'I had no idea!'

'That's okay, Mrs Wollstonecraft, we weren't implying that you did. But we do need to get in touch with next of kin for both Marianne Chadwick and Harry Leadbetter, if you could let us have their details, please.'

'Of course, Inspector. I'll just get them for you.' She went to the grey filing cabinet and quickly found two patient files. She took a pink form from each and put them into the printer to copy.

'We also suspect that he may have been responsible for Felicity's murder,' Dan said gently, scrutinising her reactions as he spoke.

'Brian murdered Felicity?' She sounded incredulous. 'Are you sure?'

She handed the photocopies to Viv, before putting the originals away as if on autopilot.

'I'm sorry, I know it's a dreadful shock.' Dan waited until she was seated again.

'We had enough evidence to arrest him for questioning about the jewellery,' he explained, 'but we're still waiting on other evidence that may lead to additional charges. We need Brian to answer our questions under an official caution, so he'll be held at Salisbury police station for up to twenty-four hours.'

'I see,' she said tonelessly.

'If there's anything else you can tell us?' he asked. She shook her head slowly.

'Very well, we'll let you get on with your day, Mrs Wollstonecraft. We're just going to go and talk to Mrs Thornton for a moment, then we'll be out of your way.'

She muttered a farewell but seemed far away and distracted.

✿

Dan and Viv made their way upstairs without talking, Dan only realising as they reached the top that he'd forgotten to ask anyone for Mrs Thornton's room number. He was relieved to see Sally just emerging from the room nearest to the stairs.

'She's quite decent,'Sally informed them, 'and apparently she has something she needs to tell you.'

Viv and Dan exchanged knowing looks, before knocking lightly and entering. Meg was semi-reclined on the bed, well supported by pillows, a blue tartan blanket draped neatly across her legs. 'Come and sit down, Inspector.' She indicated a chair at the dressing table, which Dan pulled across to sit beside her bed.

'There's a stool in the bathroom, if you'd like it, Sergeant,' she offered, but he politely declined and leant against the wall by the door instead.

'How are you feeling, Mrs Thornton?' asked Dan solicitously.

'I won't deny feeling a bit bruised and battered, but I'm perfectly well, thank you.'

'In that case, can you explain to me how you came to fall?'

'I'll tell you the whole story, Inspector, on the condition you don't tell me what a stupid old fool I've been.'

Dan smiled. 'I don't think you're anybody's fool,' he replied.

Meg told them everything and they listened patiently at first, then with greater interest, and finally with concern when she told them how she'd fallen.

'Mrs Thornton . . .' began Dan.

'Meg,' she said firmly, 'please call me Meg. You make me feel like a teacher back at school every time you say Mrs Thornton.'

'Meg,' Dan smiled again, 'you have an amazingly deductive brain, working out where the crucial evidence might be, but I do wish you'd not gone investigating on your own.'

'I know,' she said.

'It's not just the fall,' he explained. 'Someone in this

home is a murderer, and I wouldn't want them finding out that you've been investigating.'

'I completely understand,' she replied, 'but I didn't tell anyone what I'd been up to. I told them I'd gone downstairs to fetch a book I'd left in the day room.'

'Good.' He turned to Viv. 'Can you call forensics to come as soon as? Meanwhile, you'd better go and stand guard outside the treatment room.'

Viv hurried quietly out of the room.

# Chapter Forty-one

'You have some questions for me, Inspector,' Meg stated, once the door had closed again.

'I do, but only if you call me Dan.'

She was about to protest then realised that he was only doing what she'd insisted he do, in using first names. 'Very well, Dan, what do you need to ask me?'

'First of all, did Felicity Trainer have any kind of regional accent?' he asked.

'Yes. She did her best to conceal it, but there were times when she sounded unmistakably scouse. Which fits with her being born in Liverpool.'

'And just how do you know that?'

'I suspected it from her accent, so I did a little research.'

She showed him the typed pages from Lauren, without revealing how she'd got them. He glanced through them, shaking his head incredulously. 'You know almost as much as we do,' he mused.

'Thank you. I presume this confirms that Ms Trainer was indeed Mrs March?'

'We believe you are right, yes,' agreed Dan.

'Have you confirmed what happened at The Cadnum Lodge? Did she murder those residents there?'

'That's still under investigation,' he replied cautiously, 'but we are taking all of your concerns very seriously.'

'And where, I wonder, is Mr March?'

'We intend to find out, Meg, don't you worry.'

'What about Harry and Marianne?'

'We'll need to wait and see what evidence turns up from the treatment room.'

'There is something else I wanted to tell you.'

'Go on.'

'I think it was insulin that I saw someone drawing up into a syringe the night before Marianne was murdered. I initially suspected something more like morphine, but there wasn't any in the treatment room that I could find. But there was a bottle of insulin in the fridge in the treatment room.'

'Yes, I believe Jack is on insulin,' replied Dan thoughtfully, 'but he'd be unlikely to need it at that time of night. If it was administered in a high enough dose, especially during the night, it would cause hypoglycaemic shock.'

'That's what I thought.' Meg took a sip from a glass of water on the bedside locker. 'If you interview Dr Baker, as I presume you will, would you ask him if any of Jack's insulin has gone missing?' Dan nodded. 'And you might want to ask him what he meant when he told Brenda that he'd do whatever he could to protect her.'

'He said that?' Dan asked. 'When?'

Meg explained.

'There's something you want to tell me, too, isn't there?' she asked.

'Yes, we've arrested Brian Wollstonecraft on suspicion of theft and handling stolen goods.'

'Oh, I see.' She paused. 'May I ask what evidence you have?'

He paused. He wouldn't normally give out details during an investigation, but he felt confident he could trust a DCI's widow to be discreet. 'In the strictest confidence?' he asked. She nodded.

He explained how they'd recovered a gold locket and chain from Felicity's dressing table, which Brian acknowledged giving her. Also, the boxed engagement ring in Brian's bedside locker that he'd proposed to her with. Both of these purchases, it transpired, could not be accounted for on any of Brian's bank statements. Therefore, the detectives had visited the jeweller's where they'd been purchased and discovered that Brian had traded various items which he claimed to be from his recently deceased mother. The problem being that Brian's mother died ten years ago.

'He was selling the items that had been stolen?' Meg surmised.

'Yes. And we were lucky enough to recover both Marianne's brooch and a signet ring that belonged to Harry Leadbetter from the jeweller,' replied Dan. 'We also found a wedding and engagement ring hidden in Brian's wardrobe that have since been identified as Marianne's. So not only was he stealing from the residents when they were alive, he was also robbing them after their deaths.'

'Are you sure it was Brian who stole all these things?' Meg asked.

'Well, he denies it, of course,' chuckled Dan, 'but the evidence all points to him.'

Meg shook her head. 'It's much more likely that Felicity stole these items, don't you think? If she stole from residents at The Cadnum Lodge and then killed them to avoid discovery, it makes sense that it was her who did that here too. It would be a most improbable coincidence that Brian just happened to do the exact same thing as Felicity had done previously! Although Brian was most likely a party to it, after the fact if not before.'

'You make a point,' Dan conceded, 'but we will be questioning him again later today, so we'll wait and see what he says then.'

'And what about Janet?' Meg persisted. 'I'm sure it was Felicity who sedated her.'

'Ah yes, you're right there,' Dan sighed. 'Janet told us it was Felicity who gave her the tablets. But sedating someone is very different to murdering them, so it could be unrelated.'

'Surely you don't believe that!' Meg argued.

Dan privately agreed but was yet to determine how all the pieces of the puzzle fitted together so he didn't comment.

'And did you find the temazepam?' Meg asked softly.

'Yes,' Dan nodded. 'It was in a bottle prescribed to Harry Leadbetter, wrapped in an item of underwear at the bottom of Ms Trainer's laundry basket!'

'I think that rather proves my point; don't you agree? Clearly, jewellery wasn't all that Felicity was stealing from residents.'

Dan agreed, before bidding Meg goodbye. 'And, please,' he added, 'take care of yourself. No more investigating. And if you should think of anything else,' he took a card from his jacket pocket, 'contact me directly. Immediately, please.'

Meg watched him leave, content that perhaps things might be moving in the right direction now.

❀

On that Wednesday afternoon, whilst the inspector was busy investigating at The Cedars, Lauren was doing some investigating of her own. She'd caught the bus home after leaving Meg at the hospital, grabbed a couple of rounds of toast and Marmite from the kitchen, along with a bottle of Coke, and gone to her room. She opened up her Chrome notebook. Now then, where to start? She decided to dig a bit deeper into the mysterious Robert March. Using the details from his marriage certificate to Frau Flic, she trawled Facebook for him. Unfortunately, there were rather more people called Robert March than there had been Felicity Trainers. But, eventually, she found one with a matching date of birth who also listed his profession as 'accountant'.

From the photo, she was surprised to see a slightly greying but otherwise handsome enough bloke. There were numerous photos of him with an attractive brunette and a couple of children. For a moment, she wondered if she'd got it wrong and Robert and Frau Flic had got divorced after all. Or perhaps this wasn't the right Mr March. But, to her relief, his status was 'in a relationship', not 'married'. Phew! He was living in Aberdeen, apparently ... and there was a mobile phone number.

Lauren sucked in her breath and debated. Should she, or shouldn't she? 'Nothing ventured, nothing gained,' she muttered to herself, and snatched up her phone. It rang several times and she was beginning to think that her call was going to be rejected, but then a deep rich voice answered with a wary, 'Yes, who is this, please?'

'Hi there, is that Robert March?' asked Lauren.

'Yes. Who's this?'

'You don't know me. My name's Lauren Peachy and I'm, um, a private investigator.' She somehow thought that 'care assistant' wouldn't sound so impressive.

'What's this about?'

'I'm looking into someone who my client believes used false references to get a job.' Lauren crossed her fingers. 'I believe you may once have been married to her. Her name is Felicity Trainer now, but she was formerly Felicity March, née Hampton.'

There was a pause and for a moment she thought he wasn't going to answer. 'I don't know the first surname you said, but ... yes, unfortunately, I do know the other two names. If it's the same woman you're talking about.'

'So, you were married to her?'

'I still am, for my sins.' Lauren punched the air in delight. 'I married Felicity Hampton in 2015, and it was the worst mistake I ever made.'

'But you've never divorced?'

'Not for the want of trying,' he said grimly, 'but, after we separated, she disappeared without a trace. Try as I might, I could not find an address for her so that I could send her the divorce papers. Of course, the bloody pandemic didn't help matters.'

'Can you confirm a few details for me, just to ensure we are talking about the same woman?'

'Yes, okay then. What do you need to know?'

'What was her middle name?'

'Julia,' came back the answer, without hesitation.

'And where was she born?'

'Liverpool.'

'And where was she working when you separated?'

'At The Cadnum Lodge Residential Care Home, in the New Forest.'

Lauren punched the air again with each answer then tried to curb her excitement. 'Thank you, sir. That confirms that we are talking about the same woman.'

'But she was kicked out of that job,' he continued, 'just as she was kicked out of the previous two jobs before that.

In every case, there were rumours of her stealing but, of course, she denied it. Claimed she was being victimised, set up, or whatever. The first time, I believed her. The second time, I think I knew the truth, but she could be so damn persuasive.'

'I bet,' muttered Lauren.

'But The Cadnum Lodge? That was the final straw! There were rumours of patients dying mysteriously, for goodness' sake! She was sacked and I got as far away as I could just as quickly as I could! I engaged a solicitor straight away, but all his attempts to correspond with her failed, and no one seemed to know where she'd gone. In the end, I gave up and moved to Scotland permanently. It was the best move I ever made!' He sighed. 'Do I even want to ask what the hell that blasted woman has done now?'

Lauren bit her lip. It wasn't really her place to tell him, was it? 'I'm sorry, sir, I can't go into the details of my case. But I think that if you contact Salisbury Police Station and ask to talk to a Detective Inspector Bywater, he will be able to give you some information.'

'Just tell me one thing ... do you know where she is?' he asked.

'Yes, sir, I do. But the police will be able to tell you that.'

'Okay, then. This all sounds very mysterious.'

'Just contact DI Bywater, Mr March. I think you'll be glad you did. And thank you for taking the time to talk to me.' Lauren ended the call and sat lost in thought for a long time.

# Chapter Forty-two

*Thursday 15th September 2022*

The next morning was overcast and a fresh wind rustled the leaves in the garden. Lauren arrived at The Cedars bright and early, refreshed after her days off and eager to compare notes with Meg. Paul arrived soon after, so they went into the kitchen together. 'Morning, Andy,' Paul said brightly. 'Do y'know if Brian's still at the police station or is he back yet?'

'What!' Lauren exploded before Andy could reply, so Paul explained about Brian's arrest. She wasn't surprised to learn he'd been arrested for the thefts. 'But what about the murders?' she demanded.

'Murder, singular,' corrected Paul, 'and don't you start up again about Meg's crazy ideas. I'm beginning to think she's losing her marbles, y'know. She had a fall Tuesday night, coming down the stairs to look for something or other!'

Lauren was about to leap to Meg's defence when she remembered she wasn't supposed to know anything about that. 'Is she okay?' she asked.

'She was checked over in hospital and came back here yesterday afternoon. She was very lucky not to have broken anything, y'know, but she's in quite a lot of pain and not as mobile as she was.'

'Aye,' agreed Andy. 'Brenda's already been in to ask me to prepare a tray to take up to Meg as she'll not be down for breakfast.'

'How's Mrs W holding up?' asked Paul.

'The strange thing is, she's a bit more like her old self this morning,' mused Andy. 'She said that Brian was still at the station and considering the week she's had, I'm amazed she's even functioning.'

'Yes, indeed,' agreed Paul.

Lauren was itching to go and pass on this titbit to Meg, but she'd have to wait for her chance. She and Paul made their way to the office to find Brenda working at the computer composing a letter.

'Ah, good, you're here,' smiled Brenda. 'I've arranged for two agency carers to come in this morning as there's something I need to do. That means you'll have to take charge this morning, Paul. Milana and Bridget are upstairs, so if you could go and relieve them, they'll fill you in on anything you need to know. The agency carers should be here within the next halfhour. I won't go out until they get here. You know David, of course. He's worked here several times and knows what's what, so he can work with Lauren. If you could work with the other girl, Paul,' Brenda checked a note on the desk, 'her name's Anya and it's her first time at The Cedars.'

'Okay, Mrs W,' grinned Paul, pleased to see his boss more like her normal self. Lauren thought it odd that she should be so cheery with her husband under arrest at the police station, but she didn't comment.

They made their way upstairs and, after a brief handover from the night staff, they checked in on Muriel and Sylvia before going to assist Janet. Lauren was impatient to get to Meg but annoyingly Paul asked her to take Janet downstairs and then stay to supervise breakfast. She heard the other carers arriving and Paul bounding down the stairs to greet them both. It was clear that Paul was already friends with the tall, dark and handsome David. The other carer, Anya, was also quite tall and slender, with long blonde hair tied back in a ponytail. She seemed quiet and reserved as she meekly followed Paul upstairs.

'Hi, I'm David,' the dish greeted her as he came into the dining room, before waving to the residents and calling out a cheerful, 'Good morning, how are we all today?'

'Ooh, it's the lovely David,' beamed Annie.

'Lauren,' she said, shaking hands with David. 'Um, do you mind staying here if I go and sort out the day room?'

'Not at all.' He looked around the dining room. 'Only six residents this morning?' he enquired. 'Where are Meg and Marianne?'

For a moment, Lauren was floored. 'You don't know?' she asked.

'Know what?'

'Oh, crikey,' she began. 'Um, you'd better come into the hall with me.' She dragged him far enough away to be out of the residents' hearing, before telling him about the events of the previous week. David looked upset when he heard that Marianne had died – Lauren didn't mention that she had probably been murdered – and shocked to hear of Felicity's murder. 'And you say Brian's been arrested ...' he was saying incredulously just as Brenda came out of the office.

'Shouldn't at least one of you be supervising breakfast rather than standing in the hall gossiping,' she scolded. They both jumped.

'Sorry, Mrs Wollstonecraft,' said a rueful David. 'I've just heard the awful news. I'm so sorry to hear about your husband.'

'What will be, will be,' said Brenda, tight-lipped. 'Right, I need to get ready to go out. I suggest you both get on with your work.' She watched as David hastily returned to the dining room and a subdued Lauren collected a duster from the treatment room, before going into the day room. Then she went down to her flat and returned a few minutes later with a light raincoat on.

❀

Lauren watched from the day room as Brenda walked purposefully towards the kitchen. She dusted the sill of the bay window until she saw Brenda's small blue hatchback round the corner of the house and turn right out of the drive. *I wonder where she's off to*, she thought, as she tiptoed cautiously to the office, pushing the door behind her but not closing it completely. She didn't turn the light on, not wanting to draw attention to the fact of someone being in the office. Luckily, there was just sufficient light coming through the frosted window. Silently, she opened the left-hand drawer of the desk and found the key to the filing cabinet. Gingerly, she opened the bottom drawer, sitting herself on the floor beside it so she would be pretty much hidden if anyone happened to glance into the office. As long as they didn't come right in and turn the light on.

One by one, she searched the staff files until she found Felicity's. She glanced quickly over each page, before using her phone camera to capture the most relevant ones. Then she replaced each in the file, taking care to keep them in order. Twice her nerves jangled as she heard voices in the hall but, each time, they passed the office by and faded into the day room. Breakfast must be nearly finished but she still had a few more pages to look at. Then she heard Paul's voice as he and Anya came downstairs and stopped at the dining-room door. They called out to David, asking where she was, but she couldn't catch his reply. Paul laughed and then she heard Paul and Anya move closer until they were chatting right outside the office door. She held her breath, hoping like mad that they wouldn't come in.

'You go and join Lauren in the day room while I just return Meg's tray to the kitchen,' she heard Paul say. She gulped. Time was running out!

Quickly, she snapped the last couple of photos and returned the file to the cabinet. She locked it, replaced the key and went to the door, listening for sounds outside. She froze as she heard someone walk past. Then silence. She slipped across the hall and into the treatment room to grab a bottle of antibacterial spray. A moment later and she'd have blown it, as Paul was returning from the kitchen when she went back into the hall.

'Hey, Pixie, I thought you were in the day room,' he grinned.

'I was,' Lauren replied, 'just nipped out to get some spray for a stain on the table.' She kept her fingers crossed as she went to the day room. After a quick glance to check where everyone was, she headed for the table in the bay window, which was fortunately unoccupied, and pretended to tackle an imaginary stain.

David looked up from settling Janet into her habitual position and pulled a puzzled face. 'Where did you get to?' he asked.

Anya looked up at her from the settee, where she was helping Annie to sort out her balls of wool just as Paul followed her into the day room. Lauren realised that all three were looking at her and waiting for her reply. She swallowed nervously, desperately trying to think what to say.

She was saved by the doorbell chiming. Paul spun on his heels to answer it, so she waved the antibac bottle at the other two and muttered, 'Just fetching this.'

Anya seemed satisfied, but David looked at her long and hard, and she knew that he was suspicious. She'd have to be more careful in case he said anything to Brenda.

# Chapter Forty-three

It was PC Daly at the door. He asked to speak to Mrs Thornton in private, so Paul escorted him upstairs, announced his arrival to Meg and offered him a cup of coffee, which was politely declined.

Meg was delighted to see the constable and signalled to Paul that it was okay for him to leave. 'Ah, do come in and sit down,' she said to the PC. 'Do you have some news for me?'

He thought she looked a little pale and slightly frailer than she had on Sunday. 'Sorry to disturb you in your bedroom, ma'am, but I know how anxious you were to be told if I found out anything, so I came to see you just as soon as I could find a minute.'

'Please don't worry. I'm just resting after a silly fall. Nothing serious.'

'Well, I hope you make a speedy recovery,' he said sincerely as he settled his not-inconsiderable bulk onto the delicate dressing-table chair.

'Do tell me ...' she encouraged. 'Did you find out what happened to Mrs March?'

'Yes, I did, ma'am. I must apologise for the time it's taken me to handle this, but I was off duty on Monday and spent most of Tuesday attending an accident up on Countess Roundabout that kept me busy beyond the end of my shift.'

'I quite understand,' sympathised Meg, impatient to know what he'd discovered.

'Right, well, yesterday, I made a couple of phone calls and very interesting they were too. First, I phoned your friend Patricia Wilton at The New Forest Care Home. She confirmed your story, which, of course, was just as you'd explained it to me. The only new bit of information was that, according to her, the care home investigation into the death of her sister Mary concluded that Mary died as the result of an accidental overdose. Not that she agreed with its findings.'

'No! I'm sure she wouldn't!' exclaimed Meg.

'Mrs Wilton didn't know what happened to Mrs March, so I made a second phone call, to The Cadnum Lodge Residential Care Home. I asked to speak to the member of staff who had worked there the longest. As it happens, that was the matron, Mrs Collingbourne, who's been there nearly thirty years.'

'Good initiative,' said Meg, impressed. 'What did she have to say?'

'Essentially, it amounted to there being lots of suspicion about the senior care assistant, Mrs March, but no actual evidence. Apparently, she wasn't well liked by either staff or residents. Several residents accused her of stealing from them, but there was never any proof. The death of Tony, full name Anthony Fairford, was put down to natural causes when the post-mortem didn't find any signs of foul play. But Mrs Collingbourne said all the staff thought it very convenient, him dying just as he was about to make an official report against Mrs March. But when Pat's sister Mary Abrahams died such a short time later, it was a coincidence too many for the matron, and that's why she asked for the investigation. Mary's post-mortem found elevated levels of temazepam in her blood, which she was prescribed but in a much lower dose. However, the investigation couldn't prove that Mrs March had deliberately administered it, so they had to conclude it was an accidental overdose.'

'But the matron didn't agree?' asked Meg.

'No, ma'am, she didn't. Mrs March was given her marching orders, and no reference neither! Sorry, no pun intended. Furthermore, Mrs Collingbourne flagged her concerns about Mrs March on some carers' website, but there wasn't much else she could do.'

Meg heaved a great sigh of satisfaction. 'Thank you very much, PC Daly.'

'Well, all of that in itself doesn't prove that your Ms Trainer is one and the same as Mrs March. But I spoke with Detective Inspector Bywater this morning and he confirmed that they've already got evidence that Felicity March is indeed the same person as the Felicity Trainer who was murdered here in the early hours of Monday morning.'

'Yes, so he said.'

PC Daly coughed. 'If you don't mind me saying, ma'am, I was a bit surprised when the inspector told me I could tell you all of this. Usually, detectives keep things very close to their chest in a murder case.'

Meg smiled. 'It transpires that his father worked with my late husband back in Bournemouth CID. I think you'll find I can be trusted.'

'Oh, I'm certain of that, ma'am. The inspector wouldn't have allowed me to speak to you otherwise.' PC Daly stood up and stretched. 'Now, I'd best leave you to get that rest you need,' he said, pausing to gently squeeze her hand, before leaving the room.

Meg leant back against her pillows, satisfied that some things were becoming a lot clearer.

✣

Barely a quarter of an hour later, Meg's ruminations were interrupted by a knock at her door. Lauren came in bearing a cup of coffee and an air of excitement.

'How are you?' she enquired politely, clearly bursting to share something.

'A little bruised and battered but much more rested than yesterday, thank you.'

'Was that the same PC as came on Sunday?' Lauren asked.

Meg told her everything but warned her not to say a word to anyone else. 'What we now know is that Felicity Trainer no doubt changed her name because she would never have got another job in a care home as Mrs March. What I don't understand is why on earth Brenda employed her with no references.'

'I can answer that one,' Lauren announced proudly. 'I got a look at Felicity's personnel records earlier. Haven't had a chance to look through everything yet, but I can tell you that

Frau Flic had first-rate references.' She pulled her phone out and showed Meg the photos she'd taken.

'That writing is much too small to make anything out,' Meg grumbled.

Lauren showed her how she could zoom in. Meg shook her head in wonderment.

'What about her employment history?' she asked.

Lauren scrolled through until she found the relevant page. 'There's a three-year gap between her last care home in Liverpool and this job here. But these days you have to account for any gaps in employment history ...' She scrolled a bit further. 'Yes, there's a note here that she was looking after her dying mother during that time.'

'That's clearly a lie,' commented Meg. 'I remember Felicity being most upset one day after receiving a letter, and I asked her what was wrong. Apparently, her mother had just decided to sell the family home and move into a warden-controlled bungalow.'

'Worried about her inheritance, no doubt,' sniffed Lauren.

'Possibly. Those places certainly aren't cheap,' Meg agreed, 'but now we are wandering into the realms of pointless speculation.'

'Well,' surmised Lauren, 'I've got some more news for you.' She explained how she'd tracked down Robert March and spoken to him.

'Oh, well done, my dear. That is very interesting. It explains a lot, don't you think?'

Lauren agreed. 'So, what we know now is: Frau Flic stole from residents in at least three care homes that she worked in, before this one. In Cadnum, she also murdered two residents, before getting dismissed. She lied to get the job here and continued stealing from the residents, killing Harry and Marianne when they were going to report her.'

'Very succinctly put, my dear,' nodded Meg, 'even if we are lacking in sufficient proof to give to the police.'

'The big question is: who on earth murdered her?'

Meg didn't get the chance to answer because at that moment David walked into the room.

'Ah, there you are, Lauren,' he said, giving her a strange look. 'I thought we were supposed to be working together?'

'Um, yeah, of course,' agreed Lauren, leaping up and pushing her phone out of sight.

'Well, Mrs Wollstonecraft wants us to deep-clean Marianne's old room in readiness for a new resident who's arriving tomorrow.'

'She what!' exclaimed Lauren.

'I'm surprised she's concerned about taking in a new resident with her husband in custody,' remarked Meg thoughtfully.

'Not my place to comment,' replied David, 'but there's something very weird going on in this home. You could cut the atmosphere with a knife!' He shrugged his shoulders and held the door open for Lauren, before following her out of the room.

Meg sipped her coffee thoughtfully. They'd managed to find out plenty about Felicity's past, and she was now certain that Felicity had murdered four times. But she hadn't made much progress on who killed Felicity. Both Albert and the inspector seemed to be in agreement that it was Brian, as Janet had suspected. But she was convinced his grief had been genuine. It all came down to the psychology of it, she thought. Felicity was a nurse and she had been humane in her method of killing. An overdose of sleeping tablets or an injection of insulin. A peaceful death, not a violent one. But whoever murdered Felicity had bashed her over the head and hidden her body in a freezer. That was more like a crime of passion, wasn't it?

# Chapter Forty-four

Meg asked to be taken down to the dining room for her lunch, so Lauren and David fetched a wheelchair and padded it as much as they could with cushions and her tartan blanket. Even so, she nearly changed her mind as a sharp pain shot through her hip when they helped her to move. And the padding did little to cushion the movement of the wheelchair. She gritted her teeth, as she was determined to speak with the others, but her plans were frustrated by Brenda's presence in the dining room. 'I'm surprised to see you, Meg,' Brenda fussed around her, 'you must be in a lot of pain still.'

'Not too bad,' lied Meg.

'Just let me know as soon as you need to go back to your room.'

Meg tried stoically to eat some lunch, but the pain was making her feel nauseous, which didn't escape Brenda's notice. And she was unable to discuss anything of interest with Albert or the others with Brenda hovering close by her the whole time. To her exasperation, after only a few minutes, Brenda insisted on taking her back up to her room.

'I think you need some stronger painkillers,' she insisted, as she tucked her into bed comfortably. Meg didn't have the strength to argue.

❁

Lauren had noted Meg's frustration in the dining room and privately vowed to do whatever she could to continue the investigation in her stead. So, when the doorbell chimed just after Brenda had taken Meg upstairs, she rushed to get there first to open it.

'Good afternoon,' smiled the detective inspector politely.

'Inspector, Sergeant,' beamed Lauren. 'Come straight

into the office.' She led the way, hoping the other carers would not interfere until she'd had a chance to pump them for information. Fortune must have been on her side, for there was no sign of Paul, David or Anya as she shut the office door.

'Can I help you?' she asked breathlessly.

'We need to speak with Mrs Wollstonecraft again,' the inspector replied.

'I'm afraid she's busy at the moment. Can I take a message?'

'Thank you, Miss Peachy, but we really need to speak with Mrs Wollstonecraft.'

'Ooh, does it concern Wol—' She bit off the word. 'Mr Wollstonecraft, I mean.'

'I really couldn't say.'

'We're all so worried about Mrs W,' continued Lauren blithely. 'It's as if the home is in limbo with everything that's happened. Do say Mr Wollstonecraft will be back here soon!'

'I'm sorry,' grimaced the sergeant. 'That's unlikely to happen for—'

'Like I said, we need to speak with Mrs Wollstonecraft directly,' the DI interrupted.

Lauren took the plunge. 'Look, Meg is stuck in bed and can't do any sleuthing. But I've been helping her all along, you know. I know you trust her, and now you need to trust me too.'

The detectives exchanged glances. 'I'm guessing it was you who did the internet research,' surmised Viv.

'Meg doesn't even have a mobile, let alone a smartphone, so, no, she couldn't have accessed the internet on her own.'

Dan thought for a moment. 'Okay, Lauren. I really can't say much as it would be breaking all sorts of regulations, but I will say that we now have sufficient evidence to question Mr Wollstonecraft about the murder of Felicity Trainer. But keep that strictly under your hat.'

'I will,' promised Lauren, 'but it's okay to tell Meg, right?'

'Meg and no one else,' warned Dan. 'And on the subject

of sleuthing, there is absolutely no need for Meg or you, or anyone else for that matter, to do anything now that Brian is in custody. We'll handle it from here on.'

Lauren pulled a face and would have argued, but the office door opened.

'Inspector,' said Brenda, as the smile fell from her face, 'have you got news for me? Have you released Brian yet?' Her voice sounded genuinely concerned, but Lauren noted the hopefulness in her eyes.

'If we could have a word in private,' suggested Dan.

'Of course! Run along, Lauren. Surely you have work to do.' Brenda turned her cold eyes on Lauren, who read the veiled threat.

'Of course, Mrs W, I'm just off now.' She slipped out of the office and bumped immediately into David.

'And what are you up to?' he asked, giving her a piercing look.

'Nothing,' she grinned cheekily. She tried to step round him to head for the day room, but he caught her arm.

'Look,' he said, 'something is going on and I want to know what.'

Lauren was mindful of her recent promise to the inspector. 'I can't tell you,' she whispered.

'Listen,' he hissed back at her, 'either you're up to something for a good reason or you're skiving off work and I should report you. Now, which is it?'

'Please, just trust me,' Lauren implored.

At that moment, there was an unearthly wail from the office and they both froze. Viv appeared at the office door and looked around. 'Lauren,' he said urgently, 'could you go and make a cup of tea for Mrs Wollstonecraft. I'm afraid she's a bit upset by our news.'

Lauren nodded and hurried towards the kitchen, whilst David was left with no option but to return to the day room still ignorant as to what on earth was going on. 'This isn't over yet,' he muttered under his breath.

Lauren returned with a cup of hot, sweet tea and knocked on the office door. When Viv admitted her, Brenda was hunched over in the swivel chair, dabbing at her eyes with a tissue and giving occasional little sobs. 'Here you are, Mrs W,' she said kindly, as she offered her the cup. Brenda glanced up at her with suspiciously dry eyes then quickly looked away, but not before Lauren had concluded that the show of grief was nothing more than a sham. She left the office and ran as quietly as she could up the stairs, knocked lightly on Meg's door and entered, without waiting for a reply.

'Lauren?' murmured Meg sleepily.

'Are you okay, Meg?' gasped Lauren, rushing to her side.

'Sleepy,' she murmured again. 'Brenda gave me some stronger painkillers.'

'That's okay,' soothed Lauren. 'You probably needed them. The rest will do you good.'

'But the murders ...' began Meg, agitatedly.

'Shh, it's okay, Meg. The detectives are here again, and they told me they have enough evidence to question Brian about Felicity's murder.'

'No!' objected Meg.

'You don't think Brian murdered Felicity?'

Before Meg could reply, there was a knock at the door. 'Here,' she whispered urgently. 'Call Dan directly if you need to.' She pressed a card into Lauren's hand, who concealed it in her palm as she stood to face David, who had entered the room.

'Lauren, what are you doing?' he asked urgently.

'Just seeing if Meg wants a cup of tea,' she lied, 'but she's really sleepy, so I think we'd better check back later.' Lauren slipped the card into her pocket, turned a startled David around and pushed him out of the room ahead of herself. She closed Meg's door and turned to face him.

'Please,' she urged, 'you've got to stop interfering, or you'll ruin everything.'

'I don't understand,' he growled. 'Look, I want to help but I can't if you won't tell me what's going on.'

Cautiously, Lauren outlined their suspicions that Brian

and Felicity had been stealing from former residents and then murdering them to keep them quiet.

'If that's true,' he interjected, 'then who killed Felicity?'

'That's what Meg and I have been working on.'

'I suppose it must've been Brian,' he said thoughtfully. 'Perhaps he wanted a bigger share of the profits.'

Lauren was about to explain, when they heard voices in the hall below. She put a finger to her lips and moved to the top of the stairs, straining to hear. David moved up so close behind her that she could feel the heat from his body. She heard the two detectives taking their leave and the front door close behind them.

'I'm on your side, Lauren,' David whispered into her ear. She felt a shiver of something run down her spine that was not at all unpleasant. She shook herself mentally to get rid of the distraction. 'Just back me up, then. Please?' she implored. She sensed him nod and made her way downstairs, David following.

'Lauren? David?' Brenda asked warily from the hall. 'What are you two doing?'

'Just finished off preparing Marianne's old room,' answered Lauren cheerfully.

'Yes,' agreed David. 'It's all ready now.'

'I thought you'd already done that,' she snapped. 'Never mind, the late staff are due to arrive soon. Perhaps you could start the afternoon teas while I do handover and then get yourselves off duty a bit early for once.'

'Yes, of course, Mrs W.' Lauren hid her disappointment. David helped her prepare the tea trolley and wheel it to the day room. Barely had they started pouring teas than Sally arrived and told them to get themselves off home.

They walked to the pantry together to discover Anya and Paul already getting ready to leave. 'Hey, Pixie!' smiled Paul. 'Nice to get off early for a change, eh?'

'Pixie?' asked Anya.

'Yes, it's what I call Lauren. Y'know? She looks like a pixie.'

'I not understand this word,' Anya replied in her broken English. 'Perhaps this is compliment, yes? She is ... pretty, I think.'

Paul chuckled and agreed that it was something like that. He offered to walk down into town with Anya, and the two of them left together.

David smiled at Lauren, who had coloured slightly at Anya's words. 'I'd have to agree with Anya,' he said softly, which only caused her to blush even more.

'Better dash,' she said brusquely. 'Or I might miss my bus.' She fled from the house in such a hurry that she didn't hear David offering to give her a lift in his car.

# Chapter Forty-five

Brenda watched from the hall window as Paul and Anya walked out of the drive chatting easily together. Then Lauren hurried around the corner of the house and took off down the road. And, finally, David left in his car. She returned to the office, where she sat with her elbows on the desk and her head in her hands, going over what the detectives had told her. Brian had confessed to finding a book and a signet ring of Harry Leadbetter's in Felicity's room. They said that Brian had sworn he'd had no prior knowledge of the thefts and that he claimed he'd been going to return the items to Harry's family. But the silly idiot hadn't, had he? He'd knowingly sold stolen goods so he could buy presents for that bitch Felicity. She squirmed inwardly at the thought of the two of them together in the upstairs flat. *No point dwelling on that anymore*, she told herself firmly.

The DI also said that Brian had confessed to stealing from Marianne. He'd said he needed the money to buy yet more presents for her. Stupid idiot! Couldn't he see that she was using him? She couldn't believe for one moment that the bitch had genuinely loved Brian. She was too much of an ice princess for that.

The police had charged him with theft and handling stolen goods and implied that he might have been released on bail had they not applied for a warrant to hold him for further questioning. Of course, she'd protested and asked why. She had to at least pretend that she wanted Brian back even if the truth was that she didn't. They'd explained that the evidence now pointed towards Brian murdering Felicity; would you believe it? They said they were waiting for the results of some forensic tests before they could charge him. She could but keep her fingers crossed! If he was sent to prison for a good long time, she could carry on running her care home without any interference. She began to daydream about all the things she could do without Brian around.

❖

Lauren arrived home to find her mother resting on the sofa watching a quiz show.

'Hi, Mum. How are you feeling?'

Her mother paused the TV and smiled at her. 'Thanks for asking, love. I'm a little tired after my hospital appointment but otherwise okay.'

'D'you want me to get dinner tonight?' Lauren offered.

'If you don't mind. There's a couple of pizzas in the freezer, if you fancy them.'

'Great, that gives me time to do a bit more research. D'you want a cuppa?'

'Only if you're making one for yourself. What research is this?'

'Hang on a mo.' Lauren wandered into the kitchen, filled the kettle and flicked the switch. 'Right,' she said, plonking herself on the end of the sofa near her mother's feet, 'you remember me telling you about the murder at The Cedars?'

'Yes, I'm really not all that sure I like the idea of you working there if there's a murderer on the loose.'

'Mum!' Lauren rolled her eyes.

'Go on, love, what were you going to say?'

'Well, the police have arrested Wolly for nicking stuff from the residents, but now they're holding onto him on suspicion of murdering Frau Flic too!'

'Well, that's good, isn't it? If he's the murderer, then there's nothing to worry about with him being in custody.'

'Yeah, that's what I thought at first. But . . .'

'But what?'

'Well, Meg doesn't think Brian did it!'

'Meg? She's one of the residents, right?'

'She's the nice one I told you about.'

'The retired teacher? Do you think she might be right?'

'I'm not sure. I can see why the police might think it was Brian.' Lauren leapt up, hearing the kettle boil. Returning a few minutes later with a mug of weak tea for her mother and a strong black coffee for herself, she set her mother's drink down on a side table. 'I'm gonna head off to my room for a while. Be back in an hour or so to cook those pizzas.'

She clattered up the staircase and settled down on her bed with her notebook. Right, where to start? Well, who was the most likely suspect for Frau Flic's murder, if it wasn't Brian? She worked her way through the staff, and only one name stood out. Brenda. The jealous wife. Brian had proposed to Flic, even if she wasn't free to marry him. It was clear that he loved her, and no wife was going to stand for that, were they? She tried googling Brenda's name but couldn't dig up anything at all relevant.

*Okay, think it through. What was it the police needed to prove someone a murderer? Means, motive and opportunity; that's what Meg said.* She wrote those three words at the top of a Word document.

Means. Frau Flic was bashed over the head with a frying pan then stuffed into a freezer. Brenda certainly had access to the kitchen and would've known where to find the frying pan. And she looked like she had enough strength to do the deed. And, as a nurse, she was trained in how to lift people, wasn't she? So, she had the means.

Motive. Her husband was having an affair with the victim, and she knew about it. Being the jealous wife was a really strong motive, surely. What's more, it was possible that Brenda was also having an affair with that doctor. Could they have done it together? Brenda could've let the doctor in the back door, and he could've helped put the body in the freezer. Yeah, Brenda definitely had motive.

Opportunity. Brenda lived on the premises, so she was there that night. What was her alibi? She was in bed asleep. Could she have got up, done the deed and gone back to bed without Brian noticing? Hm, tricky one that. And how would she have got Frau Flic to go to the kitchen with her in the middle of the night? That was the really sticky question.

*So how can I find out more?* Lauren spent the next half hour jotting down ideas, before closing her notebook and going downstairs to cook the pizzas.

# Chapter Forty-six

*Friday 16th September 2022*

Meg took breakfast in her room again the next day as the pain in her hip was still quite bad, and the painkillers made her feel as though she just couldn't wake up. She was dozing on and off when a gentle tap on the door was followed by Sally's cheery face. 'Morning, Meg,' she said brightly, 'how are you today?'

'I wish I could say I was feeling better, but the truth is the pain seems worse today than it did yesterday,' she sighed.

'That's only to be expected,' replied Sally. 'It's quite common after a fall for the swelling and bruising to take a couple of days to fully develop. I think it's best if you ring for help if you want to get out of bed. We don't want you falling again, do we?'

Meg groaned in frustration.

'Don't worry! We'll pop in and out frequently to check on you,' she said reassuringly.

A little later, Lauren brought her a cup of tea, not too strong and with only a little milk, just how she liked it, as well as lots of sympathy. Shortly after that, Brenda brought her some more painkillers. When both David and Anya had separately popped their heads around her door to enquire anxiously after her health, she was beginning to feel especially well-cared for. All that was necessary now was to solve the case of who murdered Felicity and all would be well in the world.

✺

Meg was dozing when there was another tap at the door and Lauren asked her if she was up to having a visitor. 'It's the inspector,' she whispered theatrically.

'Of course, come in, Dan,' beamed Meg. She struggled to sit up, but moving her hip forced a sharp cry of pain and Lauren rushed immediately to her side.

'Please don't sit up on my account,' Dan urged, as he came in and shut the door. 'I've really come to see Mrs Wollstonecraft again, but I wanted to let you know where the investigation's got to. I hoped a bit of good news would cheer you up.'

'Yes, indeed it would, Dan. Thank you.' Meg lay back against her pillows with Lauren's help. Dan hesitated and looked questioningly at Lauren, but Meg insisted she remain. 'She's been no end of help, Dan,' she told him. 'It's only fair she stays.'

He nodded. Lauren offered him the dressing-table chair and brought the stool from the bathroom so that she could perch on the other side of the bed, holding Meg's hand reassuringly.

'Right, well,' Dan coughed. 'This is all a bit irregular. I trust what I say won't go any further than this room.' He glared pointedly at Lauren.

'I know when to keep schtum,' she replied hotly.

'I trust Lauren implicitly,' insisted Meg.

'Yes. Well, I wanted to let you know that we've had the preliminary results of Felicity's post-mortem through. They've opened up a new line of enquiry. You see, the pathologist found that there were signs of recent sexual activity.'

'Do you mean she'd had sex?' supplied Lauren.

'Yes, exactly. Within an hour or two at the most of her death. It will take time to get DNA confirmation, of course, but it seems reasonable to assume that it was with Brian. And that creates a huge inconsistency in his story, because he said he hadn't seen Felicity after six o'clock on Sunday evening. You see, the pathologist puts the time of death as between midnight and 3am.'

'Very interesting,' remarked Meg.

'Yes. We questioned him again this morning, under caution. At first, he persisted in denying having seen her that evening, but when faced with the pathologist's report, he admitted going up to her room at about eleven-ish. He admits that they made love, but he claims that she was alive and well in bed when he left her.'

'I suppose that could be possible,' Meg began.

'Fat chance!' snorted Lauren.

'Ahem,' interrupted Dan. 'We have a witness statement claiming that Felicity was seen on the first-floor landing, going downstairs, at about 11.55pm.'

'Ah yes, that would be Sonia, I think?' supplied Meg.

Dan smiled wryly. 'Yes, it was. She says Felicity was still dressed in the same clothes that she'd been wearing all day, which suggests Brian was lying. What is rather more perturbing is that we have examined both Brian's and Felicity's phones. They show that Brian sent Felicity a text message at 11.26pm asking her to meet him in the kitchen at midnight.'

'That implies that she was on her way down to meet him when Sonia saw her,' Meg said, frowning.

'But why would he send a text asking her to meet him after he'd already had sex with her?' protested Lauren.

'Precisely,' Dan agreed. 'It is our supposition that Brian sent her the text, met her in the kitchen, had sex with her there and then killed her.'

'That makes sense,' nodded Lauren enthusiastically.

'But why?' puzzled Meg.

'Why? There's any number of motives,' protested Dan. 'She had manipulated him, involved him in stealing and pestered him for presents. Then she'd rejected his proposal and threatened to kill him.'

'No, I meant why would he meet her in the kitchen for sex? Why didn't he just go up to her flat where it was more private and a great deal more comfortable?'

'Perhaps because you'd already seen him once going up to her flat. Perhaps he was wary of being seen again,' Dan suggested.

'Or perhaps he hadn't intended to have sex when he sent the message,' put in Lauren.

'A good point,' agreed Meg.

'Yeah. Perhaps he met her to talk after their argument. They kissed and made up, which led to unplanned sex. Then they fell out again and he bashed her over the head with the first thing that came to hand. Then he dragged her dead body across the floor and shoved it into the freezer,' Lauren finished triumphantly.

'That's roughly what we thought,' Dan admired Lauren's clarity, 'except that she wasn't dead when she was put in the freezer.'

'She was frozen to death?' gasped Lauren.

'I rather suspect she suffocated,' suggested Meg, and Dan nodded at her.

'Yes, she suffocated,' he confirmed.

'What physical evidence have you got that Brian was the murderer?' asked Meg.

'At the moment, it's not conclusive,' he admitted. 'There were three sets of fingerprints on the murder weapon: Brian's, Andy's and Brenda's. And all three of them could have quite legitimately used the skillet. But the CSIs found some hairs in the blood on the freezer lid, two of which did not belong to Felicity. It was dark brown hair, which probably eliminates the chef, who is a natural blond. We took a sample of Brian's hair this morning, and the lab has promised a visual comparison later today. That should clinch it.'

'Brenda has dark brown hair too,' Meg pointed out.

'Yes, but with all the circumstantial evidence, the text message, the timing, the motive, and so on, I think we've got our murderer,' pronounced Dan.

'Will you humour an old lady?' asked Meg. 'Will you take a hair sample from Brenda too?'

'I suppose I could. It would certainly please my superintendent, who likes to have all the i's dotted and the t's crossed,' Dan conceded. 'If the sample from the freezer matches Brian's hair and not Brenda's, that conclusively nails him at the same time as excluding her as a viable alternative.'

'Thank you, so much,' said Meg, wearily. The inspector took his leave, realising that she was tired. Lauren squeezed her hand and whispered, 'Well done for getting him to test Brenda's hair too,' before also leaving. Meg smiled. It looked as though Lauren was beginning to think along the same lines as herself.

# Chapter Forty-seven

Dan knocked on the door to the basement flat and Brenda eventually opened it. 'Inspector,' she greeted him warmly, although Dan noticed that the warmth didn't extend to her eyes. 'What can I do for you?'

'I won't take up too much of your time, Mrs Wollstonecraft,' said the inspector, pleasantly enough. 'Perhaps I could talk to you in private.'

'Of course.' She took him into the office and smiled, whilst her stomach was doing a double somersault and her heart was pounding against her ribs.

'Mrs Wollstonecraft,' the inspector began. He sounded very serious, and Brenda felt on the verge of throwing up.

'I need to tell you that we have now formally arrested your husband on suspicion of the murder of Felicity Trainer, so he will be detained in custody. I'm confident that we'll be charging him some time later today.'

'Brian killed Felicity?' she asked, wanting to be certain that she'd heard him correctly.

'Yes, that's how it looks.'

'And he won't be coming back here anytime soon?'

'I'm afraid not.'

Brenda suddenly felt as though a huge weight had been lifted off her shoulders. She would be able to continue running her care home just as she wanted to without Brian or Felicity spoiling it for her! She wanted to celebrate but thought better of it.

'Oh my God,' she gasped, sinking into a chair and covering her face with her hands. Perhaps the inspector was lacking in sympathy, or he had seen through her charade; either way, he continued talking without acknowledging her apparent distress.

'Meanwhile, I'm just tying up some loose ends. Dotting the i's and crossing the t's, so to speak. I need to ask if I can take a sample of your hair for comparison, please.' He smiled reassuringly as she looked up, surprised. The weight was suddenly pressing down on her shoulders again.

'I suppose so,' she muttered, her mind racing. Why would he ask that, if they were sure Brian had done it? Oh God, they just had to pin it on Brian! Dan pulled a couple of hairs from her head and dropped them into an evidence bag, after which he said goodbye.

Brenda escorted him to the door then returned to the office, feeling quite shaky. He had to suspect something, surely. Why else would he take her hair for analysis?

✿

Meg was going over everything Dan had told them in her head. It wasn't until she got to thinking about the text message that it occurred to her. The police had both phones and had seen the message that was sent from Brian's phone to Felicity's phone. Then she remembered Lauren offering to let her use her phone. Just because the message was sent from Brian's phone didn't automatically mean that Brian himself had sent it. Oh! She must tell Dan that immediately, because it could only mean one thing. She pressed her call bell and waited impatiently for one of the carers to answer it.

It was David who hurried in and asked if she needed some assistance.

'Yes, you must get the inspector back immediately,' she commanded. 'He not long ago went downstairs to talk to Brenda, so he might still be here. Quick, you must catch him!'

David didn't argue but hurried downstairs as fast as he could.

✿

Brenda had pulled herself together and was leaving the office when David flew down the stairs and almost collided with her. 'Whatever's going on?' she demanded.

'That inspector,' panted David. 'Is he still here?'

'No, he left a few minutes ago,' Brenda said, frowning.

'Oh dear, Meg wants to talk to him again.'

'Again?' Brenda asked sharply.

'Er, yes, that's what she said.'

Brenda frowned. Evidently, the inspector had talked to Meg before coming to her. Did she have something to do with him taking her hair sample? Surely, she couldn't have. But perhaps she'd better make sure that nosy old so-and-so didn't get another chance to talk to the inspector.

'Don't worry about it, David,' purred Brenda calmly. 'I'll pop up and talk to Meg and then I can pass on anything she wants to say to the inspector.'

He nodded gratefully, recovering his breath as he watched Brenda go upstairs.

✽

Meg was lying in bed waiting anxiously for Dan to return but, to her horror, it was Brenda who pushed open the door then quietly closed it behind her.

'Now then, Meg,' she said softly. 'I understand you wanted to talk to Inspector Bywater. That's really not necessary, you know. He's just informed me that they're going to charge Brian with Felicity's murder. So, there's no need for you to get involved, is there?' Meg swallowed nervously as Brenda approached the bed.

'Can I help you out to the toilet?' she enquired solicitously. 'Or maybe you need some more painkillers?'

Meg hesitated. It was true that she was in a lot of pain, but Brenda had only recently given her some tablets. Although, all they had done was make her feel incredibly drowsy. She shook her head.

'Very well. I'll leave you in peace to get some rest.' Brenda smiled at her then leant forward and whispered in her ear, 'And I think it's better if you don't go telling the inspector any more of your silly suspicions, don't you?'

Meg lay rigidly still, waiting until Brenda had left the

room. She tried to stay awake, hoping that either Dan or Lauren would return but, despite her disquiet, she simply could not keep her eyes open.

✿

Meg woke up some time later. She felt muzzy-headed and her hip was throbbing, like someone was pounding on it with a mallet. She tried to move, and an agonising shard of pain shot through the joint. She'd lost track of time but was vaguely suspicious that she'd missed lunch. Then she remembered that she wanted to talk to Dan. Something about Brenda? She couldn't think straight.

She was about to press her call button when someone turned the door handle and she held her breath, hoping it was anyone other than Brenda. To her amazement, the door rattled as someone pushed against it heavily and yet it didn't open. She could hear voices outside the door but couldn't distinguish what they were saying. She tried to call out to them, but her mouth was too dry. With a sense of rising panic, she realised that whoever had been there had given up and gone. Everything fell silent.

✿

David and Lauren stampeded downstairs and burst into the office.

'Mrs W! Why on earth is Meg's door locked?' demanded Lauren furiously.

'I had to lock it for Meg's protection,' Brenda explained calmly. She could see that Lauren was about to argue. 'Trust me, I had my reasons.'

'You can't lock someone in their room! What if there's a fire?' Lauren shouted, exchanging a worried glance with David.

'Listen,' Brenda said more firmly, 'Meg is pretty much bedbound now with her hip, so we'd have to help her to evacuate, if it came to that. Same as Janet. Trust me, Meg just needs some time to rest undisturbed. Meanwhile, I've had some news from the police that I need to share with you all, and it would be easier if I only had to say it once. Can you make sure everyone's in the day room, please. I'll be in very shortly.'

David looked at Lauren questioningly before answering. 'I think most of the residents are in the day room already, apart from Janet and Meg.'

'Don't worry about them. Just go and make sure all the staff are in the day room too, please, David.' He shrugged at Lauren, who nodded at him to go. 'And don't forget to get Andy from the kitchen,' Brenda called after him.

As soon as David had left, Lauren rounded on Brenda. 'What have you done to Meg?'

'Are you questioning my authority?' Brenda asked menacingly. 'You seem to forget; I am the boss here and you could find yourself out of a job very quickly if you're not careful.' Lauren faltered and Brenda pressed home the advantage. 'Now, go to the day room as I asked, and no more arguing.'

As soon as Lauren left, Brenda drew in a long deep breath. She knew that there was really no choice now. She needed to act immediately.

When Brenda walked into the day room a few minutes later, she looked round to check that everyone was there, before encouraging them to sit down, thus ensuring that she alone was standing in the doorway. Then she simply uttered the one word, 'Sorry,' before leaving the room, pulling the doors closed as she went, and quickly locking them. It was amazingly simple. By the time anyone realised what was happening, they were all trapped.

# Chapter Forty-eight

Meg must have dozed again because when she next opened her eyes, it was to find Brenda staring down at her. She tried to move, but the pain was worse than ever.

'I wouldn't move, if I were you,' advised Brenda, an odd expression on her face.

'Why?' she managed to gasp.

'Why what? Why were you locked in your room? Why are you in so much pain? Why are you struggling to stay awake? Why am I here now? Eh?' Brenda was leaning over her, taunting her.

'Why?' she managed to repeat croakily.

Brenda sat down heavily on the edge of the bed and Meg cried out in pain.

'You just had to poke your nose in, didn't you?' Brenda explained calmly. 'It was nearly the perfect crime. I got rid of that bitch Felicity, and Brian was going to get the blame. It was the sweetest of all acts of revenge. I would have been able to continue running my home just as I wanted to. But you worked it all out, didn't you? And you had to tell that inspector.'

'I don't understand.' Meg's brain felt as though it was swirling in fog.

'The police were convinced it was Brian, so why did they want a sample of my hair? Eh? Answer me that!' Brenda continued. 'Did you put them up to that?'

The memory came flooding back and Meg gasped.

'If they wanted my hair for comparison, that can only mean one thing: they've got a hair from the murderer to compare it to,' Brenda said sadly.

'You!'

'Yes, you knew it was me, didn't you? When Brian told me how much he loved Felicity, that he wanted a divorce, and that he wanted me to move out – me to leave my care home – my whole world fell apart. This home is everything I've ever wanted.' A slow tear trickled down one cheek. 'I spent all of Saturday desperately trying to think, what could I do? And in the end, there was only one answer. Get rid of the bitch!'

'No!' Meg gave a strangled sob.

'Hell, yes,' said Brenda, suddenly turning around and thrusting her face uncomfortably close. The movement caused another shaft of pain, but Meg bit her lip against crying out.

'I followed Brian upstairs on Sunday evening and saw him going into that bitch's room again. It was the perfect time to put my plan into action, so I went back to the flat and found his phone. Then I hid in the treatment room, waiting for him to return. As soon as he'd gone back down to our flat, I sent a text from his phone asking Felicity to meet in the kitchen. My only doubt was whether or not she would come. But she came all right, thinking lover-boy Brian had sent the message.'

'You killed Felicity?' Meg managed to whisper.

'I hit her with the frying pan, as hard as I could. But when I looked at her lying on the floor, I realised she wasn't dead. Part of me wanted to hit her again and again and again ... but when I saw the blood on her head, I just couldn't do it. That's when I had the idea of putting her in the freezer. She was unconscious anyway, so she wouldn't have known what was happening.'

Meg felt incredibly sickened by Brenda's callousness and the look of detachment in her blank eyes. This was a woman who had gone over the edge, driven by entirely understandable circumstances but now out of control. Her stomach roiled with fear. What would Brenda do next?

'I knew the post-mortem would show she'd had sex just before death and that the police would find the text message on Brian's phone. I thought that would be enough. And it nearly was.' Brenda suddenly sobbed and rocked to and fro on the edge of the bed, her hands covering her face. The movement was agonising, and Meg gritted her teeth so hard she thought her dentures might break.

Suddenly the rocking stopped and Brenda stood up. 'I just wanted to stop you from talking to the police,' she said apologetically. 'I didn't want to hurt you.'

She suddenly knelt beside the bed and stroked Meg's hair gently. 'I'm so sorry. I didn't know what else to do. I gave you sedatives instead of painkillers. I thought you'd be less likely to get up and walk around if your hip was painful. And the sedatives would keep you drowsy, which should have stopped you thinking as clearly. But you're in so much pain now. I can see it in your eyes. Please forgive me. I didn't want you to suffer like this, truly I didn't.'

Meg couldn't reply; her teeth were chattering with fear, waves of sickness sweeping over her from the pain. And yet a small part of her felt sorry for Brenda.

'Come on, it's time we went.' Brenda got up slowly from the floor and brought the wheelchair close to the bed. With some difficulty, she helped Meg from the bed into the chair, tucking the blanket round to keep her warm.

'Here, take these before we go,' she said, thrusting two tablets into one of Meg's hands and a glass of water into the other.

'What are they?' Meg asked suspiciously.

'Painkillers. Either take them or don't, but we have to leave now.'

Meg took the tablets, hoping that they were indeed painkillers.

'Where?' she asked.

'We're going out for a nice drive,' Brenda replied, as though this was a special treat.

Meg was vaguely aware of being taken down in the lift and pushed out through the kitchen and the back door. Brenda's car was parked close by. Meg wanted to struggle and shout, but she seemed oddly incapable. Brenda put her into the passenger seat and strapped her in, then abandoned the wheelchair and got in beside her.

'Let's go,' she said, slipping the car into gear.

# Chapter Forty-nine

In the day room, there was chaos.

'What the devil was that all about?' demanded Albert, perplexed.

Sylvia was crying, whilst Annie did her best to comfort her. Andy went immediately to the door and tried to open it but found that it was securely locked. Muriel was repeatedly demanding that someone explain what had just happened.

David moved swiftly to the French doors but discovered they were also locked and the key was missing. He looked at Lauren and nodded; she understood and tried the bay windows, but they too were tightly fastened and the key nowhere to be seen. 'It's no use,' she said, 'we're locked in!'

'Do you mean to say, there's no way out?' asked Annie.

'What now?' demanded Albert, looking from Lauren to David and back, hoping one of them had an answer.

'Oh, whatever are we going to do?' wailed Sylvia.

Lauren whistled to get their attention and waited whilst they quietened down.

'There's no need to panic,' she said, bringing her mobile phone out of her pocket. 'I can phone for help!'

She searched her pocket for the card that Meg had given her.

✿

At Bourne Hill Police Station, Dan and Viv had been over all the evidence again.

'We've got Brian for handling stolen property, theft and murder. We've just about wrapped this one up, haven't we, guv?' asked Viv.

'So far as Felicity's murder is concerned, yes. I'm sure the forensic results will confirm what we already know.' Dan nodded thoughtfully. 'Although I wish I could work out what's niggling me.'

'I think your Miss Marple is getting under your skin,' teased Viv.

'She's Mrs Thornton to you,' frowned Dan, 'and I can't help thinking she's spotted something we've missed.'

'Not about Felicity's murder,' insisted Viv. 'Although, yes, it looks as if she might have been right about the earlier murders,' he conceded. 'I can't believe the pathologist has managed to identify an injection site concealed in a natural skin blemish on the back of Marianne's hand. It was a good job we were able to request a post-mortem before her funeral took place. And if we can get permission to exhume Harold Leadbetter's body, we might well find the same.'

'If he wasn't cremated,' said Dan, darkly.

'But even if forensics can find the evidence among the stuff they took from the treatment room to prove that Felicity murdered those two, it makes very little difference as she's dead. And even if Brian was involved, he's going down for a very long time anyway.'

'Yes, you're right. I just wish I could feel more confident that Felicity's murder has been properly put to bed.'

'The lab promised to do a visual comparison on the hairs as soon as possible and phone us with the results. Maybe that'll help?'

'Yes, if we get a match to Brian, that will make it pretty conclusive,' agreed Dan.

The phone in his pocket rang. 'That was quick!' he exclaimed. But it wasn't the lab.

'DI Bywater? It's Lauren here. You know, Lauren Peachy at The Cedars.'

'Yes,' replied Dan, a puzzled look on his face.

'You've got to come quick!' she insisted urgently. 'Meg is locked in her bedroom, Mrs W's acting all weird and she just locked everyone in the day room! Something is seriously wrong, and I think Meg's in danger.'

'Slow down!' urged Dan, jumping to his feet and tensing

his muscles. 'What do you mean, everyone is locked in the day room? Who exactly? And how?'

'Mrs W asked me to bring all the staff and residents to the day room, except Meg and Janet, who are still in their rooms. She said she needed to speak to us all together. But she only said one word, then she went out and locked the doors.'

'What word did she say?'

'Sorry, just that, nothing else.'

'What about the French doors or the windows, can't you find another way out of the day room?'

'No, everything is locked and the keys are all missing.' Lauren's voice was beginning to rise with panic as she tried to impress the urgency of the situation on the detective. 'Look, you've got to come quickly. Meg was locked in her room, and I think Mrs W went upstairs after she locked us in. What if she's doing something dreadful?' Lauren's voice broke off with a little sob.

'Okay, okay,' said Dan, his heart racing, 'I'll dispatch a patrol car immediately and Viv and I will be on our way too. Just try not to worry.'

Dan ended the call and dialled the control room, issuing curt instructions. 'To the car, Viv, quickly!' he commanded, as soon as that was done.

Viv could tell from the look on Dan's face that something serious was up. He grabbed his car keys and raced after Dan without questioning. Only once they were in the car did he speak. 'To The Cedars, guv?' he checked.

'Yes, and get a move on,' said Dan, grimly. 'I think we've made a mistake. It's Brenda, not Brian, who killed Felicity, and now Meg's in danger.'

He quickly repeated what Lauren had told him as Viv sped the car along Escourt Road and round the roundabout onto Churchill Way.

'I don't understand, guv. Everything points to Brian. Where did we go wrong?'

Dan told Viv about Lauren's call and added, 'Then I remembered what Meg said about not underestimating Brenda, and the penny dropped. We proved that the text asking Felicity to meet him in the kitchen was sent from Brian's phone, and we stupidly assumed he sent it. That's what's been niggling at the back of my mind.'

'You think Brenda sent it?'

'It's the only explanation, if you think about it. She has a very strong motive. She's the only other person with easy access to his phone. It would explain why Brian was so insistent that he didn't send the text and he didn't murder Felicity. And it explains why Brenda seemed so relieved when we told her we'd arrested Brian. And so worried when we took her hair sample.'

'Do you mean to say that Brian's been telling us the truth?'

'Some of the time, at least.'

'Shit!'

# Chapter Fifty

It was all well and good, the inspector telling her not to worry, but Lauren was worried. And she had no intention of sitting back and waiting for the police to arrive.

'Listen,' she spoke to the now silent room. 'The police are on their way, but we really need to get out of this room, right now.' She looked around hopefully.

'Stand back,' said Jack, pushing his way to the day-room door. He stooped and peered into the lock. 'Good, she's taken the key,' he declared.

'How is that good?' demanded Lauren.

'It's harder to pick a lock if the key's still in it,' he explained. 'All I need is a hairpin ... anyone?'

Albert stood open-mouthed as Annie lunged at Sylvia and pulled two hairpins from her neat coiffure.

'Thanks!' Jack took the pins and knelt in front of the door, inserting the pins and jiggling them about. It seemed to take an age.

'Oh no!' cried Lauren, who was still standing next to the bay window and had spotted movement out of the corner of her eye. 'That's Brenda's car! And that looks like Meg in the passenger seat ... where's she taking her?'

David hastened to her side and whipped a scrap of paper from his pocket. He just managed to scribble the registration number down before Brenda pulled out into the traffic.

'There you are,' said Jack, standing back from the now-open door.

'I say, well done, old fellow,' applauded Albert.

'Quick.' David grabbed Lauren's hand. 'To my car! We can follow them!'

The pair ran as fast as they could down to the kitchen and out through the back door. Lauren cried out when she saw Meg's wheelchair, but David pulled her away from it.

'Get in!' he commanded, throwing open the passenger door of his car. In little more than a minute after Brenda, he was pulling out of The Cedars and accelerating towards the Harnham roundabout.

'There she is!' he exclaimed, as they slowed to a stop behind a short queue of cars waiting at the red lights. Lauren leant out of her window and could just see Brenda's blue car about five cars ahead of them at the head of the queue.

At that moment, a police patrol car, lights blazing and sirens blaring, came off the roundabout and headed towards them. It quickly passed them, and David could see in his mirror that it turned into The Cedars.

'They'll be able to help the others,' he said, 'but we need to help Meg.'

Lauren quickly pressed redial on her phone and waited for it to connect them to the inspector.

✤

Viv concentrated on weaving his way through the traffic, wishing that they were in a police car rather than his own so that he could turn on the blues and twos. Fortunately, traffic wasn't overly heavy in the middle of the afternoon, and he squeezed round College Roundabout without too much delay, although they did attract a blast on someone's horn.

Dan's phone rang as Viv approached the next roundabout and was once again forced to slow down for traffic. 'Yes,' he answered curtly.

'It's Lauren. Brenda's taken Meg in her car and David and I are following. She's at the lights for the Harnham roundabout ... oh! They've just gone green!'

'We're at the Exeter Street roundabout,' replied Dan, as Viv neared the front of the queue. 'Quick, I need to know if she's heading towards town!'

'No, she's going round the roundabout.'

'Left, left, left,' Dan yelled to Viv, who had paused at the roundabout waiting for instructions. Then they were on the approach to the Harnham junction themselves.

'She's heading towards the hospital!' squealed Lauren.

'Keep your eyes on her car until we catch you up,' commanded Dan, 'and stay on the phone!' He could see a number of cars queuing at the lights ahead and groaned. 'Take the outside lane,' he told Viv, 'and step on it, if you can.' He grabbed their police radio from the console and contacted the control room.

✿

Brenda's car was momentarily held up at the next set of lights, allowing David to close the gap to just one car between them as the others turned off either towards town or onto the Ringwood road. They followed Brenda as the lights changed, and she drove off at an unhurried pace, apparently unaware that she was being followed.

On her phone, Lauren could hear the inspector speaking rapidly but apparently to someone else, not her. 'Inspector?' she asked. He continued as though he hadn't heard her, so she tried again, a bit louder.

Dan issued a brusque 'Hold a minute' and then explained to her that he was talking to Control on the radio. 'Just update me if Brenda turns off,' he said.

A moment later, Lauren interrupted him again to say that Brenda was at the next roundabout. 'But she's going straight ahead,' she cried. 'I really hoped she was taking Meg to hospital but she's not! Where the hell is she going?'

'Let us worry about that,' Dan replied calmly. 'Keep following her but don't get so close she can see you,' he warned.

Lauren watched as the car in front of them turned off, leaving them directly behind Brenda now as they too negotiated the roundabout and headed south.

✿

Dan shared Lauren's concern: just where was Brenda taking Meg? And, more importantly, what was she planning to do? He'd finished briefing Control and told them to put all units on alert by the time Viv was able to get across the Harnham junction. To his dismay, there was no sign of any cars ahead of them. He put Control on hold again and raised his phone to his ear. 'Lauren, are you still there?'

'Yes,' came back her tense-sounding voice.

'Can you tell me what car you're in, please?' he asked. He heard her repeat the question and then a male voice shouted out his car details. *So that's David*, he thought.

'Thanks,' he replied. 'What about Brenda's car?' To his surprise, David came back immediately.

'It's a royal blue Renault Clio.'

'Don't suppose you got the reg number too?' Dan asked hopefully.

'Yes, if Lauren can reach into my tunic pocket,' David replied.

There was a brief pause and then Lauren reeled off the number.

'Well done, you two,' Dan said in admiration. 'I'll pass this on to Control and get back to you. Tell me immediately if she turns off anywhere.' He lowered the phone.

'Step on it, Viv,' he ordered, 'we're looking for a silver Peugeot 105. That's the car Lauren and David are in.'

He picked up the radio again and updated Control. 'Confirm suspect Brenda Wollstonecraft is heading south on the A345, leaving Salisbury towards Coombe Bisset. She's in a Renault Clio, index WB 19 HOT, that's Whiskey-Bravo-One-Nine-Hotel-Oscar-Tango. She has a possible hostage in the car with her. It's being followed by two civilians in a Peugeot 105, index FW 61 HGL, that's Foxtrot-Whiskey-Six-One-Hotel-Golf-Lima. They are in phone contact with us, and we're hoping to have eyes on them ASAP.'

He listened. 'Confirm, we will take over the pursuit as soon as it's safe to do so.'

'Look,' cried Viv, as he spotted the silver Peugeot ahead. Dan waited until Viv had closed the distance enough for him to confirm the registration before informing Control then raising the phone to speak to Lauren again.

'We're coming up behind you now, Lauren,' he said, as they spotted Brenda's car in front of the pursuing Peugeot. Good, there were no other cars in between.

'Lauren, you need to take the next turning off and leave us to follow Brenda now.'

'No way!' came back the angry retort.

'Lauren, Control is organising a block further down the road to stop Brenda. But it's important that you are safely out of the way before that happens.'

'If you overtake us, couldn't we just follow you at a safe distance?' pleaded Lauren.

Dan was about to argue but realised there was little he could do to stop her.

'Okay,' he said more softly, 'but keep well back.' He ended the phone call.

'David should let you overtake as soon as he can,' he told Viv. 'Keep eyes on Brenda but don't get too close. Control is going to get the chopper up to track her. And they're going to try to get Traffic out to Handley Cross in time to set up an intercept.'

'There's plenty of places she could turn off this road before then,' remarked Viv.

'We just have to hope she doesn't!' said Dan, grimly.

# Chapter Fifty-one

Meg was clutching the door handle to try to stop herself being shaken from side to side with every twist and turn of the car. Her mind was still in a fog, and every bump in the road jolted her hip terribly. She just hoped the painkillers would kick in soon. If, indeed, Brenda had given her painkillers and not something else.

She was relieved to note that Brenda was keeping to the speed limits, even though she appeared to be almost in a trance and driving on autopilot. Brenda didn't speak and neither did she, not wanting to distract her.

Meg struggled to keep herself awake, determined to make a mental note of the route they were taking in the slim hope that she might get a chance to tell someone. She thought at first that they were going to the hospital, but Brenda had taken the road towards Blandford instead. Where on earth was Brenda taking her?

She dozed for a moment then was jerked awake when Brenda slowed down. She saw a 30mph sign and one telling her they were entering the village of Coombe Bissett. Meg vaguely noticed a pub on the left and tried to read its name. She didn't notice the silver Peugeot, which had been behind them for some time, pull into the pub car park and then pull out again behind a dark blue Vauxhall Astra.

She watched houses pass by and a church as the road twisted and turned several times. They didn't appear to have left the main road. Meg didn't know if that was good or bad.

🌼

'Suspect still on A345 heading south, just leaving Coombe Bissett now.' Dan gave a running commentary to the control room. He hadn't seen the chopper yet, and he just hoped Traffic could get to Handley Cross before they did.

Just then, his phone rang and he picked it up quickly. 'Lauren?' he asked, then froze as an altogether different voice spoke briskly. He listened for a while then said, 'Understood, ma'am.' He put the phone down and looked at Viv. 'That was the superintendent,' he said.

'What?' spluttered Viv. 'She got on to this quickly, didn't she?'

'I'd swear that woman has her own special radar antenna sometimes,' said Dan. 'She knows that we're in pursuit of Brenda.'

'What did she want?'

'She thought we'd like to know that Brenda's hair sample was a perfect visual match to the hairs found in the freezer.'

'You were right, then.'

'A little late in the day, but yes. If only I'd paid more attention to Meg. How long until we get to Handley Cross, do you reckon?'

'About ten minutes, maybe a bit more. She's not speeding, which is one good thing.'

☸

Sixpenny Handley, or rather Handley Cross roundabout, is well known to travellers in the area. It is infamous as a black spot every August bank holiday weekend when the Great Dorset Steam Fair takes place in fields just to the south. Approaching Handley Cross from Salisbury, the road runs straight and high, with views of open farmland to both sides, and the horizon seems huge. The roundabout marks the intersection of the main A354 north-south route with the B3018 Shaftesbury to Ringwood road. And if not for the signposts informing you, it would be hard to see that there is a roundabout ahead until you are almost upon it, thanks to a handful of trees lining the hedgerows at the final approach. This makes it an ideal place to intercept a suspect vehicle.

Traffic police had stopped vehicles approaching the roundabout some one hundred metres or so back from three directions, much to the annoyance of businessmen on their way to their next appointment, van drivers held up with their deliveries and a local farm tractor. A police car was parked discreetly out of sight on the first exit, so that a driver coming onto the roundabout from Salisbury would not see it. Trees in the centre of the large roundabout kept the road straight ahead out of view until the cars rounded the roundabout. Police were, of course, stationed strategically on all three exits, just in case. But the betting was that she would follow the A354 south, so that's where the roadblock was.

※

Meg had nodded off despite her best intentions and only awoke as Brenda braked slightly before pulling onto the roundabout, causing the car to jolt awkwardly and Meg to cry out in pain. She looked around, confused, trying to work out where they were. Looking out of the side window as Brenda passed the first exit, Meg was sure she glimpsed a police car hidden some way back along the road. Her spirits rose for a brief moment then crashed again. They were probably there for some completely unconnected reason. But suddenly Brenda swore loudly. 'Shit!'

Meg could see police cars on the road straight ahead in the direction Brenda was currently heading.

※

'Shit! Shit! Shit!' exploded Brenda, almost in tears. She slammed the brakes on hard and hauled on the steering wheel, trying to continue round the roundabout instead of taking the exit. The back wheels skidded, and the car drifted sideways with a squeal of rubber on tarmac. Meg screamed. For a moment, Brenda thought she might just make it but too late saw the yellow and white bollard on the island rush up and crash loudly into the passenger side of the car with an ear-splitting screech of ripping metal. The airbag deployed, hitting her like a sack of flour at 30mph, and the seat belt bit into her chest, knocking all the air out so that she was winded. After the magnitude of the crash, the aftermath was momentarily and eerily silent.

❁

Dan saw Brenda pull onto the roundabout and watched anxiously, hoping she would go straight ahead. Viv followed cautiously, hanging back a bit, aware that the roadblock was in place. In a moment of pure horror, they saw Brenda's brake lights flash on and watched as the blue car swung wildly to the right, before skidding sideways to impact a bollard with a colossal bang. Viv stopped the car and Dan was out and running almost before he knew it. He rounded the back of the Clio and, seeing the ugly dent in the rear passenger-side door, heaved a sigh of relief when he realised that had borne the brunt of the damage, and that the front passenger door was relatively unscathed. He carefully eased the door open and caught Meg as she started to slip sideways, moaning softly. He brought his body in close, trying to stop her from moving, fearful of broken bones and spinal injury.

'It's all right, I've got you,' he crooned as he steadied her. 'Don't try to move.'

He was aware of wetness on her cheeks. As soon as he felt that she was no longer trying to move, he wiped the dampness gently away, relieved to see that it was tears and not blood. He kept repeating the same words over and over: 'It's all right. I've got you.'

❁

Viv jumped from his car just fractionally after Dan and, seeing him go to the passenger side of the Clio, he headed instead for the driver's side. Brenda was sitting upright, staring straight ahead, her face pale and her eyes vacant. He wondered if she was unconscious for a moment then realised that she was in a near catatonic state. He opened the door cautiously, but she didn't move a muscle.

'Brenda?' he said softly, not wanting to alarm her, but there was no response.

'Brenda, can you hear me?' He tried more strongly. Still, she remained frozen in position, her back rigid and her eyes unfocussed. He felt for a pulse, more to reassure himself than anything, and was pleased to feel it strong and regular.

He straightened up and looked around him. Several uniformed traffic cops had raced towards the crashed vehicle and then held back when they saw Dan and Viv beat them to it.

'Is there an ambulance on its way?' he called to one of them.

'Two minutes out,' another replied.

He stooped and looked through the car to see Dan supporting Meg.

'Is she okay?' he asked.

'I hope so,' Dan replied.

Viv straightened up and looked round to see a horror-stricken Lauren running towards him from David's car, which had pulled up behind his own. Tears streamed down her cheeks.

'It's okay,' he called, 'they're both okay.' Lauren seemed not to hear him as she rushed up behind Dan to see for herself.

※

The paramedics duly arrived, assessed the situation and decided to take Meg straight away, radioing for a second ambulance so that Brenda could be accompanied to hospital under arrest. Lauren climbed into the back of the ambulance, insisting on accompanying Meg. She gently clasped Meg's hand, concerned at her pale face and worried what injuries she might have sustained in the crash. Her stomach was still churning from the moment when they'd rounded the roundabout and she'd seen Brenda's car in its unnatural position, Dan at one door and Viv at the other.

Viv followed the ambulance in his car and David followed

behind him, leaving Dan to travel with Brenda when the second ambulance eventually arrived.

At the hospital, Viv paced between Meg's cubicle and the A&E entrance. He knew Dan would require an immediate update on Meg's condition.

Eventually, the ambulance pulled in and the paramedic opened the doors. Dan swiftly climbed down. 'How is she?' he demanded, as Viv approached.

'It's all right, guv, nothing too serious. No broken bones, no head injury, no spinal injury. She's shocked and in pain. No doubt she'll be as bruised as hell tomorrow, but that is one tough old bird. She wants to know what took you so long!'

# Epilogue

Some weeks later, Dan went to visit Meg in her new care home; it was becoming a weekly routine and, truth be told, he looked forward to these visits. She was sitting in a well-padded cane armchair in a large conservatory, looking relaxed and chatting to an old lady he didn't recognise.

'Dan,' she cried out with pleasure as soon as she saw him.

He presented her with the book she had asked him to bring and gave her a familiar peck on the cheek. She grabbed his hand and squeezed it.

'This is my honorary grandson,' Meg announced proudly to her companion, 'Detective Inspector Dan Bywater. Dan, this is Jeannie. We've just discovered we share a passion for jigsaw puzzles.'

'Pleased to meet you,' he said politely then looked down at Meg with concern in his eyes. 'And how are you?'

'I'm fine, thank you. I had a check-up at the hospital yesterday and they're very pleased with my new hip and the progress I've been making with the physio. They said I should be able to get rid of these fiddlesome sticks very soon.' She gestured impatiently at the offensive crutches leaning against the coffee table.

Jeannie excused herself and, as soon as she was gone, Meg looked Dan in the face.

'Well, are you going to tell me this time?' she asked.

'Yes, I can tell you now,' he said, sitting down.

'You were right, of course. Felicity almost certainly killed Tony and Mary at The Cadnum Lodge Care Home. Unfortunately, we'll never be able to prove that. Then she changed her name from March to Trainer and forged her references so that she could find another job. But you knew all that, didn't you?' Meg nodded with a slight smile.

Dan smiled back before continuing. 'Brian says that

Felicity stole from Harry Leadbetter and subsequently killed him. We've got the results of the post-mortem that was carried out following the exhumation of Harry's body, and the pathologist found a very well-hidden injection site. Unfortunately, toxicology was unable to identify what had been injected, but I'm told that if it was insulin, as we suspect, it would have disappeared from the body very quickly. Dr Baker confirmed that a vial of insulin had gone missing from the treatment room.

'We only have Brian's testimony that it was all Felicity, and he wasn't involved. But I'm inclined to believe him. He says he found the book and Harry's signet ring in her room and challenged her about them. She then used their affair to blackmail him into keeping quiet. As you know, he later decided to sell the items so that he could buy presents for Felicity. We've charged him with handling stolen goods.

'You also know that Brian confessed to stealing the brooch from Marianne and to taking her rings after her death. All so that he could afford an engagement ring to propose to Felicity, who would never have accepted him anyway. He's been charged with theft for that. Apparently, Felicity grew suspicious when Marianne asked her to call the police, so she pressured Brian into telling her what he'd done. He says that it was her decision alone to kill Marianne. I don't know about that, but I suspect he knew. However, we've only been able to charge him with being an accessory after the fact. Thanks to you, we found a speck of blood on a needle from the sharps box that was a match to Marianne and a trace of insulin inside the needle. We also found a pair of gloves with a smear of Marianne's blood on the outside and Felicity's fingerprints on the inside. That confirms it was Felicity who administered the insulin.

'The most remarkable thing about Felicity's murder is that it was not directly connected to the other murders. Everyone apart from you was convinced all the murders had to be committed by the same person. After all, do you know how rare it is to have two different murderers operating in the same place?'

'But they weren't entirely unconnected, were they?'

suggested Meg. 'Brian would never have done what he did if it wasn't for his affair with Felicity. And Brenda would never have acted if Brian hadn't threatened to leave her for Felicity. I think that unpleasant young woman was responsible for everything that happened, in a way.'

'Well, thanks to your persistence, we got there in the end.'

'What will happen to Brenda now?'

'She's being held in a secure psychiatric hospital indefinitely. If she is ever judged to be fit to stand trial, she'll be charged with murder. But I somehow doubt that will ever happen.'

'Do you have any idea where she was taking me that day in her car?'

'I'm sorry, no,' he lied. 'She isn't talking to anyone.'

There was no way he was going to tell her that Brenda had admitted that her intention had been to drive the car off the cliffs at a Dorset beauty spot called Durdle Door with the two of them inside. Meg didn't need to know that.

THE END

PLEASE leave a REVIEW if you possibly can online at the store where you bought this book or on Goodreads – reviews really matter!

And if you have time – check out my website:

https://www.the-salisbury-murders-by-wendy-boynton.com

If you enjoyed reading this book ... watch out for my next one!

# COMING SOON

## *The Mystery of the Missing Wallet*

### The Salisbury Murders: book two

Meg has settled into her new care home in Britford, a village just outside Salisbury. One January day she is delighted to be reunited with an old friend but dismayed when a wallet goes missing in suspicious circumstances. When the wallet's owner is brutally murdered that very night, Meg experiences a sense of déjà vu. But are these two events connected?

The discovery of the wallet thief leads to the dismissal of a member of staff and the arrival of Lauren at Britford Lodge. Back in tandem, Meg and Lauren turn their investigative skills to the murder, pitting their wits against DI Dan Bywater, who is once again infuriated by their persistent interference in his case. But his impatience with the pair is tempered by the warmth of his feelings for Meg, who regards him as an honorary grandson. And how can he be cross at her when she keeps handing him clues on a plate? Matters are further complicated when a budding romance sparks between Lauren and her sexy sergeant, DS Viv Williams.

A second grisly murder occurring in nearby Wilton is quickly linked to the case and the police are now on the hunt for a dangerous murderer out for revenge. Meg and Lauren turn their investigation to the question of his accomplice: there must be an insider in the care home who let the murderer in for his first kill. What Meg and Lauren don't realise is that the murderer will stop at nothing to protect his accomplice, and they are now facing a very real threat to their lives.

# Glossary of Abbreviations

| | |
|---|---|
| A&E: | Accident and Emergency |
| A-levels: | Advanced levels (school exams) |
| BIC: | Bournemouth International Centre |
| CID: | Criminal Investigations Department |
| CSI: | Crime Scene Investigator |
| CV: | Curriculum Vitae |
| DBS: | Disclosure and Barring Service (replaced the Criminal Records Bureau) |
| DC: | Detective Constable |
| DCI: | Detective Chief Inspector |
| DI: | Detective Inspector |
| DS: | Detective Sergeant |
| GCSE: | General Certificate of Secondary Education (school exams) |
| NVQ: | National Vocational Qualification |
| PC: | Police Constable |
| WPC: | Woman Police Constable (now an obsolete term) |